THE WAR GIRLS OF GOODWILL HOUSE

FENELLA J. MILLER

Boldwood

First published in Great Britain in 2022 by Boldwood Books Ltd.

Cover Design by Colin Thomas

Cover Photography: Colin Thomas

A CIP catalogue record for this book is available from the British Library.

Paperback ISBN 978-1-80162-826-6

Large Print ISBN 978-1-80162-822-8

Hardback ISBN 978-1-80162-821-1

Ebook ISBN 978-1-80162-819-8

Kindle ISBN 978-1-80162-820-4

Audio CD ISBN 978-1-80162-827-3

MP3 CD ISBN 978-1-80162-824-2

Digital audio download ISBN 978-1-80162-818-1

Boldwood Books Ltd
23 Bowerdean Street
London SW6 3TN
www.boldwoodbooks.com

For Marie and Kevin – they know why.

1

GOODWILL HOUSE, STODHAM, KENT, JANUARY 1940

'It's snowing again, Mummy, and there's already more than a foot on the ground,' Sarah said as she gazed despondently out of the drawing room window.

'Thank God, darling, we don't have to go into the village today. Imagine how cold it must be for your father, wherever he is in France.' Joanna was collating a pile of papers ready for the WVS meeting that was being held, as always, at Goodwill House.

The strident ring of the telephone in the grand hall made them both jump. Despite the fact that the room they were in was a considerable distance from the wretched thing, the noise of the bell echoed down the wide corridors and could be clearly heard. Her husband, David, had insisted they had one installed before he left with his regiment and, although incredibly useful, Joanna wasn't comfortable with using it.

Her daughter didn't move and neither did she but Betty Smith, the housekeeper, must have left her duties in the kitchen and hurried out to answer it for them as the nasty jangling noise of the bell stopped abruptly.

They no longer used the drawing room as it was far too expensive to heat and too cold to use in the winter – she and Sarah now preferred the smaller, more comfortable room that had once been Joanna's sole domain.

She couldn't remember David ever disturbing her when she was in here doing her embroidery or writing letters.

Betty appeared in the doorway. 'My lady, it's my Bert, he's had a nasty fall and Dr Willoughby thinks he might have broken his ankle.'

'Oh dear, how absolutely dreadful. You must go at once and help him. Sarah and I can manage for ourselves until you can return to us.'

'Thank you, my lady, that's ever so kind of you. There's a nice chicken pie ready to go in the oven and the veg are peeled and ready to cook. I've not got around to making the afters.'

Sarah was on her feet and rushed across and, quite inappropriately, hugged Betty. 'Don't worry, I'll do it. Mummy's hopeless in the kitchen but I've been well trained by you. Take care on the drive, it's snowing again and absolutely freezing.'

'You're a good little cook, Miss Harcourt, and no mistake. The pantry's full, so is the vegetable store. It's a good thing we were able to stock up before rationing started last week.'

Betty dashed off and Sarah followed her. At seventeen, Joanna's daughter was almost a young woman. She had taken her higher certificate a year early and intended to take up a place at Oxford to study medicine in October. Until then, she was doing everything she could to help the war effort and was now a fully trained member of the St John Ambulance Brigade.

Joanna was proud of her lovely daughter, of course, but did sometimes wonder if Sarah was a little too independent.

Goodwill House had been in the family for centuries. It was a C shape – the original part of the house had been built three hundred years ago and formed the west wing. An ancestor of David's had added a corridor and extra doors and walls so one no longer had to walk through one room to the other. The Georgians had added the central part of the house with well-proportioned, high-ceilinged rooms and then the Victorians had added a Gothic monstrosity which made up the east side.

There were over a hundred rooms in this mausoleum of a place and it was far too big for one family to live in comfortably. Perhaps in the days when the family could afford two dozen or more inside staff it might have been bearable. As it was, they only had Betty, and Mary who came in to do the laundry and heavy work twice a week.

Joanna had tried to persuade David to sell the house, as it wasn't entailed, and buy something more manageable and modern in the village. Currently, they were marooned on the outskirts, having to walk a mile to see anyone. The only thing she did like about her home was the fact that the acres of park and woodland were mainly at the rear and the house was easily accessible from the road that ran into the village.

When she'd first met and married David, Joanna had been swept away by the glamour of it all, by the thought of becoming a lady and living in the big house. Her family weren't aristocrats, merely middle-class, as her father had been a bank manager in Ramsgate. But she had come to realise soon after the marriage that she wasn't actually in love with her husband. She was fond of him, but at forty-one, only five years older than herself, David was very old-fashioned in his outlook and manners. He was an excellent husband, loved her and their daughter as he should, but was undemonstrative and treated them both like delicate porcelain ornaments unable to make decisions for themselves.

When he'd been recalled to his regiment – he was a reservist – he hadn't hesitated. Without a second thought to the chaos and confusion his sudden departure would create, he'd donned his uniform with pride and driven away two months ago, leaving Joanna and Sarah to cope with the running of Goodwill House.

She had no idea when bills were paid or to whom, as these things had been dealt with by him. She didn't even have access to his bank account but had been left with a pile of postal orders which she had to present at the post office each week in order to withdraw the housekeeping money.

The wireless was playing a dreary concert and she got up and turned it off. It would be far warmer in the kitchen, which was probably why Sarah had dashed off so readily.

When walking through the grand hall, her breath steamed in front of her – it must be well below freezing in this vast space. In fact, the entire house was hideously cold as there just wasn't enough fuel to light more than the kitchen range and the fire in the small drawing room. The bedrooms were unbearable and the only way to keep warm was by taking two hot-water bottles to bed and having an extra eiderdown.

She was almost running by the time she reached the kitchen, so desperate was she to get into the warmth. 'Something smells quite wonderful, darling. When will it be ready?'

'About an hour, I should think. I much prefer eating in here, although Daddy would be horrified at the lowering of standards.'

'Then it's a good thing he's not here. What time is your meeting?'

'All St John's meetings are cancelled because of the snow. I doubt anyone will need bandaging in this weather anyway.'

'I don't know why you couldn't just be happy being in the WVS. After all, darling, aren't you intending to be a doctor eventually?'

'I certainly am.' The kettle hissed and Joanna poured it into the waiting coffee pot. Neither of them liked to boil the coffee in the water as they thought it made it too bitter.

'It must be appalling in France for the British Expeditionary Force, and they sounded like they were having such a jolly time when the weather was good. Fraternising with the French, drinking wine and eating wonderful food. I almost envied your father – but I no longer do.'

'Apart from the rationing, and the conscription coming in for men between nineteen and twenty-seven, you wouldn't know there was a war on.' Her daughter stirred the coffee pot and strained it into the mugs. The good china had been put away for the duration.

'How can you say that? Everybody's walking around with a gas mask around their necks, the windows of the shops are taped up, there are Anderson shelters in people's back gardens and a public shelter in the village. All very depressing and hopefully unnecessary.'

Sarah looked at her mother in astonishment. 'Unnecessary? Hitler's determined to conquer the world and he won't stop until he has. It hasn't even started yet.'

A gust of wind blew snow against the kitchen window. 'Your father's quite confident the Maginot Line will hold. North-east France is well protected from the Germans and if they can't get to that coast then they can't invade England, can they?'

'Then let's pray his confidence isn't misplaced. Sometimes I wish the

Germans would drop a bomb on this house so we could move somewhere warmer and more comfortable.'

For a horrible moment Joanna thought her daughter was serious. 'Maybe we can persuade the War Office to take it over as accommodation for the RAF at Manston. After all, the base could be said to be at the bottom of our garden.'

'Daddy would never agree. I was surprised that he even spoke to the man from the Ministry of Agriculture when he came last October.'

'He spoke to him but he didn't agree that the park could be ploughed up to plant potatoes. I expect he won't have a choice eventually and there'll be a law passed that makes landowners do things they don't really want to do.'

'If the Germans did invade, Mummy, it's the Kent coast where they'll land. I'm surprised they haven't evacuated the children from the village as we're likely to be a target for any bombs when they do start falling because of Manston being so close.'

'I won't have any more of this gloomy conversation, Sarah. Hitler will be defeated in no time and your father will be back here safe and sound and life can continue as usual.'

Her daughter stared at her over the rim of her mug. 'But do you really want it to, Mummy? Wouldn't you rather have a little more freedom, independence? I'm not saying I don't want him to come home – of course I do – but I think it would be good for both of us to be able to organise our own lives for a change and not have to refer to him before we make any decisions.'

'I suppose sometimes I do feel a little trapped and stifled by his overprotectiveness. However, I doubt I'm capable of organising anything for myself. Remember, I'd only just left school when I married your father so just went from one set of rules to another.'

Sarah put her mug down so hard the coffee slopped onto the table. 'How can you say that? You're in charge of the WVS and more or less run the WI as well.'

'That's quite different. It doesn't involve dealing with patronising men, paying bills, speaking to government officials – I find it very difficult to get my point across in those circumstances.'

'If you can keep control of a room full of noisy women then I'm certain you'll have no difficulty dealing with bank managers and so on if you have to.'

Sarah had already cleaned away the coffee stain and refilled both their mugs. The telephone jangled loudly – it wasn't often that they got two calls one after the other.

'Don't look so worried, Mummy, I'll answer it. It's probably Betty.'

A few minutes later she came back smiling. 'You'll never believe who that was. It was the wing commander from Manston – he wants to know if we can accommodate some WAAF as they have no appropriate accommodation ready.'

'I hope you told them we couldn't possibly do so without permission from your father.'

Joanna wasn't used to having others in the house and certainly not strangers.

'No, I told them we'd be delighted to help. Mummy, we'll get paid for doing so which means we'll actually have money to spend on what we like. And Daddy will be none the wiser!'

* * *

Sarah knew that if she'd let her mother speak to the wing commander these girls wouldn't be coming. She'd neglected to say there would be six of them and these poor girls might well be thinking they were being sent somewhere very grand, but were in for a horrible shock.

'As you've already said yes, Sarah, there's nothing I can do about it. But what are we going to do for food and so on? We don't even have Betty at the moment.'

'I'm an excellent cook and we'll have their ration books. Someone is coming over from the base to tell us what we have to supply, what we'll be paid, and anything else that we need to know. Our guests won't be coming until tomorrow morning so we've ample time to get things ready.'

'They won't be our guests, darling, they will be our boarders. I wonder if whoever comes will be able to arrange for us to have extra coal. It's more than two miles by road to the base and those girls are going to have to walk in both directions every day. Absolutely beastly in this weather.'

'It's only fifteen minutes if they go across the park. The RAF wouldn't be sending them here if they didn't think it was suitable. We would be overrun with evacuees and their families if we weren't so close to Manston and the coast. The man from the base will be here this afternoon to check the accommodation is suitable.' She grinned as she hastily rinsed the mugs and left them upside down on the wooden draining board in the scullery.

'This might be a very large, cold house but it has to be better than one of those huts the poor airmen have to sleep in.'

'You're right, Mummy. Shall we light the fires in three of the bedrooms in the west wing? I expect there'll be icicles on the inside of the windows at the moment.'

* * *

Bates and his son – who wasn't very bright – took care of the horses, chickens and other miscellaneous poultry. Another even more ancient duo, brothers from the village, looked after the grounds and especially the kitchen garden. Sarah donned her rubber boots, thickest coat, hat, gloves and scarf and went in search of them. She found the two of them sitting by the paraffin stove in the tack room. It was a great deal warmer here, although rather smelly, than it was in the house.

'Good morning, miss, you'll not be going out on your mare today,' Bates said with a toothless grin.

'No, obviously not. I was wondering if I could ask you both if you could possibly help out in the house today?' She briefly explained the reason and Bates nodded.

'We'd be happy to, miss. Don't seem right to be sitting about doing nothing and being paid for it.'

'Thank you so much. Could you start with the fires in the bedrooms we're going to use?'

She stomped back, almost losing her balance several times as her feet slipped from underneath her in the thick snow. Fortunately, it was no longer falling and the stable yard had been swept clean. She paused to fuss

Starlight, her grey mare, and then did the same for Brutus and Othello, the two hunters that belonged to her father.

The stable cat meowed and wound itself around her legs in the hope there might be something tasty in her pocket. 'Sorry, Sooty, I haven't got anything for you today.'

It was marginally warmer indoors than out but not by much. She just had to hope these poor girls coming tomorrow had plenty of warm clothes and a positive attitude. If they were the most important family in the neighbourhood then why did they live in such unpleasant conditions? Any lodgers were going to need to be resilient living here. At least the food would be good and plentiful – but everything else was going to be far from luxurious.

From the clatter she could hear in the west wing, her mother was already there. 'Mummy, Bates and Billy are going to light the fires. I hope the chimneys are safe as they've not been swept for years.'

Her mother was head first in the linen cupboard. 'Everything in here is perfectly dry. I expected it to be damp and mouldy so that's a bonus. Here, darling, you take these sheets and pillowcases and distribute them to the beds. Exactly how many are we expecting?'

'Six – it makes sense to bring in single beds from elsewhere in the house. They'll be far warmer three to a room.'

The passageway was surprisingly warm – much better than the grand hall. The ceilings here were lower as this part of the house was ancient and maybe that helped somehow. The doors to the six bedrooms on this floor were kept shut and with some trepidation she opened the first one.

'Golly, where's the furniture?' The room was empty but at least there were curtains at the window which looked okay. 'These are double thickness so I think they'll do as blackouts as well. But that doesn't solve the problem of no beds or anything else.'

'To be honest, I don't think I've ever been in these rooms. Your father only showed me around the central part of the house and the east wing. Shall we check the others?'

None of the bedrooms up here had furniture either but they all had usable curtains. 'I'm surprised it's not cold and damp as I doubt that anybody's used these rooms for fifty years.'

There was the sound of heavy footsteps approaching and Bates and his son came in each carrying a hod full of coal.

'It's the walls, my lady, they're double thickness this side. They just built around the original house to make it fit in with the Georgian style.'

Sarah was astonished that Bates was so knowledgeable. 'That explains why in here the ceilings and walls are beamed and so uneven. We should move in here ourselves, Mummy, it's much warmer.'

'No, the family has always lived where we are now. Bates, do you think you could find the necessary beds, a chest of drawers and so on? There's more than enough room for three girls in a bedroom.'

'I reckon there'll be things in the attics, my lady. Me and Billy will go and have a look after we've got these fires going.'

'Is there any way of knowing if this is clear before we light the fire?' Sarah asked as she tried to peer into the darkness of the chimney.

'You leave that to us, miss. Which two rooms do you want getting ready?'

* * *

By the time the man from the base turned up, the rooms were ready, lovely and warm, and even the antiquated geyser in the bathroom had reluctantly rumbled into life. Sarah was just on her way down the stairs when there was a thunderous knocking on the front door.

Mummy was sitting in the drawing room looking like the lady she was, not a hair out of place, looking as young and beautiful as ever. It was a great shame, but Sarah had been told many times by well-meaning visitors that she didn't take after her mother but her father.

This meant she was tall and slim with nondescript features, mid-brown hair and, in her opinion, only her eyes were worth complimenting. Her father had these spectacular cornflower-blue eyes too.

She opened the door, expecting to find someone her father's age, but instead there was a tall, red-headed, green-eyed, devastatingly handsome young flight lieutenant standing in front of her.

2

'Flight Lieutenant Angus Trent here to see Lady Harcourt.' Angus had caught a glimpse of the delectable Lady Harcourt in the village and this wasn't her. The girl standing in front of him must be a servant of some sort as family members wouldn't answer the door themselves.

'I'm Miss Sarah Harcourt, my mother's waiting to see you in the drawing room. Shall I take your greatcoat and so on? Hanging it in here won't make it much drier. It would do better in the kitchen.'

'Delighted to meet you, Miss Harcourt.' He quickly shrugged off his outer garments and looked around, expecting to see a maid or housekeeper ready to take it.

'There's no one else, Flight Lieutenant, only myself and my mother live here. We do have a housekeeper but she's not here as her husband's had an accident.'

With some reluctance he handed over his dripping coat, unwound his scarf and rammed it and his gloves up one of the sleeves. His cap was already pushed through the epaulette on his shoulder.

'Thank you, much appreciated.'

The girl vanished, leaving him standing in the huge, freezing hall not sure exactly where the drawing room was as there were several doors, and all but two were closed.

'In here, young man. I'm not coming out to greet you as it's far too cold.'

He strode across and through the double doors from which the voice had come. Lady Harcourt was even more beautiful face to face – quite breathtaking – and didn't look old enough to have an adult daughter.

'Sarah has gone to make tea. Won't you sit down? There's no point in you beginning your explanation until she's here as having the girls is her idea and, therefore, she will be managing everything.'

Angus followed her to the fire and took the seat she indicated. There were elaborate, black lacquered screens around the seating area. If these were to make sitting here more comfortable, then they'd failed spectacularly.

His breath condensed in front of his face and she laughed. 'It's absolutely beastly here, isn't it? I thought I should speak to you in the drawing room as that's what my husband would expect. However, I've changed my mind and will do what my daughter suggested. Follow me, young man, I'll take you somewhere you won't freeze to death.'

'I'm a fighter pilot, ma'am, and I'm more warmly dressed than you are.'

Her tinkling laugh echoed in the draughty passageway as she dashed along in front of him and into a much more pleasant and far warmer room on the opposite side of the house.

'Miss Harcourt will wonder where we've gone.'

'No, she told me it was silly to sit in the drawing room and I'm forced to accept that on this occasion she was right.'

Angus looked around the room with interest, never having been inside the house of an aristocrat before. It looked no different to his own family sitting room – polished wooden furniture, comfortable well-worn chairs, sofas, and a variety of watercolours and oils on the walls.

'Lady Harcourt, we really appreciate your offer to house the six WAAF arriving tomorrow. We didn't know we were getting any girls – we certainly didn't apply for them.'

'I'm sure there'll be plenty of things they can do that you now have men doing – such as in the catering departments, admin positions and so on.' She sat, neatly folding her ankles, every inch an aristocrat even though she'd not been born one.

'It's not that there aren't duties they can fulfil adequately, it's the fact that having females about is just unnecessary. Better for the men to keep their minds on the job and not be worrying about women and be competing for their attentions.' Even to himself he sounded like an arse, and he was quite sure she must agree with him.

Miss Harcourt came in and put the tray down rather more vigorously than was necessary. She had obviously heard his last comment. Should he apologise or just pretend he hadn't said something so crass?

'I'm going to be a doctor, Flight Lieutenant Trent. Are you suggesting that I wouldn't be able to do my job as well as a man?'

He ran his finger around his collar, which had become unaccountably tight. 'No, of course I'm not. There are just some things that a man can do more efficiently than a woman – nothing to do with intelligence, but physical differences.'

She ignored his reply. 'Are you also suggesting that a WAAF isn't professional enough to do her duty without chasing after any airman she might happen to see?' She handed him a plain china mug of tea, milk already in, without offering him any sugar.

He was tempted to hand it back and say he drank it black with sugar rather than white without but decided he'd already dug himself a deep enough hole. He followed her lead and ignored her previous remarks – pretended nothing untoward had been said by either of them.

He thought he'd better explain exactly what was happening on the base. 'Until a few months ago we were an RAF training base. There's a squadron of Hurricanes and some Aussie chaps in Blenheims. The War Office expects us to be used for emergency landing in the future as well as an active fighter base.' They exchanged a puzzled glance so he continued. 'In other words, ma'am, we're still sorting ourselves out. Wing Commander Billings and myself are the senior officers plus a few dozen others, less exalted, at the moment, which is why I'm here.'

'I take it that you're a regular and not a volunteer?'

'I am, my lady, I've already served five years. I'm here to get things organised and will then have my own squadron of Spitfires but I doubt I'll be based here.'

The girl was apparently unimpressed by his account. 'I take it you intend to get to the point eventually?'

'I thought I'd made myself clear – but obviously not. We don't need WAAF getting under our feet at the moment but it seems that we're getting them anyway. Hence the necessity for billeting them with you.'

Lady Harcourt frowned at her daughter. 'And we're very happy to be able to help out. We've got more than two dozen unused bedrooms in this vast house.'

He decided to plough on with his rehearsed speech and ignore the girl's unhelpful interruptions.

'Miss Harcourt, Lady Harcourt, I came here to thank you for your generous offer to take these WAAF in until we can organise something on the base. They will be expected to do their own chores. You will provide them with suitable accommodation and breakfast and dinner.'

'What time do they have to be on duty and what time will they be returning? Will they keep regular hours or be working on a shift pattern?'

'Good question, miss, but I've no idea of the answer. I'm sorry, as we didn't even apply for any, we've not got things in place. We don't know what these girls have been trained to do, we don't know exactly what they'll be doing or when. I'm hoping you'll keep them here for a week or so. I think it highly unlikely they'll be working nights, but who knows?'

'In which case, Flight Lieutenant, shall we say that breakfast will be served at seven o'clock and supper at the same time in the evening?'

'That seems reasonable, Miss Harcourt. They will, no doubt, get a day off at some point and will then want something at midday. Will that be a problem?'

Again, the girl answered. 'As you don't require them for a week at least, we'll have to provide luncheon. I hope our remuneration will reflect this?'

Lady Harcourt visibly shuddered at the mention of something so vulgar as money.

'It certainly will.'

She nodded her thanks. 'We've turned one of the bedrooms into a sitting room for them. They can use that if they're not going out. If any of them can ride, then, when the weather's not so beastly, they can come out with me if they want to. We have two hunters as well as my own mare that need exercise.'

The remainder of his visit was less fractious and they both seemed delighted with the payment they would get for each boarder. He was more than satisfied with the accommodation offered and thought it was a great deal better than the unfortunate girls would get on the base once things had been arranged for them.

Lady Harcourt had remained in her sitting room and the girl had shown him around. She wasn't exactly pretty, but there was something striking about her and she was certainly intelligent, and lively company. Her eyes, however, were spectacular.

'If you look across the park, flight lieutenant, you'll see some woodland. If the girls go through there then they'll be at the base in a fraction of the time it takes to walk along the lanes. Mummy was upset when your squadrons arrived, thinking you would be constantly flying overhead with those noisy fighters. Fortunately, we don't appear to be on the flight path.'

'No, you're not, as the runway is parallel to your boundary. Therefore, we take off and land alongside rather than flying across. I can't promise it will remain like that once the balloon goes up.'

'What balloon? Barrage?'

'No actual balloons involved, it just means when the fighting starts.'

'I see. Anyway, whatever happens, there's a war on, and we'll just have to jolly well lump it. Now, have you seen enough?'

'Absolutely. The girls will arrive in transport of some sort, sometime tomorrow. I'll have a few hundredweight of coal delivered to you in the morning. You're going to need it.'

He wasn't sure if he should offer to shake hands but she kept hers firmly in the pockets of her very unflattering dungarees, so he did the same. His greatcoat was pleasantly warm. He was about to shove his arm through the sleeve when she laughed and grabbed it.

'Just a minute, your gloves and things are up there. Let me take them out for you.' She deftly removed his scarf and gloves and handed them over with a smile.

'Thank you, Miss Harcourt.'

She opened the door for him and, as he was walking out, he remembered there was going to be a dance in the mess that weekend to welcome the new arrivals.

'I hope you'll accompany the WAAF to the dance at the base on Saturday. We'll be sending transport for the girls. Do you think you could persuade Lady Harcourt to come too?'

'Good heavens, I should think not. She wouldn't dream of going out without my father. I might come, but it depends if I'm busy.'

'Busy?'

'I have to look after your WAAF as well as everything else unless our housekeeper is back.'

'They will only want feeding. Surely that's not going to take up all your time?'

* * *

There was something about this officer that grated. He was too sure of himself – arrogant even – it was probably because he only had to raise an eyebrow to get a girl to do what he said.

'If the weather's as bad as it is now then it hardly seems sensible to hold a dance at all. The girls would be better off remaining here. Good afternoon, flight lieutenant.' She stepped back and closed the door on him.

Her mother had drifted into the grand hall and observed the exchange with some amusement. 'I thought him rather sweet, certainly good-looking, but obviously not to your taste.'

'The last thing I want to do is put on a fancy frock and go outside in freezing temperatures just to prance around a makeshift dance floor being pawed and ogled by sex-starved members of the RAF.' She hadn't meant to reveal that, despite the efforts of her father to keep her cloistered, she wasn't entirely ignorant or innocent.

Instead of being shocked, her mother laughed. 'Well done, darling. As far as I'm concerned, the decision is yours – if you want to go, then do so. But let's not dawdle here any longer or we'll freeze.'

* * *

Angus stared at the closed door in astonishment. He thought the aristocracy were supposed to have good manners. He regretted his impulsive invitation to the informal dance they were holding on Saturday. With any luck she'd decide not to come.

He'd travelled from the base in a camouflaged Hillman Minx. This unexciting vehicle had got him here in one piece and he hoped would do the same on the return journey.

Win Co had persuaded him to take this posting, promising that once things were up and running at Manston then he would have his own squadron to command. He'd had a minor prang which meant he couldn't fly for a few weeks so he'd agreed – reluctantly. Manston was part of Fighter Group 11 but would be used mostly as a forward base and the squadrons would only stop to refuel on their way to France or to fight the Germans in the Channel.

He'd been trained on both Hurricanes and Spitfires and much preferred the latter. They could be compared to a racehorse, whereas the Hurries were the carthorses. Who wouldn't want to be in the fastest, most manoeuvrable fighter if they had a choice?

The drive was mercifully short and when he turned on to the road that led into the village he carefully steered the car into the tracks that ran down the centre. There'd obviously been at least one other car along here this morning. What he needed was a stiff drink and with any luck the pub would be open.

The car skidded to a halt on the gravel outside and he scrambled out and made a dash for the door. It was locked. The window opened above his head and the landlady, Vera, poked her head out.

'We don't open until six, Flight Lieutenant Trent, you should know that by now.'

He was given no opportunity to answer as she vanished and the window slammed shut. What was it about Kentish women that made them so belligerent and disobliging? He kicked the snow from his shoes, wishing he'd not bothered to put on his best blues and had worn his flight suit and flying boots, which would have been far warmer.

He crashed the gears, which didn't improve his temper, and by the time he arrived at the base he'd barely recovered his good humour and headed for the officers' mess – if it could be called that. Until the refurbs were done, they were using empty offices. The other ranks fared better as they had a brick-built mess and decent accommodation.

The dance would be held there and he was quite certain the airmen had already invited most of the village to attend. The brown jobs that manned the guns built around the base had their own barracks and there was very little fraternisation between his men and the army. He doubted they would have been invited to this dance – he hoped not as he'd been told there was usually trouble when they did intermingle at village functions.

* * *

Once Sarah and her mother were safely in the warmth and comfort of the kitchen, she produced her notepad and began to jot down how much it might cost them to feed and house the six girls. When she totted it up and put it against the amount they were going to be given, she was astonished.

'Taking into account the fact that they will be eating food we already have and didn't have to pay for, as well as the free coal that's going to be delivered tomorrow, we're going to do really well out of this arrangement, Mummy.'

'It's going to make a lot of extra work, for you especially, as Betty might not be back for a few days. You also have the horses to exercise and the chickens to take care of.'

'If I'm not here at mealtimes then I'm quite sure you can manage to boil an egg, make the tea, or put a saucepan of stew on the range.'

'It's about time I learnt to cook. Your father didn't like me to come in here. I don't suppose you remember, but when you were very small not only did I have a nanny to take care of you, there was also the cook, two housemaids and the housekeeper. Outside there were half a dozen journeymen as well as the grooms and gardeners.' She was counting on her fingers as she spoke. 'There was also a chauffeur and a Bentley for him to drive.'

Joanna rather thought she preferred the present circumstances, despite the lack of comforts, as she'd never been comfortable being waited on. But it was a worry that at any moment the bank could refuse to honour her cheques.

'I can vaguely remember there being a lot of servants in black frocks and white pinnies dashing about the house. When did it change?'

'Although your father never discussed such things with me, I think he lost a lot of money in the depression a few years ago. Certainly, that's when we cut back. Your father kept the car but drove it himself. As far as I know it's still sitting in the barn gathering dust.'

'Well, he's not here now to tell us what to do. I know he loves us but I felt smothered, controlled, and I'm going to enjoy being able to make my own decisions. Do you realise how hard it was for me not being allowed to mix with the villagers? I've never had friends my own age and actually, although I hated my boarding school, I often used to think that it was preferable to being here.'

'Oh, Sarah, I'm astonished to hear you've been so unhappy. I'd no idea you felt this way. I'm sorry you weren't comfortable at home.'

'I've not been exactly unhappy, Mummy, I've been lonely, bored, but never really dissatisfied with my life. Something that's always surprised me is the fact that Daddy agreed to my going to university to become a doctor. It doesn't really fit, does it?'

'I was surprised when he agreed. He told me that he wanted you to follow your dream. Even though he didn't really agree with women working, he didn't want to stand in your way.' She was silent for a few moments and then continued. 'I lived with my parents until I married, as all girls did. I thought my life was perfect, after all, hadn't I married into the aristocracy and now lived in the biggest house in the neighbourhood?'

Joanna was glad Sarah was going to have the opportunities she didn't as things were different now as there was a war on.

Sarah jumped to her feet. 'Did you close the curtains in the sitting room? It's dark, and when we put the lights on to go upstairs we'll have the ARP warden in the village ringing up and complaining again.'

'Of course I did, darling, I'm not stupid. What I don't know is if the drawing room doors are shut and they need to be.'

'I'll go and check. There's soup and the rest of the pie for supper. I'll get it ready when I get back.'

As expected, the doors were shut. The melting snow from the officer's coat had frozen on the tiles and Sarah narrowly avoided completing her mission on her backside.

* * *

The next morning, Sarah was up before light and rushed about lighting the fires in the three rooms that were going to be used by the visitors. There was no need for them to be chilled to the marrow if the RAF were supplying the fuel needed for the fires.

She'd drawn up a rota for the six incomers. As she didn't know their names, she had referred to them by number until she got to know them better. They would have to keep their own rooms tidy and launder their clothes. There was an excellent laundry room with a huge copper boiler that was lit by Bates on a Monday. There was a mangle and raised racks upon which to hang the clothes when they were washed.

It occurred to her that Mary might well be glad of the extra work and there was certainly sufficient money to cover her wages if she chose to do the laundry for the girls. She smiled to herself. She was referring to them as girls and yet they would probably all be older than her as one had to be seventeen and a half to volunteer. She was considering joining the WAAF if she didn't go to Oxford.

Having six WAAF here would give her the opportunity to find out more about life in the service and see if it might appeal if she didn't, for some reason, go to Oxford in October. The girls wouldn't be staying long enough to become friends, but making friends wasn't something she was bothered about. Being an only child had made her resilient and happy on her own.

From last week they were supposed to hand over all the eggs apart from the few they were allowed to keep but so far they hadn't done so. There weren't many eggs at this time of the year, even from two dozen hens, and a lot of those that were laid had shells so thin they cracked. This would make them substandard so they couldn't be sent anyway.

No doubt some officious person would arrive in the next week or two to ensure that Goodwill House was following the new rationing rules. There were rabbits and pheasants in the extensive woodlands so nobody here would go short of meat. Mummy and she had discussed what they would do with the surplus but now they would need it to feed the new residents.

3

Joanna hated the winter. The house was cold even in the summer but at least one could take a bath or have a wash without freezing to death. Her morning toilette was brief and she raced to the warmth of the kitchen clutching last night's hot-water bottles under her arm.

She emptied these in the scullery and hung them up from the hook at the bottom that protruded through the cosy crocheted cover. Where was her daughter? The table was laid for two – the kettle was simmering and yesterday's bread was sliced and ready to be put on the end of the toasting fork.

It was just after eight o'clock and they always breakfasted together at this time. The skies were grey, heavy with snow, and she feared there would be a further fall before this cold weather was over. On the news last night, she'd heard that the River Thames was frozen over. If there wasn't a war on, perhaps people would skate on it as they had done hundreds of years ago.

David was somewhere in northern France doing his bit and he wouldn't be at all bothered by the weather. He'd been a reservist and when he was recalled in September he'd not hesitated. Perhaps he found a quiet country life as boring as she often did.

Sarah had insisted they be paid with a postal order which meant they could cash it at the same times as David's housekeeping money and not have to involve the bank. David had said before he left that he'd be back in a few months but as nothing had happened so far, she doubted she'd see him before the autumn at the very earliest. There were only enough postal orders to last until the summer – God knows what they would do for money after that as their boarders would be long gone by then. The money she withdrew weekly was not only for food, it also paid the wages of those who still worked here.

The boot room door banged and a gust of icy wind blew through the kitchen. Sarah was back from wherever she'd been.

'Mummy, sorry I wasn't here when you came down. The coal arrived and I had to show them where to put it. I'm surprised you didn't hear it rattling into the coal cellar.'

'I've only been here a few minutes. Shall I make the tea? I'll be glad when this wretched snow has gone and we can get into the village again. We won't be able to go to church on Sunday and that will be the second week we've missed the service.'

'I'm sure God won't mind. He's got better things to do than worry about us.'

Joanna laughed. 'I'm not bothered about the Almighty taking exception to our absence, I'm more concerned with what the vicar might say when we do finally turn up. He'll probably mention us by name in his sermon – public humiliation isn't something I'd enjoy.'

'You're above reproach – you're the lady of the manor and everybody looks up to you. He wouldn't dare do anything to upset you. One word of complaint from you to the bishop and he could find himself in the East End of London.'

'I'm sure that's not true, darling. If it was your father making the complaint that would be quite different.'

'There's something I've been wanting to ask you about. I know you don't like talking about money but do you think there'll be enough for me to go to Oxford?'

This was the question Joanna had been dreading and she had no option but to tell her darling daughter the truth. 'I've not been able to entirely clear the accounts we have with the butcher and grocer each week. I hate to keep them waiting for what we owe but it's becoming increasingly difficult to manage with what your father's provided for us. I don't have access to your father's bank accounts, obviously, so I don't actually know.' She decided she might as well explain it all. 'Your father expected to be home by the autumn and only left me enough to run the house until then. He made no mention of providing fees for Oxford.'

'Is that a roundabout way of telling me I can't go to university? I'd already guessed as much.'

'I'm afraid it is. Does that mean you're going to volunteer for one of the services instead?'

'I'm veering towards being a WAAF but thought I'd wait until I've spoken to those that are going to stay here. If not, then probably the Land Army as I know more about farming, horses and so on than I do aeroplanes.'

'I don't think you have to know anything about planes, darling, that's left to the men. Whilst we are on the subject, I think we're going to have to let the horses go because there's really not enough money to pay for two grooms or the feed.'

'If *we* can't afford to keep them then I think it highly unlikely we'll be able to sell them to anyone despite the fact that all three of them are thoroughbreds. I can take care of them so we can let Bates and his son go, as long as you're prepared to help in the house.'

Joanna didn't hesitate. 'There's nothing I'd like better than to have something useful to do. Will you promise me not to volunteer for anything until next year? You won't be eighteen until September so why not wait a few more months and sign up in January?'

'They don't really need me at the moment and you do. Do you want me to speak to Bates or will you do it?'

She was going to let Sarah convey the bad news but decided it wouldn't be fair. 'No, I'll do it, but not until the weather improves. This largesse from the RAF is an absolute godsend – I'll be able to clear the bills next time I go into the village and I can't tell you how happy that makes me.'

Bates had worked for the family for decades so it was sad they were going, but inevitable. If only David had been honest with her, prepared her for what was coming, things would be so much easier to deal with.

* * *

Angus volunteered to take the thirty-hundredweight lorry to the station in Ramsgate and collect the unfortunate women posted to Manston. He rather thought he was the only bod on the base who wasn't overjoyed to have them. Females of any sort were in short supply.

He now had the list of names, numbers and duties that these WAAF were trained to do but as yet had no idea why they were being sent to his base. Someone at Victory House was trying to find out but until then they were stuck with them.

God knows why someone at the Air Ministry had decided they needed six women to run the office. All of those he was collecting were designated as clerks – both general duties and accountant. This meant they had office and bookkeeping skills. They were all recently qualified, not even an NCO amongst them, so some poor sod would also be responsible for their discipline and well-being.

The sooner he was reassigned to the job he was trained to do, the better. Footling around the way he was at the moment was making him bad-tempered. He wanted to be flying and preferably in a Spit.

Win Co had agreed Lady Harcourt could be paid in advance and he had a generous postal order in his pocket. The lorry lurched and bumped over the packed snow but he arrived with no mishaps outside the station twenty minutes after the train from Charing Cross was due to arrive. This was a considered decision as trains rarely ran on time especially with so much ice and snow around.

He didn't want to turn the engine off as the vehicle wasn't a good starter and in this weather it might stall and it was too damn cold to be stuck outside today. He hoped the girls would have the common sense to keep an eye out for him so he didn't have to go inside. This station was spacious and hopefully considerably warmer than the forecourt.

His breath condensed in front of him, the inside of the windscreen was steaming up, and he leaned forward and rubbed it clear with his glove. As he did so, he saw puffs of smoke approaching the station. The train was only half an hour late which was bloody good considering the circumstances.

He opened the door and dropped to the ground. Probably wise for them to see him in his RAF blue greatcoat standing beside the lorry in case they didn't realise the brown-and-green-painted vehicle was waiting for them.

Shortly after the train had arrived, the girls emerged. They were wearing what looked like a groundsheet over their grey-blue uniform – no sign of a thick coat at all. Bloody hell – they were hardly equipped for this weather. The fact that they were also lugging a massive kitbag didn't help either. One of the girls was dragging it through the snow as she was too short to carry it over her left shoulder as the others were doing.

He strode across and grabbed the bag. 'Flight Lieutenant Trent, welcome to Ramsgate. Your carriage awaits, ladies.'

They were too cold and miserable to do more than nod and smile weakly. He tossed the bag he was carrying into the back of the lorry and then picked up the owner and lifted her in. This gallant gesture did raise a smile.

'Cor, ta ever so, mister, I'd 'ave been showing me knickers trying to get in,' the girl shouted back happily.

'It's sir, not mister. Right, you lot, in as fast as you can. From the look of you, you need a hot drink and somewhere warm to thaw out and you won't get that at Manston. I'm taking you to your billet.'

There was a mumbled chorus of thanks and so on as with various degrees of elegance and efficiency the other five scrambled into the back. There were two slippery wooden benches, one on either side, for them to sit on.

As he was hooking the rear flap to the tailgate, he called in to them. 'Put your kitbags in the middle so if you fall off the bench you've got a soft landing. I'll do my best not to tip you off too often.'

It took him over half an hour to negotiate the slippery roads, make his way through Stodham and reach Goodwill House. Someone had been busy, he noted, as the snow had been cleared in the turning circle in the front of the house.

Again he left the engine running, jumped out and ran around to the back. He unfastened the canvas flaps, dropped the tailgate and looked in. The girls looked somewhat dishevelled but a lot happier and warmer than they had when they climbed in.

'Sorry, from the looks of you I didn't manage to keep you on the benches.'

'Don't worry about it, sir, it was jolly good fun. Shall we chuck out our bags?'

The speaker, from her crystal-cut diction, was a member of the upper classes, a bit older than he'd expected, and her blonde hair was swept back into an arrangement that allowed her to pin her uniform cap securely to her head.

'Toss them to me. Be quicker and more efficient.'

In rapid succession the six bags hurtled towards him and without his excellent reflexes he would have been flattened. The girls tumbled out and even the little one jumped down without needing his assistance.

The racket they'd made had obviously been heard and the front door opened. Both Lady Harcourt and her daughter came out to greet their temporary paying guests.

'Welcome, ladies, please come in as quickly as you can. I don't like to leave the door open too long.'

'Yes, ma'am, thank you for having us,' another of the girls replied as she snatched up her bag and headed for the door.

Miss Harcourt came down to speak to him. She was unusually tall for a girl – only half a head shorter than himself and he was over six foot. 'Thank you for bringing them, flight lieutenant. Are you coming in for coffee and cake? We've got plenty.'

He shook his head. 'Sorry, if I turn the engine off it's a bugger to get it started again. I'll be down tomorrow to see how they've settled in and give them some sort of idea what they're going to be doing once we've got things organised.'

'I look forward to it.' She smiled and he thought she was really quite pretty when she wasn't scowling at him.

* * *

Sarah pointed to the magnificent carved oak staircase that dominated the far end of the grand hall. 'Dump your bags there, girls, I'll take you up to your rooms when you're warmer. There are two coat stands for you to hang your – whatever that is you're wearing – on over there by the passageway that leads to the kitchen.'

She stood aside as they did as she requested which gave her a few moments to look at them without being observed herself. There was one pretty girl who didn't look more than five foot tall and, from the sound of her, came from the East End. The others were various shapes and sizes, but none of them were particularly memorable.

'Follow me, we're going to congregate in the kitchen as it's the warmest place in the house. It's where we eat as well.'

Mummy had greeted the girls and then dashed off to pour the boiling water onto the tea leaves waiting in the largest teapot they owned.

The kitchen was more than thirty feet long and almost as wide and for the first time in Sarah's life it didn't seem empty. The scrubbed pine table that dominated the centre of the room had ten chairs spaced around it and the girls each pulled one out and sat down chattering and laughing, happy to be finally warm again.

After two mugs of hot sweet tea and two slices of cake, the atmosphere was relaxed and she was beginning to put names to faces. Eleanor, an elegant blonde girl aged twenty-one, seemed the leader of the group. Ada, the Londoner, was the group joker. She was also the only smoker and would probably be found lurking in a corner smoking one of her Woodbines. The other four were pleasant enough but didn't seem interested in sharing information with her or Mummy, they preferred to talk amongst themselves.

'Right, I don't know if you're aware of it but you won't be going to the base to work for a bit. Think of this as unofficial leave. Flight Lieutenant Trent said they didn't expect you to arrive so swiftly and they're not ready for you.'

'We've been frantically busy these past six weeks so it will be wonderful to have time to write letters, catch up, get to know the area a little,' Eleanor said, and the others agreed.

'If you've finished, I'll take you upstairs. Three of you in a room and you all share a sitting room. You have your own bathroom and WC.'

This was greeted with exclamations of delight. It seemed for the past few weeks they'd been obliged to dash across freezing concrete to an ablutions block which was used by hundreds.

Sarah returned to the kitchen, satisfied the girls would be happy upstairs. All of them had been thrilled to find they'd got an actual mattress and pillow with real cotton sheets. Heaven knows what they'd been sleeping on up to now but it put her off the idea of becoming a WAAF herself.

She'd better start making enquiries about joining the Land Army next year.

4

It took a couple of days for Sarah and the new residents of Goodwill House to settle into a routine. She was frantically busy organising things, teaching her mother to cook the basics and keeping the vast house reasonably tidy.

Flight Lieutenant Trent had called in whilst she was busy elsewhere but he hadn't stayed long. Mummy was very taken with him but she certainly wasn't. He'd seemed too sure of himself, overconfident, and had been rather patronising when speaking to her. In the lull between serving luncheon and starting to prepare supper, Sarah was sitting in the kitchen ticking off today's list of jobs.

'I've been thinking, darling, that if the weather improves sufficiently to make it viable then I'll accompany you to the dance. I rather like the sound of this Wing Commander Billings – it would be wonderful to have the opportunity to dress up and dance with a suitable gentleman.'

If her mother had announced she was going to run naked around the house, Sarah couldn't have been more shocked by this announcement. 'I wasn't intending to go, Mummy. They won't be our sort of people.'

'Good heavens, when did you become such a snob? Weren't you telling me just the other day how much you resented not being able to make friends with the girls from the village?'

'I'll rephrase that. There are probably fewer RAF officers at the base – which means the bulk of the men wanting to dance with us will be ordinary airmen. I'm not saying they won't be perfectly pleasant, but they won't be like us.'

'I'm not quite sure what you mean. One thing I do know, my dear, is that they won't step out of line with us. Are you worried they might want to kiss you?'

Sarah shuddered at the thought that any man would want to kiss her. 'No, of course not. It's just the thought of having a stranger's hands on me that puts me off. As you know, I don't really like being touched by anyone.'

'Then you can dance with the handsome Flight Lieutenant Trent. He's hardly a stranger, is he?'

'I've only spoken to him a few times so, Mummy, as far as I'm concerned, yes he is.' She smiled reluctantly. 'However, you're right, if I do have to dance then he would be better than anyone else. Our guests are all desperate to go whatever the weather so I suppose they'll think we're being unfriendly if we don't go with them. I warn you that I expect we'll have to travel in the back of that lorry.'

'You know how to drive – we can go in the Bentley. Why don't you go out now and see if it starts?'

Sarah was tempted to refuse, or to go out and then pretend that she'd tried to start it but failed so that she wouldn't have to go to the base. With a sigh, she stood up.

'I'll have a go. I rather like tinkering with engines. Daddy taught me a lot and it was the one time he treated me like a real person and not a porcelain doll.'

She pulled on the heavy canvas overalls she wore for working outside with the horses or the poultry, added a thick knitted balaclava over her head and crunched her way across the snow to the closed barn where the Bentley had sat unused for the past few months.

She'd gone in and turned the engine over and driven it around the barn several times since last September. This was something her mother knew nothing about. However, the weather had been so dire since December she'd not bothered.

It took half an hour to clear the snow from in front of the doors and she was certainly warm by the time she'd finished. Although petrol was already in short supply, her father had prepared for this and there were more than a dozen cans filled with fuel so that wouldn't be a problem.

The Bentley guzzled petrol and was really very uneconomical to run as a family car. She pulled off the three thick dust sheets covering it and was pleasantly surprised to find there was no ice on the windscreen. In fact, the car looked as good as it had when she'd covered it up two months ago.

There was no need to do more than add a little choke when she turned the key. The car roared into life, the sound deafening in the empty space, and she drove it around a couple of times just to make sure it was in full working order.

If they were going to use it tomorrow then she'd ask Bates and his son to clear a path from the barn to the drive as even the magnificent Bentley couldn't manage two feet of snow. Neither man had much to do at the moment so she didn't feel at all guilty about asking them. Most of the day they were just sitting in the tack room, keeping themselves warm around the paraffin heater.

'You thinking of using the Bentley then, miss?' Bates asked.

'Yes, Bates. Lady Harcourt and I will be attending a dance at Manston tomorrow. Please make sure there's sufficient petrol in the tank.'

'Fair enough. 'Bout time her ladyship went out and enjoyed herself. I can't remember the last time the master took her anywhere.'

This was a highly unsuitable conversation to be having with him so Sarah ignored his remark and just thanked him. She wondered if he was aware that he was going to be dismissed shortly? He must know there wasn't enough work to justify having him and his son here. This wasn't her concern, Mummy would have to deal with it, although she did feel sorry for the two of them and hoped they could manage without the meagre income they got from the family.

* * *

The blackout meant everything took place earlier than it would normally have done, therefore the dance was being held in the afternoon, not the evening. There was a feeling of anticipation in the house and Sarah could hear the excited voices and laughter coming from the west wing.

The weather hadn't improved, but the fact that she would be driving the Bentley, which had an excellent heater, meant she no longer had an excuse to refuse to dress up. Obviously, they would all wear boots and their warmest coats and change into indoor shoes when they arrived. Only as she was selecting which of her numerous frocks she should wear did she remember that everybody else would be in uniform.

In her dressing gown, she rushed to her mother's room and knocked on the door. 'Mummy, we'll be the only ones in ordinary clothes this afternoon...'

'No, darling, don't forget there'll be dozens of people from the village attending. They won't be in uniform but their glad rags.'

'Gosh, how silly of me. What are you going to wear? Have you decided yet?'

Her mother pointed to a beautiful black evening gown, cut on the bias, so no other ornamentation was necessary. 'You can't wear that, Mummy. It's an afternoon dance, not an evening one. Let me find you something more suitable.'

Her mother laughed, not at all offended at being taken to task by her daughter. 'Now it's me that's being silly. I think there's something in my closet that I wore to an afternoon tea dance at the Ritz many years ago.'

It didn't matter that the gold silk gown was unfashionable, it was perfect. Sarah hurried back to her own room in search of something similar. Daddy had insisted she got the village seamstress to make half a dozen grown-up frocks when she'd left school last year, using the best materials and London designs.

Whatever she wore, she would be overshadowed by her mother, but she didn't mind that. Eventually she selected a dress that came to mid-calf, had a wide skirt, a matching belt and a pretty heart-shaped neckline. The fact that there was also an angora cardigan exactly the same shade of blue made it perfect for a winter event.

* * *

Angus had flown a Blenheim Mk IV IF, a fighter bomber, but wasn't impressed by its speed, manoeuvrability or the fact that the flyer was so cramped that he couldn't see all the flight instruments. The engine instruments made the forward view on landings impossible. The secondary items were along the left side of the cockpit, but essential things such as the propeller pitch control were behind the pilot where they had to be found by feel alone. Not ideal, and he hoped he never had to fly one in action.

There was a three-man crew – the pilot, navigator bombardier and a wireless operator who also acted as the gunner. This squadron consisted of all Australian pilots and they seemed happy enough, although never stopped binding about the weather. He didn't need telling every time he met one of them that it would be midsummer back home in Oz.

Nothing was airborne at the moment and all the kites were undercover in one or other of the ten hangars. There were two other flight lieutenants, each in charge of a small squadron of Hurricanes, as well as a pilot officer and a flying officer. The squadrons were small so didn't require more than a couple of officers to run them. As he was adjutant he outranked all of them and thought he should wander over and speak to the mechanics who would be busy, regardless of the weather, making sure all the kites were airworthy.

This phoney war couldn't go on much longer and the kites and flyers must be ready to go at a moment's notice. The massive bitumen runway at Manston was over three thousand yards long, plus the 500-yard overshoots at each end – the fact that it was also 250 yards wide meant it was perfect to be used for any incoming damaged bombers and fighters. There was ample room for three lanes. Two for the kites based here to land and take off and the third left for emergency landings. He prayed there wouldn't be too many of those once the war in the air kicked off.

He was heading for the warmth of the office, satisfied everything was as it should be, when he thought he ought to inspect the preparations for the dance this afternoon. An RAF flight sergeant had volunteered to drive the lorry and collect the girls later so that was one duty he didn't have today.

Nobody bothered to salute him – he supposed they were rather lax on discipline here and things would have to tighten up once they were fully operational and there were several squadrons based here. He stepped into the warmth of the mess – it was shared by other ranks and NCOs – and was pleasantly surprised by what he saw.

'Angus, old boy, what do you think?' He was greeted by Flight Lieutenant James Miller, who appeared to have taken charge of the event.

'Absolutely splendid, Jimmy. Nothing like streamers and balloons to cheer a place up. Do you have a record player for music?'

'Good God, not bloody likely. You're sadly out of touch, old boy. You should come over here more often. We've got a professional fiddle, and a piano player, in my squadron. Live music all the way. Mind you, it's a good idea to have the backup of a few records. Thanks for reminding me.'

'Good show. Catering organised okay?'

'All tickety-boo. What are the WAAF like? You're the only one that's seen them so far.'

'To tell you the truth, I didn't really take much notice. There's an upper-crust girl, blonde and elegant, and a petite brunette from the East End, but as for the others I couldn't tell you anything about them.'

'It's too bad they're not going to be stationed here at the moment. Having girls around would liven up the evenings.'

'Good God, have you taken leave of your senses? They wouldn't be allowed in here – I've been checking up on places that have fully functioning WAAF on base and they have their own facilities, canteens and so on. No fraternising apart from at functions like this.'

'Bloody shame, if you ask me. Small wonder you've not allowed them here as there's absolutely nowhere ready for them. In fact, I can't see there being anything set up in the foreseeable.'

'I'd come to that conclusion myself. I've already been in touch with Victory House and the six of them will be transferred to Marham in Norfolk. There was a cock-up somewhere and they were sent to Manston by mistake. They have to remain where they are until the weather improves. I've not told Lady Harcourt or the girls, so keep mum until I've spoken to them tomorrow.'

'Righto, will do. The only good thing about this bloody awful weather is that the Luftwaffe are grounded too.'

Angus admired the bar that had been set up in the mess hall and carefully didn't ask how so much beer and other things had been acquired. 'How many are you expecting to come from the village?'

'We spread the word at the Rose and Crown and the Brewery Tavern and wouldn't be surprised if we were jammed to the rafters. The bloke collecting the WAAF is going to stop at both pubs to pick up anyone who wants a lift. They might have to do a couple of trips – I take it you've no objection?'

'You'd take no notice if I had. No, there are hundreds of men on this base with nothing much to do and a bit of a knees-up will do us all good. I feel sorry for the poor bastards stuck in northern France. There are squadrons of Blenheims, Hurries and the vile Fairey Battles, based on temporary airstrips out there.'

'The Aussies are expecting to be posted there when the weather improves. Do you think we'll get the promised squadrons of Spits?'

'God knows, for I certainly don't. The building of the new accommodation for officers and the officers' mess can't be finished until the weather improves. As soon as that's done, Win Co said, we'll be fully operational. We've already got sufficient hangars for several squadrons and the accommodation for the ground crew to maintain them.'

'Do you hope to get a flight of your own here or do you think you'll be posted elsewhere?'

'I haven't the foggiest. I'm used to being moved about the place as I've been a regular for the best part of five years. As long as I get command of a flight, if not a squadron, and preferably one of Spits, then I'll be happy.'

Billings was ten years his senior but looked younger than thirty-three. He was a good-looking man, clean-shaven, just above average height, and Angus was surprised his superior officer had never been married.

Jimmy had command of Squadron 79, Hurries. The Aussies were under the command of Flight Lieutenant Drummond. He and Billings had their own rooms but the other two had to share as accommodation was limited at the moment. The rooms they were presently occupying would be given over to admin and other equally important things once the accommodation building for them was completed.

Angus hated being inactive but there was little for him to do when there were no flights in or out of the base. There were two airmen running the office and they were adequate at their job but both of them would much rather be doing something more interesting than answering the telephone, typing letters and dealing with men who wanted a twenty-four-hour pass, a sick note or something else equally mundane.

As he was acting adjutant, he dealt with all disciplinary matters as well as everything else. His CO must be even more bored than he was with the inactivity. Angus couldn't wait to be get a clean bill of health and get his active posting. Dislocating his shoulder had been a damned nuisance but at least he was doing something vaguely useful being here.

* * *

There was more than enough room for three of the girls in the back of the Bentley and it seemed unfair not to offer to take the extra passengers.

'Why don't you draw lots to see who gets to go in the Bentley and who has to sit in the back of that lorry?'

'No need, Miss Harcourt, three of us will travel to the dance in your car and the other three will return in it,' Eleanor, the elegant blonde, said.

'I've put out some spare rugs and a few cushions for you to take. I have to ask – don't you have anything warmer to wear than that thing that looks like a groundsheet?'

Ada replied. 'No, we ain't got greatcoats like the officer what came to collect us had. Blooming cheek, if you ask me, expecting us to keep from freezing without a proper coat.'

'I heard that when the war started the new recruits didn't even have a uniform – the powers that be just weren't ready for so many of us to volunteer,' one of the other girls said. 'Anyway, we're well protected underneath.' She laughed and raised the hem of her skirt to reveal knee-length bloomers. 'These are known as blackouts – more like passion killers if you ask me.'

Sarah laughed with them but couldn't help being shocked at the freedom with which they exposed their underwear, even if it was only to each other. 'They look very warm, but certainly not glamorous.'

Ada sensed her unease. 'You wouldn't believe what we've had to do to become WAAFs, miss. We had to parade in front of them medics in just our knickers. We had to change when we got our uniforms – strip to our birthday suits – so no time to be bashful.'

Mummy had joined them, looking stunning in her afternoon tea dress, and smiled at the conversation.

'Good heavens,' Sarah said, 'sounds just like my boarding school. Communal bathing and no doors on the WCs. One gets used to the lack of privacy. It sounds as if being a member of the WAAF is very similar.'

'I'll bet you didn't get someone peering down your knickers to see if you'd got lice,' Ada said to gales of laughter from the others.

The jolly gathering was broken up as the lorry trundled in. The three going in that vehicle this time grabbed the cushions and blankets and dashed out to the front door.

'I'll lock up, Sarah, you take the young ladies out to the car,' Mummy said as she bolted the door.

They both had on thick winter boots as well as their warmest coats. It might be reasonable inside the Bentley but there was always a slight chance it would break down so it was better to be prepared. Sarah had already put a shovel, two blankets and a thermos of tea in the boot and she had a powerful torch in her bag.

'The car's in the barn over there,' she said as she pointed across the yard. 'It'll be a lot easier for you to get in whilst we're still inside.'

They scrambled onto the leather seat in the rear of the luxurious car, exclaiming in delight at what they saw. There was ample room in the front passenger footwell for both gas masks and shoe bags to be stored.

It was still light, even a little weak winter sunshine, which would make the drive easier in this direction. She was determined to note every bump, rut and danger on the way there so she could avoid them when she was driving in the dark on the way back.

The base was unfamiliar to Sarah as neither she nor her mother had accepted any of the invitations to visit. There was a huddle of brick buildings to the left of the entrance and she headed in that direction. Her eyes widened when she saw the size of the runway, which seemed to stretch for miles in both directions. She was disappointed there were no aircraft on show as she'd never seen one up close.

There was no sign of the lorry and they definitely hadn't passed it on the way. But there was no time to worry about the missing vehicle as a veritable horde of grey-blue emerged from the largest building eager to introduce themselves. It looked as if they were the first to arrive, as the Bentley was the only vehicle there so far.

Her heart thudded and her fingers closed over the steering wheel. This was going to be worse than she'd thought.

5

Angus was talking to Tony when there was a mass exodus from the mess hall. 'I think the first of the guests have arrived. As the senior officer, I think you should be the one to greet them and to make sure the chaps don't misbehave.'

'They take more notice of you than they do of me, old boy, so why don't we go together?'

A massive dark-blue Bentley had just pulled up. Good God – the Harcourt girl was driving it. Seeing that the men were about to surround the vehicle, Angus had no option but to intervene. He shouldered his way through the crush and his expression was enough to disperse the men.

There were two mechanics about to open the nearest doors. 'Clear off, you two. This isn't the way to greet our guests. Wait inside until you're introduced.'

One jumped back without argument but the other ignored him. He stepped up and gripped the man's shoulder. 'That was an order. Remove yourself if you don't want to be on a charge.'

For a horrible moment, Angus thought he'd misjudged the situation and the man he had hold of was going to swing a punch. Then the matter was resolved by Lady Harcourt pushing open the door.

'Good afternoon, Flight Lieutenant Trent, thank you for coming out to meet us,' she said brightly as she swung her booted feet to the concrete.

'Thank you for coming, my lady.' The man he had hold of shook his head in disgust and with a few muttered curses shrugged himself free and returned to the mess hall. This insolence and insubordination would have to be dealt with before it got out of hand – but not today – it could wait until tomorrow.

Then three WAAF tumbled out of the rear of the vehicle and, with a nervous look in his direction, dashed after the airmen. Tony stepped in front of him.

'Allow me to introduce myself, my lady, I am Wing Commander Anthony Billings, but my friends call me Tony.' He offered his arm as if he was someone out of a Jane Austen novel and she took it.

'Gosh, that could have been unpleasant, flight lieutenant. Thank you for intervening.'

'Happy to oblige, ma'am. Do you want me to offer my arm to take you in?' Angus asked as he turned to Sarah.

'Of course I do. As, after my mother, I'm the most important person here.' She laughed up at him and he returned her smile.

'Then let's get inside. The sun might be out but it's bloody cold.'

'Do all RAF officers swear as much as you do, flight lieutenant?'

'Probably more – do I have to apologise for using inappropriate language in your presence?'

'You do, but do it at the end of the evening as no doubt you'll offend me several times and there is little point in repeating yourself.'

This time he laughed out loud. She really was an entertaining companion. 'How old are you, if you don't mind me asking?'

'I do mind. It's just not done to ask a lady her age. However, I'll tell you mine if you tell me yours first.'

'I'm twenty-three, and my birthday's in September.' He thought she might avoid answering but was wrong.

'I'm seventeen and my birthday is in September too. I was thinking I might join the WAAF but after hearing that they have to sleep on biscuits and parade semi-naked I've changed my mind.'

Her fingers clenched on his arm and he realised that, despite her apparent confidence, she was nervous.

'Don't worry, I'll make sure nobody upsets you tonight. I'll wait here whilst you put your coat and things in the cloakroom.'

From the noise outside, the lorry had turned up with its first load of villagers. Sarah emerged, looking surprisingly attractive in a pretty blue floral frock that emphasised her tiny waist. He hadn't noticed before that her figure was excellent – she obviously wore clothes that disguised her curves.

'Come on, Miss Harcourt...'

'Please, will you call me Sarah? I feel like a schoolmistress being addressed as Miss Harcourt all the time.'

'Only if you agree to call me Angus.' He was pleased when she nodded. 'Let's move from here as, from the sound of it, we're about to be invaded by a lorry full of villagers.'

He put his arm lightly around her shoulders but she flinched and moved away. Had she been frightened by some bastard when she was younger? None of his business, but this wasn't what he'd expected. He'd never had this sort of reaction from any woman before.

The two-man band were in situ and about to start playing. The three girls who had arrived with Sarah were already paired up and to his surprise Lady Harcourt was partnering Tony.

'Will you dance with me? I've no idea what they're going to play but I'm prepared to take a chance if you are.'

'Because I'm so tall, I always had to be the male at school so am absolutely useless at any sort of dancing, apart from country dancing where it doesn't matter as much.'

The piano and violin launched into a lively polka. Sarah nodded happily. 'I can do this one – I don't see Mummy doing it with your CO. She's more a waltz or quickstep sort of person.'

He put his arm around her waist and took her hand and they were off. It was like dodgem cars at a fairground as he constantly had to change direction to avoid colliding with the others careering around the floor with as much enthusiasm as he and Sarah were. Even her mother appeared to be enjoying the experience.

By the time the music stopped, the noise of people enjoying themselves made it impossible to hold a conversation without shouting. God knows what it would be like when the lorry returned with a second load of people. He pointed to the room where the bar was and mimed drinking. She nodded and this time allowed him to steer her through the crush.

It was marginally quieter in here. 'I'm having a pint, what would you like? They seem to have a decent choice. Lemonade, ginger beer or orange squash?'

She spoke directly to the barman. 'Thank you, I'll have a weak shandy please, unless there's tea or coffee.'

'Tea later, miss, with the buns and that. So it'll have to be shandy for now.'

Once they had their drinks, he suggested that they retreat to the far side of the bar where there were a couple of tables with chairs, more or less out of the way. He pulled one out for her and was amused to see her smooth her skirt underneath her bottom before she sat down.

'I suppose I should be grateful you didn't ask for a sherry or a G & T.'

'I've tried all the usual culprits – my parents thought it better that I learned how to drink alcohol before I went to university, not that it matters now. I discovered I don't really like anything apart from dry white wine, champagne and shandy. Actually, as it's an afternoon shindig I was rather hoping there'd be coffee or tea.'

'A sophisticated palate for someone of your age. Have you changed your mind about going to Oxford to study medicine?'

'Our financial circumstances have changed, not my mind. I think I might train to be a nurse instead as I'll get paid, whereas if I study medicine it will cost a small fortune.'

'That's a shame. There are half a dozen hopeful airmen coming this way. Do you want to dance with one of them?'

Her look of absolute horror made him smile. 'No, thank you, Angus, if you don't mind, if I dance at all I prefer it to be with you.'

* * *

Joanna had found the polka rather too energetic for her taste and much preferred the waltz that followed. Tony, as he'd insisted that she called him, was an excellent dancer, far better than David. As they made their third turn of the floor, she noticed her daughter in the side room that was being used as a bar, holding half a pint of shandy and accompanied by the handsome flight lieutenant.

'After this dance, Tony, could we find ourselves something to drink? I've not been so energetic in years and I'm terribly thirsty.'

'Then we'd better go in now before everyone else has the same idea. What's your poison?'

'I prefer wine, but I doubt there'll be any available.'

'There's beer, sherry, gin and a variety of soft drinks.'

'Then lemonade would be splendid, thank you.'

He danced them all the way to the bar much to the amusement of those watching. He ordered the drinks and then nodded towards a second room, much larger, that led from this one. 'That's the canteen – there's afternoon tea being served later on. Scones, real butter and jam, a variety of cakes, and sandwiches with recognisable fillings.'

'That sounds quite delicious. I imagine that service people aren't affected by rationing as civilians are.'

'So far we've had no complaints from the men, but things might be different in a few months.'

There was a row of trestle tables at the far side of the room covered with what looked suspiciously like old curtains. Didn't they have tablecloths in the RAF?

'My husband is with the BEF in northern France. Must be absolutely beastly for them, up to their armpits in snow.'

'I don't expect the officers will be roughing it – we usually manage to find a comfortable billet. I expect Angus has told you the girls were sent to us by mistake.'

'Oh dear, no, he hasn't. Does that mean they will be leaving tomorrow?'

'Victory House said they can remain with you until the weather improves. They should be in Norfolk somewhere.'

'The poor dears have no proper outdoor clothes. I don't understand how you men can walk around in greatcoats and expect the girls to manage with little more than a groundsheet to keep out the cold.'

'That's the reason they can stay here for now. I'm told greatcoats are being provided but God knows when they will have enough for our temporary WAAF.'

Joanna sipped her lemonade, found it too sweet, but hid her distaste as she had no wish to upset her escort. It had been so long since she'd been out anywhere and she was finding it all rather exciting. David would disapprove but he wasn't here and he'd told her to get on with things in his absence. He obviously didn't mean her to go out to a dance – even if it was an afternoon dance – but she was glad that she'd come.

Tony leaned over and removed the glass from her hand. 'Disgusting stuff, you're not enjoying it. You'd be better off with a glass of water.'

'I would, but maybe a small G & T would do instead?'

'I'll see what I can do. Don't go away – I won't be long.'

Joanna hadn't been sitting by herself for many minutes when her daughter dashed in. Where had her handsome partner gone?

'Mummy, I wondered where you'd gone. Have you been abandoned by the wing commander?'

'No, darling, he's gone to replace my lemonade with a gin and tonic. I know it's rather early to be drinking alcohol but I don't want to appear unsociable.'

'I'm so glad that you're enjoying it and I wish I was too. It's a frightful crush in there and far too hot.'

'Sit down, Sarah, there's something I've just found out and you need to know.' She quickly explained about the WAAF and their imminent departure.

'We knew they weren't staying long, Mummy. If they're not going until the weather improves then they might well be here for as long as we'd originally thought. I was thinking that maybe we could make this a permanent thing. We're so close to Ramsgate and there must be plenty of female service personnel of one sort or another looking for lodgings.'

'That sounds like a splendid idea. I'll leave you to look into the possibility of us becoming a boarding house – your father would be most displeased if ever he found out.'

'Daddy shouldn't have left us without enough money to pay the bills. He won't know anything about it as nobody in the village will tell him even if they did know where to send the letters.' Sarah stood up abruptly as she saw Tony returning. 'I don't intend to stay to the end, just until after tea is served. The three girls expecting a lift back will have to decide if they want to come in comfort and leave early or remain and travel in the back of a lorry.'

* * *

Sarah was reluctant to go back into the main hall and didn't know where Angus was. She was dithering in the doorway when an airman blocked her way.

'Dance with me?'

Even if she'd liked the look of him, which she didn't, she would have refused. The duo was now playing a foxtrot and she absolutely didn't want to show herself up with a complete stranger.

'No, thank you, I'm not dancing much tonight.'

The man's expression changed. 'Not good enough for you? You posh birds think you're better than us but you're happy to let us die to keep you in luxury.'

Sarah was so shocked by his aggression she couldn't think of anything sensible to say. He was standing far too close – she didn't want to make a scene but didn't know how to get away from him.

'There you are, Sarah, I was hoping you would introduce me to some people from the village.' Angus appeared at her side and stepped between her and the unpleasant airman as if he wasn't there.

'I'd be happy to. My mother's in the canteen, so it seems that I didn't have to worry about her. I was just coming to tell you.'

This time when he put his arm protectively around her shoulders she didn't flinch away and allowed him to guide her around the edge of the heaving room to the comparative safety of the end which had been set out with tables and chairs for those who didn't want to participate in the dancing.

'Good heavens, that's Holy Joe. I do hope he's not going to get up and start preaching and wave one of his placards about.'

'Holy Joe? Which one is he?'

Sarah nodded towards the small man with pebble glasses leaning against the wall scowling at everybody enjoying themselves. 'He's got a small shop in Alma Street where he sells pink and blue paraffin, kindling and small bags of coal. Anyone who goes in there has to be desperate as they know they're going to be harangued about God and told that they're unrepenting sinners before they can escape with their purchases.'

'Do I have to worry about him causing problems?'

'I was joking when I said that. He'll behave himself this afternoon as he's come for the free food and beer. He turns up at every village event and lurks in a corner glaring. Mind you, I always hide if I see him coming towards me in the High Street.'

There were no empty seats but they'd found a quiet space where they could talk without being buffeted by the crowd and could still hear each other over the din.

'Is that when he waves his placards? Why would he pick on you? I've never seen anyone who looks less like a sinner.' Angus was obviously amused by this eccentric villager.

'He doesn't like children of any sort and doesn't seem to have noticed that I've grown up.'

'Must be the glasses he wears – they look like bottle tops.' His smile was warm and there was something in his eyes that made her cheeks flush. 'No one would mistake you for a child, especially in that lovely dress.'

'I thought you wanted to meet villagers, not talk nonsense. I'm not going to introduce you to him. Have you met the vicar and his wife or the local doctor?

'I haven't. We have church parade on the base but we don't get him, we get his curate. I don't think I told you that I've not been at Manston for long. I was only posted here in November.'

'Where were you before that? I seem to remember you said you were a regular – does this mean you joined straight from school?'

'Exactly. I was trained at Cranwell and it took them six months to decide I was fit to be an RAF officer and another eighteen for them to decide I was safe to fly a kite unsupervised. I expect things will be different as the war progresses and we need more pilots and officers.'

'Are all pilots officers?'

'They were when I graduated but not now – there are already some NCO pilots and I expect it will be commonplace if this bloody war carries on as long as I fear it might.'

'How awfully depressing – Daddy said it would be all over by Christmas when he was called back. In the olden days the heir to a title wouldn't have joined the army in case they were killed. As far as I know, there isn't anyone to take over when my father dies.'

'What happens then?'

'The title becomes extinct. Fortunately, the estate isn't entailed, otherwise I think it would go to the state. Mummy's terrified that there might be someone, a distant male cousin, who will turn up and expect to take everything.'

He was looking at her strangely and she realised she'd been talking as if Daddy's death was inevitable. 'I know it must sound callous talking like this but it's best to be prepared, don't you think? Last time millions of soldiers died.'

'That's true, but very few civilians. This war will be different – the likelihood of gas attacks isn't certain but I think the Luftwaffe will definitely bomb this country. They've already had practice doing this during the Spanish Civil War.'

'What a depressing conversation to be having at a dance. We don't have an Anderson shelter as we've got massive cellars under the house. I defy any German bomb to reach us down there. Did you know there are disused tunnels that used to take the trains to the coast in Ramsgate? I've heard that these are now going to be the public air-raid shelters in the event of an attack.'

'I'd heard something about that. I've just realised none of the visitors in here at the moment knows where our shelters are. I should have announced their whereabouts before this bun fight started. A bit late to do that now as I think there'd be a riot if I tried to stop them dancing.'

His mention of dancing made her look nervously across the room in case the belligerent airman was somewhere about. It was hard to tell one from the other as they were all dressed identically. There must have been about thirty villagers scattered amongst the crowded floor – but most of them were women. The young men had already been conscripted or volunteered, unless they were working on one of the local farms.

'I know the name of the bastard who upset you. He's a troublemaker – one of the mechanics with a massive chip on his shoulder. Don't worry, I'll deal with him tomorrow. He's a member of the Communist Party...'

'Well, good for him. Better than a member of the fascists. Let's not talk about him. I can just about manage a waltz – if you don't mind having your toes trodden on, would you care to dance with me?'

Sarah wasn't sure if she was pleased that Angus had stepped in or cross that he felt she needed to be protected by him. After all, she hardly knew him, did she?

6

Angus didn't need asking twice. He'd much rather dance with Sarah than with someone he didn't know. 'Why don't you stand on my toes and let me carry you around?'

'I'm no lightweight, even if it was a sensible suggestion you wouldn't be able to move with me standing on you like that.'

'Let's give it a go. You can always get off if it doesn't work. After a few turns around the floor I expect you'll have got the hang of it anyway.'

They both knew the idea was ridiculous but as soon as they were safely in the throng on the dance floor she carefully stepped onto his shoes. What neither of them had considered was that this meant she was now far closer to him than she would have been otherwise.

He didn't give her the chance to change her mind but held her close with one arm and gripped her other hand in his. Every inch of her was pressed against him and the softness of her breasts was having a disastrous effect. He moved a few yards and pretended to stumble.

'This won't work. Let's do it the conventional way.'

She was the correct distance so fast he had a nasty suspicion she'd been aware of his arousal. She wasn't perhaps as naïve as he'd thought.

It didn't really matter if she didn't know the steps, as it was impossible to dance properly with so many couples milling about. After a few minutes, he stopped moving and drew her a little closer but not close enough to cause the same reaction.

'Do you want to continue or shall we make a dash for the bar and refill our glasses?'

'To tell you the truth, I'm not enjoying this at all. I really don't like being in a crush and although I hate to say so, a lot of the people – including some of your airmen – would have done well to have taken a bath before they came out tonight.'

He shouldered his way to the edge of the floor and then keeping her hand in his led her into the comparative peace of the bar. 'I doubt that many here have access to a bathroom as you do.'

She was unbothered by his gentle reprimand. 'Everyone has access to soap and water.'

'It's the worst weather we've had in Britain for decades. How do you think ordinary folk can get their laundry dry?'

She stopped so suddenly he cannoned into her and they both narrowly avoided ending up on the floor. Whilst he'd been struggling to regain his balance and keep her from falling, she'd remained within his grasp, but as soon as they were steady she stepped away.

'Point taken, flight lieutenant. My mother called me a snob the other day and now you've confirmed her opinion. Excuse me, I'm going to find the powder room.'

She was gone before he could react. He watched her move gracefully through the crowd and was aware how many admiring glances she got from the men she hurried past. For some reason, their interest annoyed him.

He wasn't going in search of her – he'd monopolised her for far too long and didn't want to cause comment – but he'd keep a careful watch and make sure none of the men under his command did anything to cause her further distress.

After circulating, stopping to talk to as many from the village as he could, he returned to the tables and chairs thinking Sarah must be sitting down and that's why he couldn't see her. But she wasn't there. He was now seriously concerned as she'd been absent for almost an hour and it had just been announced that the afternoon tea was about to be served.

From his height he could see over the heads of most of the people in the room and was quite certain she wasn't there. He would find Lady Harcourt and ask her if she knew where her daughter was. She too appeared to have vanished into thin air but he saw Tony heading for the canteen and pushed his way through the crowd so he could speak to him.

'Have the Harcourts gone home, Tony? I can't find either of them.'

'The girl was feeling unwell and Joanna insisted on returning with her. They left some time ago. Don't look so disappointed, old bean, they're both out of our league. Plenty of pretty popsies here tonight for us to canoodle with.'

'I'm not interested in canoodling with anyone, Tony. I've got a couple of things I need to do in the office but I'll be back in an hour.'

He hadn't bothered to bring his greatcoat to the dance as finding it again would have proved difficult with so many other coats piled in heaps on the tables in the cloakroom. God knows how anyone would find their own belongings and boots when the event finished.

The temperature had dropped by several degrees, the cold caught his throat and he could feel the inside of his nostrils freezing. The concrete had been cleared of snow but there were patches of ice underfoot which were potentially lethal. The fact that it was now dark didn't help.

When he shone his torch to where the Bentley had been parked, he saw Tony was right – Lady Harcourt and Sarah had gone home. He didn't blame them, he was going to abandon the dance too. There didn't seem much point being there now Sarah had gone home.

He slithered his way across to the offices and his own billet and fumbled for his keys. He thought to try the door and it opened. Some silly bugger had forgotten to lock up – the petty cash was kept here as well as records and information that wasn't exactly top secret, but certainly not for general consumption.

The interior of the building was pleasantly warm but it took him a few moments to recover. It occurred to him that returning the villagers was going to be considerably more perilous than bringing them. Holding a dance in this weather had been a bad idea and he should have cancelled it and put up with the flak that would have followed from the enlisted men.

The blackouts were permanently drawn so there was no need to worry about putting on the lights although he doubted there would be any vigilant wardens about tonight. There certainly wouldn't be any Luftwaffe coming to drop bombs. So far, the only enemy kites they'd seen had been reconnaissance aircraft and most of those had been chased off.

RAF bases would be the first places to be attacked and being only a mile from the coast closest to France meant Manston was likely to get a hammering once things kicked off. He pushed the sombre thought aside and went to the cabinet to find the file he needed for tomorrow.

AC2 Frederick Jenkins had volunteered at the start of the war, which somewhat contradicted his belligerent attitude and statement that men like him were being used as cannon fodder. His membership of the Communist Party meant he would never get a commission, and was unlikely to get promotion either. If Stalin's Russia remained neutral then he rather thought anyone with such affiliations might well be in trouble with the authorities.

Angus filled out the requisite forms to put the man on a charge for insubordination and behaviour towards civilians which brought the service into disrepute. Tomorrow he would have the man arrested and brought before him. He would have Jenkins transferred if necessary. This wasn't the first time the man had been in trouble and it needed to be dealt with now. Tony had been too lax where discipline was concerned.

* * *

Sarah was relieved to reach Goodwill House without mishap. 'There was no need for you to come back with me, Mummy. I didn't want to ruin your afternoon.'

'Good heavens, darling, do you really think I would have been prepared to travel in the back of a lorry in this gown? No, I did enjoy myself but was quite ready to return.'

Her mother jumped out of the Bentley close to the side door and Sarah drove it into the barn alone. This gave her a valuable few minutes to decide exactly how she was going to explain her reasons for deciding to abandon the party so precipitously.

She wasn't exactly sure herself what had made her decide to leave. It had been a combination of the unpleasant experience with the airman and the exchange between herself and Angus. She tried not to think of herself as better than others, but her upbringing had made her see that her life was quite different from the majority of those she met.

The house they lived in was the largest in the neighbourhood by far and, until the turn of the century, she was pretty sure the family had once owned thousands of acres – had been indecently wealthy. Where had the money gone? It couldn't all have been lost when businesses crashed a few years ago. She'd been too young to be bothered about outside events and had been more interested in her pony.

A flurry of snow enveloped her as she struggled to close the barn doors. She shivered. There was definitely another blizzard on its way and she hoped the girls would get home safely. Bates had shut up the poultry before he'd left and there was no need for her to check on the horses as that was his job.

Once in the house she removed her boots, hung up her thick coat and shoved her feet into her slippers. The house was eerily quiet – surely her mother hadn't retired so soon? They'd not stayed for tea and so both of them would need something to eat.

'Mummy, I'm going to light the fires upstairs so it will be warm when the girls get back. It's snowing again.'

'There's no need to yell, Sarah, I'm in the kitchen, not the other side of the house,' her mother called back brightly.

'Put the kettle on, I'll be down shortly.'

It didn't take long to get the fires going as the girls had left them ready to light. The coal cellar was accessed from the boot room so there was no necessity to go outside to get the coal or logs to keep the fires and the range burning.

As she was already upstairs, she decided to take off her smart frock and change into her usual outfit of dungarees and jumper. Not flattering, but comfortable and warm.

The kitchen as always was the warmest room in the house and Sarah wasn't surprised to find her mother sitting at the table looking at last week's newspaper.

'Let's eat now as our guests won't want anything other than cocoa and toast. They'll have stuffed themselves with the free afternoon tea. I almost wish I'd stayed now as the thought of scones, jam and cream is rather appealing.'

'I think they should have cancelled the event,' said her mother. 'I wouldn't be surprised if there's at least one accident on the way home, not just because of the weather, but because some of those who came on foot might well be inebriated and end up dying of hypothermia in a ditch.'

'That's a happy thought, Mummy. The RAF invited them so it's up to them to get them home safely. I'll be glad when the weather improves as I've missed my weekly St John's ambulance meetings. I've been thinking, if I can't be a doctor then I'm going to train to be a nurse as having passed all the St John's exams I'm already well qualified to do that.'

'I couldn't possibly allow you to do that, Sarah. Your father wouldn't want you to do something that involved emptying bedpans and other awful things. Becoming a doctor is quite different – you would be giving the orders and the menial tasks would be carried out by the nurses.'

'I'm not prepared to sit around doing nothing, Mummy.'

'Daddy wouldn't approve and I must stand in his stead.'

'If I did decide to become a nurse, I could train at Ramsgate General. All nurses have to live in, but I'd be paid to train instead of having to pay. When I got a day off, I could come and see you, I wouldn't be able to do that if I joined one of the services.'

'I wouldn't allow you to do that either. I'm sure you have to have your parents' permission to do anything until you come of age...'

'There's a war on, Mummy, and we've all got to do our bit. Daddy has gone to fight the Germans in France and I'm quite possibly going to train to be a nurse and you will be accommodating female service personnel here. Nobody can say that the Harcourt family are slackers.'

'You can't leave me in this house on my own with six people to cater for. I only know how to make an omelette and vegetable soup.'

Sarah laughed, gently. 'Betty will be back long before I go – I can't enrol until I'm seventeen and a half and that won't be until March.'

The kettle whistled and Sarah made the tea. They had scrambled eggs on toast and bottled plums and evaporated milk. The dance should have finished and it only took fifteen minutes to drive from the base.

'I'd better unlock the front door as the girls will be back soon.'

She wasn't envious of the girls, she didn't like crowds, and certainly wouldn't accept any further invitations to the base. However, she had enjoyed talking to Angus and wouldn't object to spending a little more time with him.

* * *

The following morning there were icicles on the inside of the window. Sarah scrambled out of bed, collected her underwear and clothes, and got dressed under the covers. The girls had told her last night that they had enjoyed their outing and were delighted they could stay in comparative luxury, with absolutely nothing to do apart from domestic chores, until the weather improved.

Sarah headed downstairs to get the range riddled so she could prepare the morning porridge. She hated it – gloopy, slimy stuff – but their guests had asked to have it served so she had no choice but to stand over a saucepan of oats stirring constantly until it thickened. She made it with milk and served it with sugar and jam, but even with these sweet additives she wouldn't eat it herself.

The blackouts were left in place until after breakfast so she'd no idea if the weather had worsened overnight. Occasionally, the windows rattled so there was obviously a storm of some sort raging outside. If it was too bad, neither Bates nor Billy would be able to come so, once the guests were fed, she'd have to go out and see to the horses herself.

This was another thing she must deal with before she left – if she did pluck up the courage to go. The horses were an expensive luxury they couldn't afford. She would try to find homes for the three of them because if she didn't, they could end up at the knacker's yard. This would be a dreadful shame as they were all thoroughbreds and had cost Daddy a fortune. There had always been horses here but these two weren't hers and she couldn't afford to be sentimental about keeping them.

She pushed this horrible thought aside. There was enough fodder and bedding for one winter and as soon as it got warmer the three horses would be turned out in their rugs. If she had their shoes removed, that would be one less cost.

The sound of voices approaching meant the WAAF were on their way. Mummy had yet to put in an appearance – she preferred to get up when all the work was done. That was going to have to change if she wanted Goodwill House to survive the war.

* * *

Joanna had greeted the girls last night but left Sarah to deal with them and hear all their excited chatter about who they'd danced with and so on. She'd retreated to the small sitting room they used and had been delighted that the fire had been lit for her. She'd had a lot to think about and none of it pleased her.

If her daughter insisted on enrolling either as a student nurse or in one of the services, then running the house would be left to her and Betty. When she'd been living at home, Joanna hadn't had to do more than hang up her own clothes – everything else had been done by a live-in maid. The house and kitchen had been run efficiently by Mrs Hendry so she'd never had to take care of herself.

On her marriage, she'd been even more mollycoddled as David wouldn't allow her to lift a finger. A servant would be fetched even to open the curtains or put a log on the fire. Running this enormous house with just one inside servant was going to mean she'd have to do a lot of the menial tasks herself.

Only now did she understand just how much Sarah must have been doing to keep the household running smoothly since the war started, and without a murmur of complaint. Being chairman of the WVS and an active member of the WI was something within her capabilities, something she was confident doing, but housework, cooking and other mundane tasks didn't appeal to her at all. Goodness knows how she was going to cope if she was left in charge of running the house and it was full of boarders.

Another thing she wasn't familiar with was being in charge of finances. David had paid all the bills and taken care of that side of things and since he'd gone she was just muddling through. She was Lady Harcourt, everybody in the village looked up to her, she had standards to adhere to and couldn't let the side down.

What would people think if they knew she was so short of money she had to take in lodgers and act as cleaner and housekeeper herself? Her mind wasn't any clearer today. She recalled word for word last night's conversation with Sarah.

'Mummy, the girls have gone up and said they'd make their own cocoa later. This is the last of the coffee and I doubt we'll get any more. Even if it was available in the village stores, it's too expensive for us now.'

'Sarah, I've decided that you can't leave here until you've got permission from your father. I'm going to write to him now. The letters seem to take about two weeks to reach him and the same to return so you should get your answer by the end of February.'

'I wish you wouldn't tell him. Hasn't he got enough to worry about fighting the Germans? Wouldn't it be better just to get on with things the way we think is best?'

'It wouldn't be right for me to make that sort of decision without him.'

'Then, obviously, you'll be telling him about our arrangement with the RAF? That we've got to get rid of Bates and his son, that I'm going to sell the horses?'

'Of course I'm not going to tell him any of that. Anything to do with you is quite different, as well you know.'

'If I'm old enough to run this house, do all the things that I do, then I'm quite old enough to make decisions about my own future. Anyway, I expect unmarried women will be conscripted at some point and I don't want to be forced to do something I don't want to by the government.'

'I don't wish to discuss it any further, Sarah. Did the girls enjoy themselves? Did you tell them they'd been sent to Manston in error?'

'They had a splendid time and I think at least one of them will be seeing one of the airmen again. I didn't need to tell them they were here by mistake – they already knew that.'

Despite her daughter's reservations, Joanna had written to her husband, asking his opinion about her becoming a nurse. If she asked Bates to post it on his way home, it should reach David in a week or so. Hopefully, there would be a reply before Sarah actually applied to the hospital in Ramsgate. Was she being disloyal to Sarah or being a good wife by sending the letter? Life had been so much simpler when David had been there to make the decisions.

7

Angus put the bolshie airman on fatigue duty. There was a mountain of snow to clear from the paths and he joined two others who'd also disgraced themselves last night. It was a bit like painting the Forth Bridge – as fast as they cleared it, more snow was coming down. Serve them bloody well right. They'd think twice about stepping out of line again.

There was no point in getting the snowploughs out on the runway until the blizzard had passed. The Met report had forecast continuing snow and strong winds for the next few days. The bastard Germans wouldn't be moving either as the weather was equally appalling over the whole of northern Europe. According to the chaps who knew about such things, this was the worst storm in living memory.

The completion of the officers' accommodation, mess and recreation room would obviously be stalled until the weather cleared. According to Tony, Squadron 600, the Blenheims and their Aussie crews, should have been posted to France but they were now staying put.

There was a temporary kitchen installed in another room in this admin block with three members of the catering corps in charge. Angus had his own orderly, as did Tony, but the others had to share.

The telephone on his desk jangled and he picked it up. 'I've just had someone from the town council in Ramsgate on, sir, they want to know if we can help them out. They're desperately short of manpower to clear the pavements and roads. Everything's totally blocked.'

'We're not using the snowploughs at the moment so I don't see why not. Round up some volunteers and we'll do what we can. I'll accompany them. If they've got a flight suit and boots then I suggest that they wear them.'

Angus thought that there'd be more men prepared to brave the elements if they knew he was prepared to do so. He went in search of Tony and found him with his feet up on his desk, smoking a pipe and cradling a large mug of tea.

'What ho, old boy. Something up? You look a bit agitated.'

Angus explained what was going on but didn't bother to ask for permission. Tony was so relaxed about the chain of command he might as well not be there.

There was probably something in the rule book that forbade the wearing of flight gear for anything but flying. However, the conditions were arctic and it would be ludicrous to brave the elements in anything but the warmest clothes one had.

The lorry trundled up fifteen minutes later. Although the canvas flaps were closed, from the racket inside he knew it was full. Angus scrambled into the front passenger seat, pleased to see that Jimmy was driving.

'Anyone for the skylark? The blokes with the ploughs have already left. We need to get behind them or we might not get through. With the amount of snow falling, whatever we clear will be back before we've finished.'

'Quite probably. I spoke to the Met chaps and they say we've got another couple of days of this. Then it might be another week before the roads are sorted.'

'Bloody horrible weather even for Blighty. Pity the poor buggers with the BEF.'

There was a path to the gates where the ploughs, each attached to the front of a tractor, had gone ahead of them. The lorry lurched and bumped but appeared stable enough. Obviously, the road through the village that led to Ramsgate was also being cleared.

'There's no hurry, Jimmy, better to let the ploughs do their job. Let's hope they don't come to grief on the steep hill into the town.'

'Good thinking, Skip, I don't think this vehicle will stop safely on a hill.'

The lorry cab was freezing and Angus had to constantly lean forward and wipe the windscreen free of condensation. The men in the back were singing, more likely because they were cold than that they were enjoying the unexpected excursion. He recognised the shape of a huge building on the right which was just visible through the snow – they were passing Goodwill House. They shouldn't be anywhere near it.

Suddenly, Jimmy swore. 'Christ, that's the plough. I hope I can stop in time.'

'The silly arse has turned off the road and taken us onto someone's farm. I can see a gate blocking the path,' Angus shouted above the grinding of the gears and roar of the engine. The lorry slithered sideways.

'Hang on to something, boys, we're going to hit the tractor,' he yelled. Not a moment too soon, as with a hideous inevitability, they collided with the tractor.

They were travelling no more than a couple of miles an hour but the impact was still heavy enough to cause damage. God knows what had happened to the poor sods in the back. He'd braced himself and was totally unscathed.

From the swearing and noise coming from the passengers behind him, they hadn't fared as well. 'I'm going round to see if anyone's hurt. Are you okay, Jimmy?'

'Tickety-boo. Can't say the same for this old girl. Even if she still drives after this shunt, I'll not be able to turn round here.'

'At least the tractor won't be damaged and it can probably tow us back to base if necessary.'

By the time he got around to the rear of the vehicle the flaps were open, the tailgate down and the men were starting to jump out looking none the worse for their experience.

'Bloody hell, sir, this is a turn-up for the books. This don't look like Ramsgate,' one of the men said cheerfully.

'I'm afraid it isn't. We appear to be in the middle of a field – God knows where – but as long as nobody's hurt it's not the end of the world.'

Some wag behind him answered. 'No, sir, it ain't. It's a bleeding farm. No bugger's been injured. Can't say the same for a couple of the shovels, though.'

Jimmy appeared at his side and he grabbed his arm. 'I'm going to check on the chap driving the tractor. Why hasn't he come round to see what damage we've sustained?'

He yelled up at the cab but got no reply. He couldn't see through the steamed-up windows if the driver was in there. Was that a moan coming from somewhere in front of him? The swirling snow made visibility all but impossible.

Using the metal bars of the plough itself to guide him, he felt his way to the front. There was that sound again. His gut twisted. The man driving the tractor must have got out to open the gate and when the lorry hit the back of the tractor he'd been trapped underneath the big metal scoop.

This was an absolute bloody disaster. Why in God's name hadn't it occurred to the bloke there shouldn't be a gate across the road into Ramsgate? He dropped to his knees and shuffled forward, calling out as he did so.

'We'll get you out. Keep still until we lift the plough. Can you hear me? Are you badly hurt or just trapped?' Bloody stupid thing to ask because the poor sod could quite easily be both.

'It's me bleeding leg, sir, I reckon it's broken. I can't move – someone will have to lift it off of me. If you try and back the tractor me bloody leg will come off.'

It was Harrison – he recognised the voice. 'I'll get the men to do it. We've got more than enough here.'

* * *

The girls had asked Sarah whether mealtimes could be more flexible if they were prepared to fend for themselves in the kitchen and she'd readily agreed. This meant she only had to prepare the vegetables and so on and leave them out for the girls to cook when they were ready to eat.

It took an age to bring up sufficient fuel for all the fires but there was no one else to do it – if she was honest, she'd prefer to do the cooking and have the girls do the heavy work. Her mother drifted down at nine o'clock.

'Good heavens, darling, haven't they had their breakfast yet?'

'No, in future they're going to do it themselves when they get up. I've left everything ready. You'll have to make your own toast as I've got to go and do the horses, feed the chickens and collect the eggs, if there are any in this weather.'

'I think I can manage that. You've got smuts on your face but I don't suppose it matters if you're going to go out and shovel manure.'

'It certainly doesn't. It would be lovely to have a bath but I don't suppose I'll get the time so a strip wash will have to do.'

She had on thick woollen slacks, long socks, thick knickers and a vest as well as two jumpers. Hopefully, with her overalls on over the top of all this and then a coat, she'd be warm enough. She couldn't remember it ever having been so cold for so long and even people who liked snow couldn't be enjoying this.

The birds stayed in the barn in the winter where they had ample room to scratch and flap about. She took in the cooked potato peelings and bits and pieces from last night and then stirred in some grain. The chickens, ducks and geese greeted her with a cacophony of honking, quacking and clucking. They fussed around her feet, eager to be fed.

By the time she'd refilled the water trough – which had frozen – and collected four eggs, she was feeling warm, which was a bonus. Her next and most important job was to feed the horses and muck out the stables.

It was considerably warmer in this barn, where she was greeted with just as much enthusiasm. There were four empty stalls from the days when the family had kept teams of carriage horses as well as riding mounts.

'Good morning, lady and gentlemen. Don't make so much noise, I won't be long.' She piled fresh hay in the mangers of the three unoccupied stalls, put in fresh water and then moved each of the animals. It was much easier to muck out when there were no horses in there treading on your feet.

They were rugged up, not at all bothered about having no exercise and fresh air. They seemed to sense that they were better off inside at the moment. It was just after eleven o'clock when she finally emerged, satisfied all three horses would be fine until late afternoon.

As she was closing the door, she thought she heard voices. Who on earth could be out in this weather and why would they be in the home paddock? Fortunately, the wind had dropped a little although, with the snow falling heavily, she couldn't see more than a couple of yards in front of her.

'Hello, is there somebody out there? Follow my voice and it will bring you safely to Goodwill House.' Her voice must've carried because someone yelled back.

'We're bringing an injured man. He needs urgent medical attention and the rest of us need somewhere to thaw out.'

She recognised the voice. 'Flight lieutenant, there's enough room inside for everyone. I'll keep shouting.'

'I can see the building. Don't hang about in the snow. We'll be there in a few minutes.'

Sarah all but fell indoors, shouting for assistance. 'There are dozens of RAF arriving momentarily and one of them is seriously injured. I need everybody here.'

She wasn't sure if Angus would bring his men to the front or to the side door so she wanted somebody standing at both of them. There was no sign of her mother but all six of the WAAF arrived at the double.

'Two of you put on all the saucepans and both kettles to boil. There are three teapots and we're going to need all of them as well as all the mugs and cups you can find. We're about to be invaded.'

The other four waited expectantly to be told what to do next. No one argued with the fact that Sarah was in charge. 'One of you at the boot room door and be ready to let them in if they arrive there and someone else at the front in case they come that way.'

The remaining two she sent to light both fires in the drawing room while she went in search of her first aid kit and the bedding to turn the chaise longue into a bed for the patient. There was absolutely no chance of getting an ambulance or doctor to attend to the injured man so it would have to be her who dealt with it.

Belatedly, her mother arrived from her sitting room. 'Whatever's all the fuss? I really don't like you to shout like a fishwife, Sarah.'

By the time she'd explained the emergency, her mother was fully involved. 'I'll organise the catering and the other necessities but you'll have to see to whatever injuries this man has. Let's hope that you being a fully qualified member of the St John's ambulance is sufficient to deal with whatever injuries the poor fellow has.'

'I can bandage, splint a broken limb, put on a sling and I've watched Dr Willoughby stitch gashes so I'm pretty sure I can do that too.'

There was going to be barely time to gather everything she might need before Angus arrived. She dropped a metal tea plate, three silver needles, a pair of silver scissors, a wooden reel of silk thread and a pair of tweezers into one of the saucepans.

'These need to boil for a couple of minutes. Can you take them out without touching them and bring them in to me on the tin plate that's in there with them?'

Before heading for the downstairs WC, she stripped off her outdoor garments and dumped them in the corner of the boot room. Then she scrubbed her hands and up to her elbows with soap and water and dried them on a clean towel. She shoved her arms into one of Betty's cleanly washed and pressed wrap-around aprons. The best she could do in the circumstances.

Angus and his men had arrived at the front door. Her patient was being carried on a stretcher, made from someone's greatcoat, by four men. She hadn't initially recognised one of the stretcher bearers as Angus as he was wearing his flying gear. A blast of icy air and snow whirled through the grand hall. Then there was no time to think about anything else as the space rapidly filled with dozens of RAF – some in flight suits like Angus but others in greatcoats.

'Bring him through here. Where is he injured?'

'Badly broken right leg.'

Whilst the patient was being gently put on the bed she had made ready, she turned to the others. 'Take off your outdoor garments and boots and give them to the WAAF – they'll find somewhere to hang them until you need them. Then go to the far end of this drawing room – there's plenty of seats but I'm afraid the fire's not been alight for very long but it's a lot warmer than outside.'

Again nobody questioned her authority and one of the men in flying gear, obviously another officer, took charge of the process. 'Thank you, ma'am, your help is much appreciated.'

'The WAAF are making tea and will bring it through when it's ready.' She really couldn't waste any more time issuing instructions, she needed to examine the man with a broken leg.

To her astonishment, he was chatting away as if at a church picnic – although his language would have raised quite a few eyebrows.

'Bleeding hell, ain't this grand? Are we in a blooming palace or what?'

'I'm glad to see you're conscious. I'm Miss Harcourt – I'm the only medical help you're going to get. I'm a fully qualified first-aider and hopefully can patch you up until an ambulance can get here.'

Angus gestured that she step aside and talk to him in private before she examined the man. She ignored him. 'Use the telephone, flight lieutenant, I'm sure there will be someone somewhere who can do whatever you think is necessary.'

One of the girls came in holding the tin plate gingerly in a tea towel with the other items on it. 'Well done; put it on the table there where I can reach it.'

The screens were already arranged around the daybed so both she and the patient had privacy. The only person not bothered about being treated by her was the man with a broken leg himself.

'Right, lovey, you do what you have to. You seem to know what you're doing.'

She pointed to a hovering airman. 'Would you please remove the boot on his uninjured leg and his outer garments for me? I don't want to contaminate my hands by touching anything apart from his injury.'

* * *

Angus was seething. He could hardly pick the wretched girl up bodily and remove her but he was damned if he was going to let someone totally unqualified mess about with one of his men. Then he heard her issue her instructions and wondered if he'd misjudged the situation.

He watched from a few yards away whilst she waited for two chaps to take off Harrison's boot and greatcoat.

'Let me have a look before you touch his damaged leg.' The girl didn't touch anything but stared down at the leg.

'Make sure the laces are removed before trying to take off his boot. Cut it off if necessary. Here, use this knife to cut the seams of his trouser leg. Do it very carefully.'

It was a compound fracture, he could see bone sticking out of the wound. She shouldn't touch this or it could leave the man permanently lame.

'I'm not qualified to straighten the leg and might well do more damage, Mr Harrison...'

'Call me Sid, lovey, more friendly like.'

'Sid, I'm going to put a ring dressing around the break to protect the bone and then I'll put a clean dressing on and splint your leg. As long as you don't move too much, the surgeon at the hospital will be able to set it so you can walk normally when it's mended.'

'Is there anything I can do, apart from making unnecessary telephone calls, Miss Harcourt?'

She didn't look round. 'Nothing, thank you, Flight Lieutenant Trent. All under control here, as you can see. It might be worth ringing the hospital anyway and Dr Willoughby – the local chap – knows what he's doing and might be able to get here before an ambulance. I'd also like to speak to him.'

'Right, ma'am, I'll get on to that.'

The operator connected him with the base first and he briefly explained what had happened.

'The other lot have come back, sir, couldn't get through. Snow's drifted ten feet high and then frozen solid. They wondered what had happened to you and the other plough.'

'We're stuck here for the moment. Make sure Wing Commander Billings is aware.'

Lady Harcourt appeared and handed him a slip of paper with the telephone number of both the hospital and the local quack. He nodded his thanks and was connected to the hospital in Ramsgate. Little point really, as they were totally snowed in, but best to let them know that when things improved they would be getting Harrison to deal with.

His third call was answered immediately. 'Dr Willoughby speaking, how can I help?'

Again Angus gave a brief and clear explanation of the circumstances. 'Is there any chance that you can get to Goodwill House?'

'Not a hope in hell, flight lieutenant. However, Sarah Harcourt is a natural when it comes to medical matters. Can you get her to the telephone?'

He put the receiver down on the table and went to fetch her. 'The doctor wants a word with you. Can you come?'

'Yes, there are one or two things I need to ask him.' She smiled at Harrison who was looking a bit pale and most likely in serious pain.

'I've given him aspirin, but he really needs morphine and of course I don't have any of that.'

She rushed ahead of him and snatched up the telephone. 'I'm concerned that if his leg isn't straightened, doctor, the blood circulation will be cut off and he might end up losing the leg.'

Angus couldn't hear the reply but the girl nodded. She then went on to explain in detail what the injury looked like. She used the correct terminology and sounded just like a fully qualified medic. She listened some more and then handed him the receiver and dashed off.

'Flight lieutenant, Sarah's going to need your assistance. She has to straighten the leg and I've explained how to do it. There might well be considerable bleeding but she's quite capable of putting in any necessary sutures – she's done it a couple of times already. She has also successfully set a broken arm.'

'Jesus wept! I can't let her do that.'

'You can't stop her, young man, because otherwise this Harrison fellow could lose his leg or might well die before either myself or an ambulance can reach him. Get him to drink a tumbler of whisky – or any other spirits – this will ease the pain a little. I'll remain connected as I want to know what's going on.'

'I'm not comfortable with this but it seems I don't have any option.'

Angus had been impressed with Sarah's competence and if the medic was confident then he'd trust her too.

8

Joanna enjoyed giving instructions to others. It was doing the mundane tasks herself she found difficult. Organising the six girls was second nature to her and probably a lot easier than keeping the committee of the WVS in line.

'I expect these airmen will want their tea strong so put plenty in even if it means we have very little left for ourselves.'

'The RAF will replace it, Lady Harcourt, they'll not let you or us go without,' one of them said.

The men might be able to leave if it stopped snowing later today, but the patient obviously couldn't. Good heavens – what if the Germans decided to invade today? Manston would be unable to protect the country if the number of flight suits drying at the far end of the kitchen was anything to go by.

'Ada, there's a passageway running down the side of the drawing room that leads to another entrance into that room. I've no idea how many guests we've got – could you go and count them for me?'

It was always easy to pick out the tiny cockney girl but all the rest looked very similar as they were dressed identically. Ada vanished at speed and was back in a few minutes.

'There's the flight lieutenant, the bloke with a broken leg and one other behind the screens and sixteen at the other end of the room.'

'Thank you, my dear. They'll want feeding as well as tea – I've no idea what we can give them – we don't have nearly enough bread to make sandwiches even if we had something to use as a filling.'

'Soup, ma'am, and jacket potatoes – there's enough vegetables in that horrid cellar place to make soup for twice as many.'

Joanna had no idea who the speaker was but nodded. 'Can you make it? Sarah won't be able to help at the moment.'

'You've got some lovely big pans that will do a treat. You leave it to us, ma'am, in a couple of hours we'll be able to feed an army.'

'Just feeding nineteen RAF will be sufficient. Thank you very much. I think the tea has brewed enough so will you start tipping it into the cups and mugs?'

The WAAF had their own tin mugs and she noticed that they had utilised these. She should have thought of that herself.

'Thank goodness we've got plenty of milk and sugar. I've just remembered, there are half a dozen packets of digestive biscuits somewhere at the back of the pantry. They've been there since November but I expect they're perfectly edible.'

There were a dozen mugs and a dozen utilitarian cups and saucers – she had no intention of using the best china in case it got broken. David had inherited a massive collection of crockery all engraved with his family crest but she couldn't remember the last time any of it had been used.

The biscuits were quickly spread out on plates and then the six girls acted as waitresses, carrying the trays into the drawing room. This wasn't a task she wanted to do herself. She had yet to discover what this band of airmen were doing out in such appalling weather but she wasn't going in search of answers as she had no wish to brave a room full of noisy airmen herself.

Her daughter would know all the details and could tell her later. It was such a shame Sarah couldn't take up her place at Oxford as she would make an absolutely splendid doctor. She'd been a member of the St John Ambulance Brigade since she was in pigtails. In the long summer holidays when she was home from her boarding school she used to ride over to any gymkhana, village fête or garden party in the vicinity and spend the afternoon in the St John tent. At first she had only offered tea and sympathy but by last summer she'd passed all their exams.

This devotion to medicine had convinced David to allow her to apply to university and she wished now she hadn't written to him asking his opinion on Sarah becoming a nurse. Even if he said no, if he wasn't here then he wouldn't be able to stop her. Joanna decided that whatever her daughter wanted to do, she should have her support. If she could handle an emergency like this one with such confidence then it would be quite wrong to stop her becoming either a nurse or a doctor.

Last summer Sarah had set a broken arm and put stitches in a large gash – both patients had been journeymen so were grateful to get free medical attention. They both made a full recovery and now anyone who worked on the estate would always come to her for first aid rather than going to Dr Willoughby and having to pay.

The sight of blood nauseated her so she wasn't going anywhere near the drawing room until she was quite sure whatever was being done by Sarah had been completed.

* * *

Sarah plied Sid with the last of her father's very expensive Scotch and when she was quite sure he'd drunk enough to dull the pain she handed him a leather belt.

'Bite on this, you don't want to scream and frighten the horses.'

'Righty ho, lovey, anything for a smashing girl like you.'

Angus and Sid's friend, the one who'd removed his outer garments and had stayed with him to offer what comfort he could, were going to help her. The airman didn't need to scrub his hands as he wouldn't be touching the injury, but she'd sent Angus off to do his hands and arms. He'd removed his uniform jacket and his shirt was spotless and that would have to do.

Her instruments were set out and there were now four pairs of sterilised tweezers. Three lengths of silk thread in the needles ready for use. The splints were waiting, as were the bandages to hold them in place. She sent up a quick prayer and hoped the Almighty was listening today.

Dear Lord, guide my hands and help me to save this man's leg and his life. Amen.

'Angus, stand at the end of the bed. When I say so, grab Sid's foot and pull steadily. Don't jerk. I've got pads ready to press on any bleeders.'

The other man was going to hold Sid down whilst they set his leg. She'd already swabbed the area with gin – Sid said he preferred whisky so she'd not used that but kept every drop for him to drink instead.

'Right. Now.'

Sid's back arched but his moan of agony was muffled by the leather between his teeth. She watched the ends of the bone slide back inside the flesh. There was blood, but not anything to indicate an artery had been severed. She picked out a few splinters of bone and checked the two ends of his tibia were aligned.

She stitched up the leg confidently and applied a dressing and then bandaged the injury. The splints were ready and she carefully secured them with further bandages. Obviously, a surgeon would have to set the leg properly but the blood was now circulating to his toes which it hadn't been before. There was nothing she could do but keep him warm and comfortable and hydrated.

'It's over, Sid, you've done amazingly well. You can take the strap out of your mouth now. The pain shouldn't be too bad as long as you don't wriggle about.'

There was no answer and for a horrible moment she thought he was unconscious but he'd merely fallen into a drunken stupor.

'Angus, he might well need to empty his bladder when he wakes up. He might also vomit. You need to find people to sit with him – he can't be left alone.'

'I'll get that organised.'

She stepped away and hurried into the privacy of the downstairs cloakroom, where she burst into tears. Her hands were trembling and for a moment her stomach churned. How had she just set a man's leg with no real medical training? She prayed the man wouldn't die because of something she'd inadvertently done wrong. She washed her hands and face and, feeling calmer, returned to the hall.

She'd left Angus to set up the rota and was sure he'd have done it efficiently. Somewhat later than planned, she picked up the telephone receiver. 'Hello, Dr Willoughby, it all went very well.' She quickly explained exactly what she'd done.

'Perfect, my dear. Your patient is in excellent hands. If you've any worries at all about his condition, I'm on the other end of this line whenever you need me.'

'Thank you, that's a great help. I'll call you this evening with an update if that's all right?'

She headed for the kitchen where Joan and Ada were busy cooking a vast amount of vegetable soup. There was also bread dough proving on the back of the range. From the appetising aroma coming from one of the ovens, the jacket potatoes were cooking too.

'It all smells quite delicious. Feel free to use anything you find – we've got a well-stocked larder and pantry. Why don't you add a couple of rabbits to the stew? I can skin them for you if you like.'

'We saw them but didn't fancy preparing them,' Joan said with a grimace.

'Give me a few minutes to wash and so on and then I'll do them. I think our visitors would prefer something a little more substantial than vegetable soup.'

Half an hour later the rabbits were cleaned and skinned and Joan and Ada were busy cutting them up and dropping them into the four saucepans of soup.

Angus appeared at the kitchen door. She handed him a freshly made mug of tea and they moved into the passageway, which was only marginally warmer than outside.

'How is Sid? Is he still asleep?'

'He is, no temperature, good colour and I checked his toes and they are pink and warm to the touch.'

'Thank you. It's just possible he won't need surgical intervention if I've got it right.'

'We all owe you a huge debt of gratitude – not only for taking us in but also for your expert medical treatment. I can't believe someone of your age, with no actual training, was able to do what you did.'

Sarah smiled and managed to hide her delight at his praise. 'I've been a member of the St John's for years, as well as shadowing the local doctor. I'm going to sign up to be a nurse as soon as I'm old enough as you already know I can't now be a doctor.'

Mummy would be horrified that she was discussing something that was really none of his business. 'I'll actually get paid if I become a nurse.'

'It would be a shame if you didn't follow your dream as you're obviously meant to be a medic. If you've got your St John's qualifications you could join any one of the services as a medical assistant. You could use that experience when the war's over to become a doctor.'

'I'd not even considered that option. I must admit the thought of spending three years emptying bedpans and being told what to do by student doctors who know less than I do doesn't really appeal to me.'

'I should contact your CO in the brigade. He'll be able to give you more accurate information.'

'I might well do that, but I'm pretty sure that women are only considered to be acceptable in a nursing role, however well qualified they are.'

'I do know there's a hospital in London – I think it's the Royal Free – that's actively seeking young women to train as doctors rather than nurses.'

She shivered. 'It's too cold to talk here, let's go somewhere warmer.'

Sarah wanted to ask more about this hospital but didn't want to seem too eager. Could it be the way out she was looking for? Clutching their mugs of tea, she led the way to the private sitting room where her mother was calmly reading a magazine as if having the house invaded by a large crowd of airmen was nothing at all to worry about.

'There you are, darling, I take it from your expressions that everything went well with that unfortunate airman.'

'Yes, I did everything I could. Do you mind if we sit in here with you?'

Her mother put down her magazine. 'I'd better go and check on what's going on in the kitchen.'

Sarah frowned as her mother left her alone with Angus as if they were a courting couple. He was very attractive if you liked tall, broad-shouldered gentlemen with red hair and green eyes. She was beginning to suspect that maybe she did but as she'd not even spoken to a young man before she wasn't really sure how she felt.

'How long do you think it will be before you and your men can return to base?'

'Hopefully, the blizzard will have abated soon and we can start digging out the snowplough. I didn't have time to tell you what happened. I expect you're curious about how we came to be in the middle of one of your fields.'

When he'd finished telling her the unfortunate story, they were both laughing. 'Thank God Sid wasn't more seriously injured. I hate to ask you this, but is there any possibility the RAF will be able to replace the tea and so on that we've used?'

'That goes without question, Sarah. And to get back to your dilemma. I might be able to help as I've an uncle who is a surgeon at the Royal Free. Would you like me to get in touch with him on your behalf?'

* * *

Angus watched the play of emotions on her face. He guessed she was tempted to take up his offer but thought this was something she should do for herself.

'There's no need to make a decision about anything at the moment. One thing at a time. On another tack entirely, I'm sorry the WAAF won't be with you for very long this time.'

Her eyes widened and she looked at him with interest. 'Are you saying that we might get girls here in the future?'

'Absolutely. We're not ready for any at the moment as we've not even got sufficient accommodation for ourselves. But once the weather improves and building construction is completed then there'll be a massive influx of officers, men and kites. Manston is going to be crucial to the air defence of this country.'

'Will you go back to flying again? I thought an adjutant was usually an older person like the wing commander who was only suitable for a desk job.'

'That's right. I've not been cleared to fly after a minor mishap in November but was perfectly fit to do the job I'm doing. I'm going to be cleared for active duty as soon as I can get to Hornchurch and see a medic there.'

'That explains it. You don't look at all injured – if you don't mind me saying so.' She narrowed her eyes and viewed him from toes to crown. 'In fact, I've never seen anyone look fitter in my life.'

He knew she wasn't really flirting with him but he still rather enjoyed her close scrutiny.

'I dislocated my shoulder for the third time and it had to be sewn back together. Flying a fighter is perfectly possible with one hand but they refused to let me do so. I doubt they'll be as fussy once the sky is full of Messerschmitts and bombers.'

'So, it looks as though both of us will be moving on in a few weeks. You to active duty and me to begin a medical training of some sort. I've decided that I would be grateful if you could ask your uncle how they would view an application from an impecunious young woman, but I'm pretty sure you have to be at least eighteen.'

'Maybe you could do nursing duties and get paid whilst you train, but I don't know enough about it. I do know that surgeons are gods at the hospitals they work in so if Uncle George is in favour of you coming then the board won't argue.'

Her smile changed everything. It lit up her face and suddenly he saw her as a potential girlfriend and not an irritating schoolgirl. If he was honest with himself, he hadn't thought of her like that for some time. How could he not see her as an equal after what she'd just done?

'There might be a scholarship or bursary of some sort I could apply for because, even if they agree to train me for nothing, I'll still need money to live on. From what I've read, a medical student doesn't get any free time so offering my services as a nursing assistant wouldn't work.'

'I shouldn't worry about it at the moment. Let's get through the next couple of days and things might look a bit clearer.'

'I'm afraid I can't dawdle about here as there are too many things to do with so many people in the house at the moment. I've got to dig out enough bedding for your men to be able to sleep tonight.'

'I've got plenty of fit men lounging around who are perfectly capable of doing a lot of that for you. What would you like me to organise them to do first?'

'They could fill all the coal scuttles and tend to all the fires and the kitchen range. It would be really useful if a couple of them could clear the path from the house to the stables to make it easier for me to get out and feed the horses and the birds in a couple of hours.'

'I've already got a team taking it in turns to watch Sid Harrison. I'll sort out the others and get them moving immediately. By the way, I'm impressed by the efficiency of the WAAF you've got here. My opinion of them has also radically changed.' Again, her smile made him feel ten feet tall.

'I think it's time men stopped thinking of women as incapable of doing more than run a house and bring up the children. We're going to be needed to do all sorts of things that before the war started would never have been considered suitable.'

'Radical thinking, Sarah. Women are weaker physically and therefore need our protection. I don't suppose you're suggesting they should be wielding guns or flying fighters?'

'Of course I'm not, I'm not stupid. I was thinking about driving ambulances, buses, perhaps even joining the Observation Corps. There's already the Land Army, which is women being trained to take over as the men are conscripted to fight. They will have to do all the jobs the men used to – including driving tractors and so on.'

With some reluctance, he stood up and collected both his mug and hers. 'Take a breather, Sarah, you deserve it.'

'I will – I'll put the wireless on and hope there's some jolly music to listen to.'

'I should have said, don't worry about providing actual beds if we do have to stay overnight. They can kip perfectly well on the floor if you can find a few blankets.'

* * *

The remainder of the afternoon passed more quickly than one might have expected. His men were only too happy to have something to do as they weren't used to idleness. Three of them were more than enough to take care of the fires so the rest, led by himself, braved the elements.

The snow had stopped but the skies were still grey and the wind bitter. He'd been pleased to find a couple of the blokes were familiar with horses and domestic fowl, so they were taking care of the animals so that Sarah didn't have to come out again.

'Come on, chaps, we need to collect the shovels and dig out the lorry and then see if it'll start.'

Jimmy slogged through the knee-high snow beside him, cheerful as always. 'It would be better if we could get both vehicles into the barn where the Bentley's stored. Miss Harcourt said there's more than enough room.'

It took the combined efforts of all the men to clear the snow from under the wheels of both vehicles. Jimmy volunteered to drive the tractor. 'If I can get it into reverse then I reckon I can push the lorry backwards and give myself room to turn round. Then if the lorry starts you can turn it round in the space the tractor and plough have left.'

'Sounds sensible – but I'm not holding my breath. If by some miracle both start then you could tow the lorry back to the barn. I doubt it'll get through two feet of snow under its own volition.'

The tractor started immediately. Jimmy's plan worked and the lorry slid backwards without any trouble. He tried the ignition whilst the lorry was moving and after a few coughs and hesitations the engine fired into life.

It had taken an hour and a half, they were frozen and filthy, but triumphant when the snowplough, tractor and lorry were safely in the barn.

9

The snow stopped but it remained several degrees below freezing and there was no sign of an imminent thaw. Soldiers from a nearby base had helped the RAF clear the roads so the ambulance had arrived to take Sid to hospital.

Sarah had been sorry to see the unexpected guests depart the morning after their arrival, but Angus had promised to deliver the replacement groceries himself, which cheered her up somewhat. There was still no sign of Bates or his son, therefore taking care of the livestock was still down to her.

'Mummy, we haven't heard from Betty. Do you think she might be coming back soon?'

'The roads are clear so why don't you walk down to the village and ask? I would dearly like a newspaper that isn't more than a week out of date.'

'I'll suggest some of the girls might like to accompany me; they must be sick of being cooped up indoors.'

Only Ada and Eleanor wanted to come so the three of them set out together. The sun was out, the snow was blindingly white, and all three of them were forced to admit that despite the inconvenience it did make the world look beautiful.

'I think now the roads are clear you might get sent to your correct posting,' Sarah said.

'Actually, although we've thoroughly enjoyed our stay with you, we are all frightfully bored with nothing important to do. After all, we didn't volunteer to sit on our bottoms in a stately home.'

'Speak for yerself,' Ada replied. 'I've spent all me life working and although I'm happy to do me bit, I'm enjoying doing bugger all.'

'Mummy and I are just glad that you came to us. Our intention is to continue to take in paying guests of one sort or another. If we weren't so close to Manston then I expect we'd be full of evacuees and their families.'

Ada missed her footing, lost her balance and vanished head first into a pile of cleared snow. By the time they'd extricated her they were laughing and the excursion became far more enjoyable. Sarah hadn't been into the village since before the bad weather had hit two weeks ago.

'I have to pop in and see Betty, our housekeeper, her husband had an accident a week ago and I want to know how he's getting on.'

'Righty ho. I'll get your ma's paper and see if there's any chocolate. That's what I miss worst – me, I love a bit of Cadbury's fruit and nut.'

They'd now arrived outside the detached cottage where Betty lived with her husband. It was a tied cottage supplied by one of the tenant farmers on Harcourt estate – so she supposed it actually belonged to her family.

'Did you notice that every path has been cleared? I think the soldiers and airmen must have done it for them. I suppose they're all equally bored being so idle,' Sarah said as she unlatched the small wooden gate.

'Keep an eye out for us, Sarah, we'll wait for you at this gate. I don't reckon we'll be very long – too bleeding cold to hang about.'

Eleanor winced every time Ada swore but Sarah found it amusing. She'd never use profanity or blaspheme herself, but rather admired those who had the courage to do so. After having so many men in the house, she scarcely noticed any more.

Betty had obviously seen her from the front room window and had the door open as she approached. 'I was going to come up myself later today, miss, you didn't have to walk down in this weather.'

Inside the cottage was warm, far warmer than Goodwill House, and she didn't blame Betty if she decided to stay absent from work for as long as possible.

'How is your husband? Is he home now?'

Betty drew her into the empty sitting room. 'He's been back three days. He had a nasty head injury and concussion but he's fine now. He can't go back to work until the stitches come out. Dr Willoughby is coming to do them tomorrow.'

'That's really good news. I don't suppose he likes being at home.'

Betty pulled a face. 'He thinks nobody can look after the cows the way he can. To be honest, I'll be glad when he's back at work. I can't do anything right and he's constantly snapping and snarling at me.'

'I'm sorry to hear that. Does that mean when he goes back you can come back?'

'I'd have come yesterday but he won't hear of it. He doesn't like me working at the best of times. He blames me for not providing him with the son he so desperately wants.'

'I've told you before, Betty, it's not necessarily anybody's fault. I've read about infertility and some specialists think worrying about it can aggravate the problem.'

Her mother would be shocked if she overheard this conversation as most girls her age wouldn't know anything about such things and certainly wouldn't talk so freely about them to an older woman.

Betty was more than just a housekeeper to her – she was like an older sister. Even though she refused to call her Sarah, they talked to each other as equals. Obviously, when she was younger this hadn't been the case, but for the past eighteen months things had been different.

'There's no chance I'll be in the family way now as he's moved into the spare room.'

Sarah quickly changed the subject. 'I haven't got long and there's a lot you don't know.' She quickly told Betty of the exciting events of the past week and of their plans to continue to take in lodgers.

'That's the best bit of news I've heard in an age, miss. Mr Root will be getting some land girls in the next couple of weeks and Mrs Root's refusing to have them in the house. If I can tell my Bert they can come to you, he'll be that pleased.'

'Then do so. The WAAF will be gone in a few days and I have to tell you the extra money has been an absolute godsend.'

Betty nodded towards the window. 'There's two of them waiting at the gate. Thank you for calling in, miss, and I'll be back the day after tomorrow.'

'Goodbye, then, and I hope your good news will improve things with Mr Smith.'

* * *

Angus had promised to visit but so far had failed to arrive with the promised tea, butter and sugar. There'd also been no news for the girls, who were eager to leave and begin their new life in Norfolk.

It was highly unsuitable to be the confidant of one's housekeeper, to hear intimate details of her married life, but she did so anyway. If her parents ever found out, they would be furious, and no doubt Betty would be dismissed.

Domestic staff were almost impossible to come by as the women who could work preferred to do so in factories making munitions, uniforms and so on where they would be paid far more. She didn't blame them – who would want to be a servant if they'd got an alternative? The only reason they still had Betty was because it was the only employment her husband would allow her to do.

Sarah had decided that if she ever did get married it wouldn't be to someone like him, or her father, who'd expect her to follow his every instruction and not think for herself. The girls she'd been at boarding school with had thought only of marrying well, having a grand home and a life of leisure. This had never been her aim in life – she supposed one day she would be married but being a doctor was her priority and wedded bliss, if there was such a thing, would come later.

* * *

Joanna listened to the girls laughing and squealing as they dashed about the house playing hide-and-seek. There had never been any children's games here. David had disapproved of any frivolity – he loved Sarah but believed children should be seen and not heard.

She had no friends of her own – the only women she knew were the wives of his friends and once he'd decamped for France, they no longer invited her to dinner or even contacted her to see how she was doing. As the only child of a bank manager, she'd married above her and had always suspected that David's friends merely tolerated her because of him. She was never really one of them. She was jerked from her reverie when her daughter dashed in.

Sarah tossed over a copy of the *News Chronicle* with a wry smile. 'I'm afraid that's all they'd got left. They'd sold out of *The Times* and *The Daily Telegraph*.'

'I'm sure your father would be horrified to see me reading it but to tell you the truth I rather think I'm going to enjoy seeing things from a different perspective.'

'Betty will be back the day after tomorrow. Isn't that absolutely spiffing news?'

'I'm delighted to hear that, darling. Flight Lieutenant Trent telephoned to say he would be here this afternoon.'

'I hope he brings more tea as we've completely run out and there was none to be had in the village.'

'The other girls are having a riotous game of hide-and-seek – why don't you join in?'

Her daughter looked at her as if she was speaking in tongues. 'Why ever would I want to do that? I've got lunch to prepare and I've got to light the fire under the copper in the laundry. That's something Bates usually does but he's not here again today.'

'I really don't like you doing those sorts of jobs. If only we had a larger income then I could employ more staff…'

'It doesn't matter how much money one's got nowadays, Mummy, one won't get anyone to do domestic work.'

The telephone interrupted their conversation and Sarah hurried off to answer it. Joanna carefully put the newspaper on the side table, straightened the cushions, and then followed her. She intended to offer to help with the lunch. Once Betty had returned, there'd no longer be any need for her to frequent the kitchen, which would suit her perfectly.

Sarah was replacing the handset on the receiver. 'That was Dr Willoughby. The surgeon didn't need to reset Sid's leg. Isn't that wonderful?'

'It certainly is. You'd be wasted as a nurse, darling, and I really don't think you should make any hasty decisions about giving up your place at Oxford. You never know, something might turn up so you can go after all.'

'I'm glad you mentioned that as I've not given up. I might not be able to go to Oxford but it's possible I could train at a London hospital. The fact that I'm already semi-qualified should help.'

'Are you going to apply before we hear from your father?'

'Daddy shot off without a second thought for us. As far as I'm concerned, we're on our own. I'm going to make any decisions about my future. I don't think I can go until September even if I did find a place, but I'll have to apply now.'

'Then do so, you have my full support. I've never done anything useful with my life and it will give me the greatest pleasure to know that you will become a valuable member of society.'

'You've run this house, attended numerous functions at Daddy's side, you are the most important person in the neighbourhood and everybody looks up to you. How can you say your life hasn't been important?'

'Yes, I agree that I've done all that. However, I'm not equipped to do anything to help the war effort...'

'That's not true either. We're going to run a guest house for young women who need somewhere safe to live. Which reminds me, we might well be getting some land girls very soon. How many do you think we can manage if we've got Betty to help us?'

'There are two more bedrooms available on that floor and both rooms are big enough for two or three girls to share without getting in each other's way. The room you turned into a sitting room is perfectly adequate for ten, don't you think?'

'Definitely – so we can accommodate ten at least? Imagine what a difference that will make to us. We could keep the horses. I've been wondering if the gig could be resurrected and have my mare pull it for us.

I'm really not comfortable using the Bentley when it's so uneconomical and petrol is already in short supply.'

'What a super idea, darling, I don't know why we didn't think of it before. I wonder if Daddy's hunters could be made to pull a plough?' The two women made their way to the kitchen, laughing at this ridiculous idea.

* * *

Angus had put in a requisition and was just waiting for someone to deliver the various items that he had to take to Goodwill House to replace what had been consumed by the men who'd stayed there for twenty-four hours. He'd already had the lorry deliver half a dozen bags of coal. He'd promised to take the food and so on himself but was so bogged down with paperwork relating to the incident he was beginning to feel he wouldn't have the time.

The weather report he'd studied that morning showed the unprecedented storm had moved on and things should be moving again in a few days. Kites didn't fly when it was sub-zero temperatures if they could avoid it, as the wings iced up.

Tony yelled from the office across the passageway. Why the hell couldn't he use the internal telephone or get up and speak to him like a normal bloke?

'Yes, how can I be of assistance? After all, I've got nothing at all to do today.'

'Point taken, old boy. I've just been on the blower. I'm afraid HQ wants you to remain here as adjutant for another few weeks.' He raised his hand as if warding off a blow. 'Don't glare at me, I did my best. They want you to expedite the building work so we're ready when things get going.'

'They'll need me to fly soon, so I'll just have to get on with it until then. Was there something else?'

'They don't think I'm up to commanding an active fighter base. I'm going to be transferred somewhere inland, miles away from any action.'

'I'm sorry to hear that, Tony. Do you know who's replacing you and when?'

'Not the foggiest, old bean. Unlike you, I'm happy to be out of it – when my eardrum perforated it was almost a relief that I couldn't fly.'

'We have to follow orders like everybody else and just hope the orders we get are what we want. I've enjoyed working with you these past months.'

'Same here – especially as you've done all the work. If you're going to the mess, I could do with another cuppa and a wad.'

It was hard to be annoyed with Tony as he was such a jovial fellow, even if he was the laziest superior officer he'd ever worked under. Both tractors with the ploughs attached had made good progress clearing the runway of snow and what they'd missed could be shovelled by not so willing volunteers.

There were some compensations for not getting his command immediately. It meant he could get to know Sarah better. He'd already commandeered the Hillman and was just waiting for someone from the stores to bring him what he needed.

It scarcely seemed possible that he'd only met Sarah and her mother a few days ago as he already considered them both as friends. He didn't want anyone to think that he was seriously interested in Sarah as she was still so young and he might be considered predatory. However, if he was honest with himself, he'd never met a girl who interested him more.

As Angus drove cautiously from the base to the house, he thought he might ask her if she'd be prepared to write to him when he was posted. He never received letters from anyone but his doting mother – even his older sister rarely communicated.

Having a letter from someone like Sarah would brighten anybody's day, however grim the circumstances might be. They were having a film show at the base next week – something called *The Great Dictator* with Charlie Chaplin. He'd not seen it but had heard it was good viewing and decided to ask both of them if they'd like to come.

He had a large cardboard box full of goodies as well as an extra five pounds to cover the cost of feeding twenty extra men. If Sid had been attended to by the local quack, it would have cost them another fiver. Sarah had done everything as professionally as a qualified medic, but he couldn't put a payment to her through the books.

She opened the door herself as she'd done the first time he'd met her, but this time was quite different. Her smile when she saw him made the journey more than worthwhile.

'Angus, I'm so glad to see you. I do hope you've got tea in that box as we're all desperate for a cup as we ran out yesterday. It's not as though we've got any coffee either – at least not anything worth drinking. Camp coffee is beyond disgusting in my opinion.' She stepped aside to allow him to enter and closed the door hurriedly behind him.

'Did the coal arrive yesterday?'

'It did, thank you so much. We didn't use half as much as that but it means we can be profligate with our fires now and not walk around with three jumpers and a pair of gloves on.'

'This is an impossibly large house. Why don't you close off the Gothic wing? It might make the rest of the house a bit warmer.'

'That's an excellent idea and whilst I've got the WAAF here twiddling their thumbs I could get them to help. Something in that box smells absolutely delicious.'

'I got the chef that takes care of us officers to make a cake for you. So far we don't seem to be affected by the rationing that started a few weeks ago. There are even four bars of chocolate, a tin of cocoa and two tins of coffee. Now, aren't you pleased to see me?'

Her delightful laugh echoed down the draughty passageway. 'I'm always delighted to see you, Angus, but even more so if you've got real coffee. I hope you're staying to share in these luxuries.'

'If you insist, then I certainly won't refuse. I can't be too long as I've still got things to do back at the base. We're expecting an influx of parts sometime this afternoon and I want all three squadrons to do a few practice flights.'

Lady Harcourt must have heard his voice as she drifted into the kitchen a few moments after he put the large box on the table.

'Good afternoon, Flight Lieutenant Trent, I was so happy to hear that Sid is making an excellent recovery thanks to my daughter.'

'He certainly is. I wanted to ask you and Sarah if you'd like to come to the showing of a Charlie Chaplin film on Saturday? You don't have to get out the Bentley – I'll act as your chauffeur in both directions.' He'd asked her as he thought he was less likely to get a refusal than if he'd asked Sarah directly.

'We'd love to – Lord Harcourt didn't approve of films so I've never seen one and neither has my daughter.' She turned to Sarah who was busy unpacking the box and looking suitably thrilled about the contents. 'We're going to see a film on Saturday at the base. Isn't that exciting?'

'Absolutely spiffing, Mummy. I'm going to make coffee and tea to go with this absolutely scrumptious cake. My mouth's watering just looking at it.'

The six WAAF girls were summoned and all nine of them sat around the kitchen table munching. He felt rather like a sultan with a harem, surrounded by so many attractive young women.

'I'm sorry, but I must go. I'll be here at two o'clock on Saturday to collect you.' Sarah got up to accompany him through the chilly house to the front door.

'I can only take two of the girls in the Hillman...'

'Don't worry, only Eleanor and Ada haven't already been invited. To be honest, Mummy and I were feeling a bit left out. I just wish it would get a little bit warmer so I can exercise the horses properly – just lunging them in the ménage isn't sufficient.'

'Don't you have grooms to do that for you?'

'We were going to let Bates and his son go and try and find new owners for the horses but now we've got several land girls coming next month we can afford to keep them on, at least for the summer. However, he sent a note saying he was retiring as he was too old to be out in this weather.'

'Isn't your housekeeper coming back in a few days? Hopefully, when she's working you won't have quite so much to do.'

'Your girls are bored without official duties to perform and are happy to muck in,' said Sarah. 'Actually, I'm in the process of cleaning up the gig so I can use my mare to pull it. I've put the Bentley on blocks for the duration.'

'Good idea. Have you thought any more about applying to the Royal Free?'

'I'm definitely going to do it but... but...'

'What? Why would you hesitate when it's what you've always wanted and you're damn good at it too?'

'My mother wrote to my father asking for permission for me to become a student nurse. For some reason I want to get his reply before I make up my mind. If I became a student nurse then I'd be able to come home on my day off, but if I go to London that just won't be possible. Also, Mummy's terrified I'll be blown up when the bombing starts as it'll be London that will be the target.'

'You'd hate being a nurse when you know enough already to work alongside a medic. I'm here for another few weeks, but don't leave it too long because once I get posted I might not have the time to even write a letter or make personal calls.'

He didn't want to pressure her into doing something she might not want to, but he didn't want her to miss out on an excellent opportunity. Was he becoming more than an interested friend?

'I'm glad you're staying. I really didn't like you when we met but I've rather changed my mind now.' She smiled and something changed between them and he hoped it wasn't just him that felt it.

'I just wish you were a bit older.' He'd spoken without thought but she understood immediately what he was getting at.

'You're six years older than me – that might seem a lot now but it won't in a few years' time. There's a twelve-year age gap between my parents and nobody thought anything of it.' Her expression changed to horror. 'Goodness – that came out all wrong. I'm not suggesting we should get married or anything like that.'

'Don't worry, I'm not thinking of proposing this week. And you're right, you've got more sense than most girls a lot older than you.' He reached out and caught her hand in his before she could retreat. 'Would you consider Saturday as our first date? I'd be proud to have you walking at my side and for all the chaps to know you were my girlfriend.'

10

Sarah stared at the hand on her arm and he hastily removed it. Did she want to be his girlfriend or just his friend? She detected hesitance in his demeanour, and this decided her. Perhaps he wasn't the overconfident, slightly arrogant young man she'd thought him to be.

'I would like to be your official girlfriend, but I have to warn you I'm totally green when it comes to etiquette and so on. My parents didn't approve of me having friends of any sort.'

'Not even school friends? I take it you went to an exclusive boarding school?'

She was on safer ground here. 'I did, but didn't make close friends with anyone. I jogged along with my peers but never had any wish to spend time with them away from school.'

'Your mother said you'd never been to the cinema – from what you said you've not socialised at all. Was that your first dance the other night?'

'Not exactly, as I'd tagged along with my parents to a couple of grand events, but I wasn't allowed to do more than sit in the background trying to be invisible.'

'How extraordinary. I'll make it my business to escort you to all the places you should have already visited. I can use the Hillman whenever I want, therefore, once the weather clears, and I have a free afternoon, I'll take you to London. It'll be safe enough at the moment.'

'How exciting, but I think we'd better start with just going to Ramsgate or Hastings and see how we get on before venturing so far.'

'Fair enough. I know absolutely nothing about either town. I take it you're familiar with both?'

'I know Ramsgate but not Hastings even though it's only fifty miles or so from here. I'd love to go there. I seem to recall Mummy telling me there's a rather splendid hotel we could lunch at – I'll get the details from her.'

It was possible permission would be refused for these jaunts but she wouldn't mention that to him now. This time, instead of closing the door Sarah stood on the step and watched him stride to the car and he turned and waved – well, he raised his hand which sort of counted – before driving off.

Did she really want to become anyone's girlfriend, even someone as attractive as Angus? She'd never been out on her own with a girl and now she was intending to go to the cinema with him – was she wise to do this?

* * *

Betty returned and life became much easier now she only had the livestock to take care of. Closing off the unused wing of the house had been successfully accomplished and the house was noticeably warmer.

There was an air of excitement on Saturday morning as everyone prepared for the afternoon's visit to the base to see a film.

'I wish my Bert would let me come with you,' Betty said sadly. 'He doesn't hold with films and if I'm honest he doesn't really like me listening to the wireless either unless it's the news.'

'That's a shame. I remember when you got married how happy you were. When we saw you at church you were both smiling and so much in love.'

'Things change and he certainly has. He'll be coming up to see her ladyship next week to discuss accommodating the land girls. Let's hope there are only going to be four of them initially as there isn't room for more than that.'

'We can squeeze a couple of extra beds in if necessary. Don't look so worried, Betty, you know Bert is in awe of my mother and whatever she tells him he'll be happy.'

They both stared gloomily out of the kitchen window. 'I hope those grey clouds are rain and not more snow. I've slipped on my backside three times this past week walking up here.'

'I've gone flat on my face more than that but fortunately always in a nice comfortable pile of freezing cold snow. I've started turning the horses out into the ménage now it's a little warmer. At least they can canter about and chase each other if they want to. Do you think any of the land girls will be able to ride?'

'Shouldn't think so. From what my Bert says, most of the girls don't know one end of a spade from another and it's going to be up to him to show them what's what on the farm. He'll not let them anywhere near his precious dairy herd, that's for sure.'

'I can't believe that it's already the fourth of February and I've still not seen any sign of spring. Do you think that there'll be daffodils coming out soon and we'll find patches of snowdrops under the snow when it melts?'

'I doubt it – spring's going to be late this year what with all the bad weather we've had.'

The plates on the dresser suddenly rattled as half a dozen Hurricanes roared overhead. Sarah supposed they'd have to get used to this as it was inevitable the planes would fly this way occasionally.

A flicker of unease ran through her. If the weather was sufficiently improved for action on the base then did this mean there might be unwelcome visitors from Germany coming soon? The only good thing about the snow had been the lack of worry about being bombed.

Everyone talked about what was going to happen but she wasn't sure anyone, apart from the military, really understood how horrible things were going to be when the bombs started to drop. Mummy had so far refused to go down and see the splendid shelter Daddy had made in one of the cellars.

* * *

An hour before the film was due to start, a somewhat dilapidated van skidded to a halt outside. Sarah watched with some amusement as all six girls, plus the men who'd come to collect them, somehow crammed themselves inside. Obviously, Eleanor and Ada had decided they'd prefer to travel with their friends.

Fifteen minutes later, the Hillman arrived, but there was still no sign of her mother. She flew up the stairs but her mother's room was empty; more significantly, the outfit they'd chosen together for this afternoon's excursion was still hanging on the rack in the dressing room.

Mummy must have changed her mind but an hour ago she'd been as excited as everyone else. Where was she? Had she had an accident? Her pulse skittered and she rushed to Angus who was at the front door. She flung it open. 'I can't find my mother. Help me look.'

'When did you see her last? Could she have gone outside and had an accident?'

'Absolutely not. She hates the cold. She was so happy to be coming with us but she's not been up to her room to change and the last time I spoke to her she was about to do so.'

'Have you tried calling?'

'You mean shout and expect her to answer? Nobody ever shouts in this house – it's just not done.' As soon as she said this she realised how silly that sounded. 'She won't be in the west wing so has to be somewhere downstairs. You take the main reception rooms and I'll check the others. Shout as loud as you like – I'm going to.'

* * *

Joanna checked the grandfather clock ticking intrusively, as it always did, in the drawing room and decided there was ample time for her to inspect the work done by Sarah and the girls to close off the Victorian wing.

This was yet another thing her husband would disapprove off when he came back, but he didn't have to live in the icy conditions. Her mouth curved slightly as she thought he might well be a lot colder than they were at the moment.

This part of the house was what could be considered a modern extension as it was built in 1860. This was one of the things that she and David had been in total agreement about – this wing would be better demolished than lived in. There were three towers all overdecorated with gargoyles and other unrecognisable stone animals. Even the red brick it had been built with was offensive to the eye.

On the ground floor there was a billiard room which to her certain knowledge had never been used this century, as well as half a dozen ugly rooms too large to be used by a family of three but not big enough for entertaining significant numbers.

On the first floor were half a dozen equally unattractive bedrooms and above that attic rooms meant for servants. David had installed central heating, indoor plumbing and bathrooms in both the main wing and the west wing but quite sensibly had ignored the Victorian monstrosity. Unfortunately, ten years ago the boiler that served the radiators had failed and not been replaced.

From the central section of the house, the one they occupied, one could move freely into either end of the huge building. The passageway that led between the drawing room and the dining room continued through an arch into the unoccupied section – there were no doors that could be locked either downstairs or up.

Her daughter had ingeniously constructed a thick curtain from what looked like old blankets and this had been neatly nailed from the ceiling and then side to side. She was most impressed. It was certainly a lot warmer with this screen keeping out the icy wind that usually blew straight along the corridor.

As she turned to go, she heard something. She stopped and put her ear against the material. Yes – there it was again – a definite crying, whining sort of noise. It sounded a bit like a small child but how could one have become trapped in the house? She ran to the boot room and hastily pulled on the nearest coat and rammed her feet into the first boots she could find.

The only way into the house now would be through the French doors that led out on to the terrace. These could be opened from the outside by the careful insertion of dinner knife between the two doors and then if one flicked upwards it would open the catch. She'd successfully done this a couple of times many years ago.

She'd brought a thick rug with her to wrap the child. She hoped she was wrong and it was an animal of some sort but it certainly sounded human. She was still at a loss to understand how an infant could be inside this house but was determined to rescue the baby before it froze to death. What monster would leave someone so young and vulnerable in so unpleasant a place?

* * *

Angus searched all the rooms on the left of the front door and was unsurprised to discover there was a library, a study and a further two smaller disused reception rooms as well as the drawing room, dining room and breakfast parlour. None of them contained Lady Harcourt.

He was about to head back to the grand hall when he thought he heard her from somewhere behind him. She definitely wasn't anywhere he'd looked – the only place she could be was in the Victorian part that was now separated by thick blankets nailed across the passageway.

'Lady Harcourt, it's Angus Trent, can you hear me? Are you hurt?' He was quite certain that if she was within a hundred yards then she'd hear him as he'd used his best parade-ground voice. Sarah certainly had; she appeared at the double behind him.

'Did you hear something in there?'

'Listen, was that her answering us?'

'I think it was, though I can't think why Mummy would be in there as it's all locked up. Quickly, we must rip down the curtain.'

He didn't need telling twice. They grabbed a handful of blanket each and heaved. With a horrendous ripping sound, the whole caboodle came away bringing plaster and mouse droppings down in a cloud on their heads.

Spitting and cursing, he tore the remaining nails out of the ceiling and walls and dumped the ruined blankets in a heap on the floor.

'Lady Harcourt, are you in here? Call out if you can hear me.'

His voice boomed down the empty corridor and was immediately answered. 'In here, flight lieutenant, I don't know how the poor little thing came to be trapped but he needs our assistance.'

Sarah took off ahead of him and they skidded through an open door to find not a baby, thank God, but a pathetic scrap of a dog.

'Let me see, Mummy, is the animal injured or just starving and half-frozen?'

'He is very pleased to see is all so he can't be that bad. I think he's just undernourished. I can't imagine how he got in, but I've got him now.'

Lady Harcourt, much to his surprise, wrapped the puppy in a blanket and stood up holding him close. She must be aware the animal would be riddled with fleas but was obviously unbothered, which seemed very out of character.

'Would you like me to carry him, my lady?'

'Absolutely not. I've always wanted to have a dog of my own but neither my parents nor my husband liked them. Now this little man has arrived under his own volition and I intend to keep him.'

'Sarah, I don't think we're going to make the film now. By the time you've changed it'll be too late.'

'I don't care about the film, having a puppy is far more exciting. You go if you want to, I fully understand.'

He shook his head. 'I'd like to stay if you don't mind. If you want to get into something that isn't covered in mouse droppings then I'll keep your mother company until you get back. The puppy needs a drink, food and then a warm bath. Let's hope he's not too far gone to recover.'

'I won't be long. Suggest to my mother that we call the puppy Lazarus – after all, he has risen from the dead, hasn't he?'

He caught up with Lady Harcourt. 'Do you need any help with the puppy? Sarah has gone to change and will be back in a minute.'

'No, I might never have had a dog of my own but I know enough about looking after animals to be able to take care of him. I suggest that you go into the downstairs WC and remove the debris and droppings from yourself before you come into the kitchen.'

'I'll do that. Sarah says to call the puppy Lazarus. I'll get cleaned up and then put the blankets back. Where will I find hammer and nails?'

'I believe I saw a toolbox at the back of the boot room. Sarah can help you when she comes down. I like her suggestion for a name. Lazzy is what we'll call him.'

When Sarah joined him, he'd already nailed the blankets back on both sides of the corridor and just needed to do the same across the top.

'You shouldn't stand on that chair, Angus, there's a perfectly good set of steps somewhere.'

He grinned down at her. '*Somewhere* being the operative word. I've almost finished but you can hold on to the back of the chair to keep it steady if you want.'

'No chance, flight lieutenant. If you fall off, I don't want to be crushed. I'll leave you to it. I want to know how the puppy's getting on.'

By the time he joined them, the puppy was sleeping peacefully in an old wicker picnic basket lined with what looked like a pullover. 'He certainly looks content. Did he eat?'

'We spooned water into his mouth first and then we found some left-over rabbit stew and hand-fed him some of that. He's had a bath and we combed the fleas out of his coat. There weren't that many, thankfully, probably because it's so cold,' Sarah told him as she smiled at the puppy.

This was another thing he now knew about the girl he was becoming inordinately fond of. She liked dogs as well as horses.

'What sort of breed is it?' Lady Harcourt asked as if she expected him to know about these things.

'A mongrel, but from the size of his paws I'm pretty sure he's going to be enormous. He looks as if he's got Labrador and lurcher in him.'

'How absolutely splendid – I'd much prefer a big dog, wouldn't you, Sarah?'

He was also seeing another side to Lady Harcourt. He'd never have believed she was an animal lover too.

'I prefer any dog to no dog at all. I'm going to see if I can find a couple of kittens so they can grow up together. I'm sure we wouldn't have the rodent problem we do if we had house cats. Sooty keeps the barn and stables clear, but not the house.'

'I'm not overfond of cats, but I like mice and rats even less. I think Betty said a cat at the farm had kittens a few weeks ago and they should be ready to leave their mother now. The only problem being, darling, is that without Bates to shoot game we won't have enough meat to feed them properly.'

'I'm a good shot, Mummy, so I can do it until I leave in the autumn.'

'With any luck, the cats will catch their own dinner, and so might the dog given half a chance,' he said with a smile.

Lady Harcourt picked up the basket and with a fond smile at the sleeping contents nodded goodbye and left him with Sarah.

'It seems a shame to waste the car as I've got it. Also, I won't be able to slope off quite so easily when the new chaps start arriving. It's my job to make sure they have suitable billets and understand the chain of command.'

'I must admit that I've been somewhat surprised by the fact you seem to have absolutely nothing war-related to do most of the time.'

'It's like that in the RAF – like this in all the services. Hours, days, possibly weeks of excruciating boredom and then short periods of gut-wrenching fear and activity.'

'I don't suppose there'll be much sitting about when the Luftwaffe start coming over. I heard the girls talking about a possible invasion as soon as the weather clears. Do you think that's possible?'

'The Germans are busy invading Scandinavia and Belgium at the moment. They need to conquer the whole of northern Europe before they can get to the coast closest to us. Until they do, I don't think we've got anything to worry about.' He hoped he sounded confident but really wasn't sure his reassurances were valid. He wanted to be on active duty when it started, not mooching about as assistant to Tony.

She was about to make a pot of coffee. 'Shall we go to Ramsgate? You can show me around and we might be able to get something to eat – even if it's only fish and chips.'

'I'm not very smart...'

'Nobody will see your scruffy jumper and slacks when you've got your coat on.'

'Thank you for your kind words, flight lieutenant, but I'm dressed as you so politely put it in my oldest clothes because you managed to get mouse droppings and plaster all over my smart ones.'

'We can discuss it further in the car. Are you going to tell your mother we're going out?'

'No, she might say I can't go and then I'll have to disobey. Better to ask for forgiveness than permission.'

He didn't open the car door for her, she wasn't that sort of girl. In fact, the more he got to know her, the more he thought she was his sort of girl.

11

Sarah spent most of the five-mile journey to Ramsgate bracing herself against the dashboard as the car skidded several times. Angus was an excellent driver so she was pretty sure they wouldn't end up in the ditch.

'Margate Road, the one we're about to turn on to, is somewhat steep. It goes past the station – but surely you've already been there as you collected the girls in that hideous lorry?'

'I've only been as far as the station. Do I continue on down the road towards the seafront?'

'Yes, you'll come to a junction where this road and another meet and become the High Street. Continue down this until we get to the Royal Parade. There's a smashing hotel, the Royal Hotel, right on the front and as far as I know it's still open. Although I've not been there for years, so it might not be.'

'Thank God there's not much traffic as, to tell you the truth, for the past half a mile we've been sledging rather than driving.' He turned his head for a second and grinned, his green eyes bright with excitement.

'I trust you, you're a fighter pilot. A Hillman car wouldn't dare give you any trouble.'

Luckily, they arrived in one piece and the hotel was still very much open. 'Do you think they might have afternoon tea? I warn you that it could be frightfully expensive. Perhaps it would be better to go to the Copper Kettle just along Harbour Parade.'

'Absolutely not. This is my treat and it's our first official date and I've no intention of stinting my new girlfriend.'

If he hadn't been laughing as he spoke, she would have been uncomfortable. She still wasn't quite sure if she was ready to be anyone's girlfriend. Neither of her parents had been physically affectionate – in fact she couldn't remember ever having been hugged or kissed by her father and not by her mother since she was small. This had led to her being nervous about being touched and especially by such a large, handsome, unpredictable man as the one holding the door open for her.

He offered his arm but she shook her head and immediately regretted it as her feet shot out from under her. His lightning-fast reactions saved her from a painful and embarrassing fall.

'*Pride goes before a fall*, and I just proved the truth of that. I really do need to hang on to your arm if I don't want to go flat again. I don't know why I seem so prone to slipping over.'

'I've got bigger feet so I'm less likely to lose my balance,' he said with a straight face.

The smartly uniformed doorman was ready to usher them in. 'Good afternoon, sir, madam, were you wanting to partake of afternoon tea?'

'We were. Is there a table available?'

'There are two free, sir. Allow me to call somebody to escort you there.'

She exchanged a glance with Angus and he winked and she barely managed to hide her amusement. An incredibly ancient waitress tottered over, looked them up and down as if to see if they were suitable, nodded and muttered something that could have been a request for them to follow her, but Sarah wasn't sure.

Angus put his arm around her shoulders and she rather liked the casual weight of it. She even enjoyed the feel of his shoulder pressing against hers although, to be honest, through two thicknesses of heavy winter coats and his uniform there wasn't much to be worried about.

The dining room faced out onto the Channel and there were no tables by the window, which wasn't surprising. Only then did she remember she was inappropriately dressed for such a smart place. She stopped and would have retreated if he hadn't prevented her.

'It doesn't matter what you're wearing. We don't know any of these people and they don't know us. The only people who matter are you and me. I think you'll still be the most beautiful woman in the room even in your somewhat disreputable apparel.'

Something was obviously amusing him and she was about to be offended when he nodded at the two dozen tables. Then she snorted inelegantly. There wasn't a person in there under fifty and they were all so busy talking and eating they hadn't even looked round.

'I'm certainly the youngest female and you the youngest male. You're also the only one in uniform so I can bask in your reflected glory. I do wish I'd changed into something smarter, though. My mother will be scandalised if she ever knows I came in here dressed as I am.'

'Then we won't tell her. Come on, Sarah, our waitress is waving at us.'

They hurried across and Angus ordered two afternoon teas before turning to assist her to remove her outer garments. He draped them over his arm and strode over to the coat hooks, where he deposited both their coats.

The table was the smallest in the room and when he sat down his knees were touching hers. Again, he sensed her unease.

'Well, isn't this cosy? I'll do my best not to tread on your feet, Sarah. There's another table considerably bigger over there. Shall we decamp to it?'

'No, I don't want to make a fuss. This one is tucked away nicely and the other one would have a constant flow of waitresses and so on going past. I think the waitress was doing us a favour.'

They talked at first about the puppy and this led on to his own family life.

'I have an older sister, ten years' difference, and I'm afraid we don't have a very close relationship. I was away at school when she got married and she lives in Hampstead somewhere. Her husband is in naval intelligence.'

'And your parents? Are they still alive?'

He chuckled. 'Good God, I should hope so. Dad's a solicitor in Chelmsford, he has a big practice of his own, and is still working. Mum's a leading light in the WI and WVS so we do have something in common. We had cats and dogs but no horses or other livestock.'

She rather envied his upbringing, so much warmer and more loving than her own.

'Why did you join the RAF?'

'Dad was a pilot in the last war and was lucky to survive intact. I learned to fly in my teens and was an air cadet at school. We both knew a few years ago that another war was inevitable and if I was going to have to fight it was going to be in the air.'

The waitress arrived pushing a noisy trolley. 'Here you are, young lady and gentleman. Just the ticket. My grandson's in the RAF learning to be a pilot like you.'

'That's good to know, ma'am. This looks absolutely delicious. Thank you.'

He'd not been exaggerating either. There were scones, strawberry jam and real butter as well as a selection of crustless sandwiches and three dainty pieces of cake each. An absolute feast.

'You're not allowed to cut the crusts of bread, so the leaflets say. I wonder what they do with them.'

'They make them into breadcrumbs.' Her look of astonishment at his culinary expertise made him laugh. 'I only know because the chef who made the cake for you told me that's what he did.'

'I've never been called *madam* before. I suppose it's marginally better than being called *miss*.'

* * *

The tea was as good as it looked and, despite the eye-watering amount of the bill which had been presented with the tea, Angus thought it well worth it. The more time he spent with Sarah, the better he liked her. She'd understood his disappointment that Manston wasn't going to have permanent squadrons of Spits of its own and fully supported his wish to be transferred as soon as possible.

'You said you'd been injured. What happened? You look the least injured person I've ever seen.'

He explained about his shoulder and immediately she was interested and her expression professional rather than sympathetic. 'Are you having any problems with it now?'

'No, fully functional. The surgeon did a good job.'

'As we happen to be talking about medical things, I'm going to write to the Royal Free and see how the land lies. Women in St John's aren't considered suitable to do more than nursing so I'm not sure about asking them for a reference. Dr Willoughby is more than happy to provide one, especially after I helped Sid. He's the one who taught me how to put in sutures, give injections and set bones. I got my nursing and first-aid skills from the brigade.'

'Write down everything you've done with him and with the brigade and what qualifications you've gained. As you've got a place to study medicine, I assume you got the necessary qualifications before you left school last year?'

'I have, and I got my Highers a year earlier than usual. If I'd been able to take my place last year then I wouldn't be having this conversation.'

'You certainly wouldn't, as we'd not have met. Also, isn't it better to start something knowing you can complete it? From what you've told me you would have had to leave because of your financial situation.'

'I've only just realised that we live in the grandest house for miles around, are the only titled family, but it's all pretence. I don't think there's ever been any money for luxuries. My school fees were paid for by a long-deceased grandparent, otherwise I expect I'd have had to attend the grammar school in Ramsgate.'

'Are you going to eat that last cake? It seems a shame to leave it.'

Her smile as always resonated somewhere deep inside. 'I'm not surprised you're such a large gentleman as you eat enough for two. On that subject – how on earth do you fit into the cockpit of a fighter plane? I thought only small men were allowed to be fighter pilots and the larger variety had to fly bombers.'

'I think that's the case now but when I got my wings the fact that I might have to bail out in a hurry didn't seem quite so important.' He wished he'd not been quite so explicit as her smile faded.

'Are you saying that in an emergency you might get stuck in a burning plane because you're too big to get out safely?'

'No, I didn't mean that. I'm sufficiently experienced to get out pretty damn quick if necessary. The chaps being trained now, the volunteers, don't have a choice. It was different for me five years ago.'

'I'm going to find the ladies' room whilst you pay the bill. I saw from your expression that it's considerably larger than you expected. I'd offer to pay half but you're obviously far better off than I am.'

The fact that she was prepared to discuss money so openly, something that both his parents and hers would consider exceedingly vulgar, made him like her more – if that was possible.

Perhaps he should step away now because he was in danger of falling in love with her and neither of them was in a position to become seriously involved. They both had a job to do. As he watched her weave gracefully through the tables and vanish into the foyer, he knew it was going to be all but impossible for him to keep her at a distance.

He shifted uncomfortably and hoped his arousal would settle before he was obliged to stand up. She was a complete innocent and he'd no intention of seducing her. He would do his damnedest not to do anything he'd later be ashamed of – would kissing her be stepping over the line?

He paid the bill and left a shilling for the waitress. Overgenerous, but the occasion demanded such a gesture. With the coats over his arm, he headed in the same direction, only then realising they were almost the last to leave. The blackouts had been drawn some time ago which should have warned him how late it was. The time had flown by and now they had to negotiate the steep hill, on ice, in the blackout.

'There you are, I was beginning to think you'd ordered another pot of tea.'

'It's dark...'

'Not surprising as its the middle of winter and already five o'clock. Going up that hill with only the pinprick allowed from your headlights is going to be interesting. Do you want me to walk in front waving my torch like they used to in the olden days?'

'I'm more likely to ask you to get out and push.'

'If anyone is going to do any pushing, Flight Lieutenant Trent, it's going to be you. A – I'm lighter than you, and B – you're stronger than me.'

This time she was more cautious and it was he that almost ended up on his backside. It took their combined effort to scrape the ice from the windscreen before they could even get into the car. The Hillman started after a few gasps and groans which was a small miracle in itself.

'The only good thing about leaving it so late is there's unlikely to be anything but military traffic on the road.'

'I suppose I should have rung home in case my mother's worried about me. Do you think we'll be back before the film finishes?'

'Good God, that will have been over at least an hour ago. Your girls will be home demanding their supper before we get there.'

'Betty will have left it ready for them – it'll just be something simple like soup. Now the roads are clear, will the girls be leaving?'

The car hit a patch of ice and veered dangerously to the left. A front wheel hit the frozen wall of snow that bordered each side of the road and this sent it careering in the opposite direction.

'Hang on, this could be nasty,' he managed to say as he struggled to hold the car straight. Like every driver, he knew to steer into the skid, not to apply the brakes, but when the road was virtually sheet ice there was very little he could do once he'd lost control.

The car ricocheted against the snow bank and then began to slide inexorably backwards. They hadn't cleared the rear window so they were travelling, at increasing speed, completely blind.

'Let's pray it stops before we reach the promenade. I don't fancy a dip in the sea tonight.'

'I'm going to slam on the brakes and see if I can turn round. I want to see what we're about to hit.'

His manoeuvre worked, but not as well as he'd hoped. They were sliding sideways, which was marginally better than backwards.

'I'm going to wind down the window and hopefully it'll give us some warning before we crash into something.'

Halfway down, the handle snapped off. She was about to poke her head out of the gap but he yelled at her. 'No, absolutely not. You'll be decapitated if you do that.'

Hastily she withdrew her head. He wished he could see her expression, know whether she was terrified by this potentially fatal incident. Then she laughed – not hysterically as other girls might have – but with genuine enjoyment.

'Golly, this is exciting. It's like galloping flat out towards a six-foot hedge, not knowing what's on the other side.'

'Grab hold, I'm going to try to stop. I think we're slowing down a bit.'

He spun the wheel, pumped the brakes and hoped for the best. The car shot across the road and embedded itself nose first into a rock-hard snowdrift.

* * *

Joanna heard the side door open and the voices of their guests echoing down the passageway. The puppy was still sleeping, his breathing even, and she was certain he wasn't going to perish after his unpleasant experience.

Sarah would deal with the girls so she could remain here in front of the fire keeping an eye on their new family member. Ten minutes later, there was a tentative knock on the door and Eleanor poked her head round.

'Excuse me, my lady, but we can't find Sarah and are not exactly sure what we're supposed to be making for our supper.'

'No Sarah? Did you notice if the Hillman was outside?'

Eleanor wasn't listening as she was already peering into the box, smiling like a proud mother. 'I say, where did this splendid little fellow come from? He's absolutely gorgeous, although rather undernourished.'

Joanna explained. 'To return to my original enquiry, was the Hillman there? If it isn't then Sarah has gone out somewhere with the flight lieutenant.'

'Now you come to mention it, my lady, it wasn't. We'd have seen it when the van turned round. You missed an absolutely spiffing film.'

'I expect I'll have the opportunity to see at another time. I've put newspaper underneath the woolly so if Lazzy urinates it shouldn't go through the bottom of the box.'

'If you put him down by the fire where the tiles are, it won't matter if it does. I'll see if I can find something to put in a tray for him to use as a dirt box. He certainly can't go outside.'

'You apparently know a lot more about dogs than I do. Thank you, your help is much appreciated.'

Joanna carefully put the box by the fire and then hurried down the draughty passageway to the kitchen where the other girls were waiting hopefully.

Why hadn't Sarah asked permission to go out? Being alone with a young man wasn't something David would ever have approved of, unless the man in question had already been vetted by him and considered a suitable candidate for Sarah's hand. It was very thoughtless of her daughter to abandon her duties and leave the girls without their supper.

'Betty will have left something for you. Have you checked in the pantry?'

'We don't like to poke about without permission, my lady,' one of the girls said.

'Well, you don't need to ask in future. This is your home for the moment and I want you to treat it as such. Would you mind awfully if I left you to sort out your meal? I need to see if Sarah left me a note of some sort. It's already dark and I'm concerned she's not back yet.'

There was no communication from her daughter, which was unlike her. She stared at the telephone set, willing it to ring, but then her stomach rumbled. She would eat supper with the girls and by then either Sarah and the flight lieutenant would be back or she would have rung to explain why she was delayed.

* * *

The girls retreated to their own domain and she returned to hers, pleased to see that the puppy, although awake, hadn't attempted to climb out of its box. Eleanor had braved the elements and gone to the stable and brought back a bucketful of bran which was now spread thickly in the bottom of a deep silver tray. David would be absolutely furious if ever he found out his precious family silver was being abused in this way but as he wasn't there she must stop worrying about these small things and learn to make her own decisions.

'Lazzy, I'm so glad to see you wide awake. I'm going to put you in your WC – it's where you've got to do your business, little man.'

The puppy made no objection when she picked him up and she'd barely released him when he peed.

'Good boy, clever boy, just what Mummy wants you to do.' She was being quite ridiculous talking to him as if he was a human child, but the puppy wagged his tail and began to snuffle around in the tray.

'I think you're hungry. Don't do that, it's most unhygienic.'

This time he drank from the bowl without assistance but she still had to hold out the scraps of food as he didn't seem to quite grasp how to eat it on his own.

As soon as he'd done she put him back into the tray and again he obliged by opening his bowels and his bladder. The tray now both looked and smelt quite revolting – maybe this was one job she wouldn't do herself.

The telephone rang. She was so eager to pick it up she forgot to replace the puppy in his box before she ran down the passageway.

12

Sarah was flung sideways as the car hit the snow and she caught her right leg below the knee on something hard – probably the gearstick. For a moment she was disorientated, her heart thudding, unable to react. The impact had stalled the engine. They were in total darkness. There was no moon tonight. Slowly, her head cleared and she was aware of him talking to her.

'Sarah, are you hurt? Can you open the door?'

'I'm fine, but I've hurt my right leg. I don't think it's too bad but I can feel blood trickling down my shin. I wish it wasn't so dark. My torch is in my pocket but for some reason my hands won't move.'

'Sit tight, sweetheart, I'll go over the back of my seat and out through the rear passenger door.'

She clenched her hands on her lap, trying to stem the trembling, but failing miserably. The car rocked and then somehow he contrived to get his long length over the back of his seat and into the space behind. He then kicked the door open using both feet and the next thing she knew he had reached in and picked her up.

Someone from the hotel must have heard the crash because there was now light from several torches wavering towards them. 'I'm quite capable of walking, Angus. You're likely to drop me when you slip on the ice and cause me more damage.'

He ignored her request and yelled at the approaching figures. 'We are not seriously hurt but Miss Harcourt has injured her leg. I'm bringing her in. I think somebody had better try and shove the car out of the way as it's causing a serious obstruction at the moment.'

In the flickering pinpoints of light, she saw two of the men were ARP wardens. 'Don't you worry, flight lieutenant, we'll get it shifted. You get your young lady inside out of the cold.'

She'd expected to be taken to a side room but a woman in a smart black suit conducted them upstairs and into a vacant bedroom. 'If you would care to put Miss Harcourt down, sir, we can take care of her until the doctor arrives.'

'If you don't want your beautiful bedspread and carpet completely ruined by my blood, then I need your first aid kit and we can take care of it ourselves.'

The woman took one look at the blood soaking through the leg of Sarah's slacks and spread two thick bath towels on top of the bed. Hopefully, that would be sufficient.

'Angus, you know the drill,' said Sarah. 'You saw what I did last time. What I need is a bandage and a thick pad of gauze to stem the bleeding temporarily. That should hold until you've sterilised a needle and thread and can sew me up.'

The housekeeper, the chambermaid and another man in a black frock coat stared at her with open mouths. Only Angus reacted.

'I'm not bloody sewing you up and you're not doing it yourself. We'll get the local quack to do it. I'm going to ring the base before I'm pronounced AWOL and then ring your mother and tell her we've got to spend the night here because of the weather.' He gave her a reassuring smile. 'I won't tell her you've been hurt. No point in worrying her needlessly.'

It was all very well for Angus to say they were spending the night away from home so casually. She shouldn't even be with him and to stay out all night, however innocent, was just not on.

The man – presumably the manager – nodded and disappeared. The first aid kit arrived at the double carried by a bootboy in a livery two sizes too big for him.

'I'm not going to remove my trouser leg as I might well make it worse. It's probably easier if you do it, but I'll tell you what to do.' This wasn't true as she might well exacerbate the injury by pressing bits of material into the gash. She thought if the true extent of the injury was exposed it would upset those present.

Ten minutes after their arrival, her leg was elevated on a pile of cushions and the injury temporarily taken care of. It wasn't bad enough to require a tourniquet – thank God. She was plied with hot tea with sugar, which she refused, and the young waitress willingly poured her a cup without. Sugar was good for shock but it would make her gag.

'Would you bring me a jug of water? I need to drink as much as I can to help replace the blood I've lost.'

Knowing it was good for her, she forced down two glasses before her stomach rebelled. While she waited for Angus to return, she closed her eyes and tried to force her mind away from the thought of just how badly her leg might be injured. She'd done everything she would have done if tending to an injured person at an event, apart from cutting away the trouser leg. The doctor had been sent for and the housekeeper, who proved to be friendly despite her austere appearance, had said he was on his way and would be there within a quarter of an hour.

Angus arrived before the doctor. 'Your mother was relieved to hear from us. Tony, Wing Commander Billings, hadn't even noticed I wasn't back.'

'Was she upset because I'm here unchaperoned?'

'Didn't seem unduly bothered. Your mother is a sensible woman, Sarah, she wouldn't want us to risk our lives driving in the ice and snow at night.'

Sarah rather thought she would certainly hear a lot more about this escapade when she returned tomorrow but her mother was too polite to voice her displeasure to Angus.

'Are they sending someone to collect us tomorrow? What about the poor Hillman? Will you have to pay for it or be put on a charge for writing it off?'

'Yes, no idea, and no and no.' He grinned and stretched out beside her on the double bed. As his shoes were on the bath towels, it didn't matter that he hadn't removed them.

'You're an idiot, flight lieutenant, but I'm finding I quite enjoy your company. I'm going to miss you when you go.'

'And I you, Sarah. I know there's an age difference, that my having a relationship with you is highly unsuitable, but I find myself unable to resist.'

Her blood pressure was dropping. She would have to ask them to send for an ambulance, which she hated the thought of doing. One glance at the blood-soaked bandage was enough to tell her things were bad. She was glad that she had Angus with her as she was sure he wouldn't panic and a lot of men would.

* * *

Angus noticed the temporary bandages on her leg were no longer white. If the blood had soaked through so many layers of gauze, things were worse than he'd realised. The doctor had better get a move on. Her skin was noticeably paler; when he casually brushed his fingers against her hand, he was horrified to find it cold and clammy.

He swung his legs to the floor. 'I think I can hear the doctor.'

He met the man limping his way along the passageway, his black medical bag in his hand. 'It's not good, I think I should have taken her straight to hospital. She's losing a lot of blood.'

'I've sent for an ambulance, but I'll see what I can do before it gets here.'

The doctor was efficient and professional. After scrubbing his hands at the sink, he produced scissors and cut off the temporary bandage along with the trouser leg. He deftly washed the long gash, with surgical spirit judging by the smell, and then nodded.

'Could be worse. No major veins or arteries damaged. I can stitch it up here...'

Angus had thought Sarah had passed out but she opened her eyes and interrupted. 'Don't ask the flight lieutenant, ask me. I'm the patient, not him. Here is just fine by me.'

'Right. Do you want any pain relief?'

'No – just get on with it. I'd have done it myself but I wasn't allowed to.'

Angus waited for the doctor to look horrified, patronise her, but instead he nodded. 'Probably better to have left it to me. I don't need to tell you it won't be comfortable but I'll be quick.'

Angus wasn't sure if he should hold her hand, offer her physical comfort, but she smiled at him and shook her head. He couldn't watch – didn't know why she wasn't screaming in agony.

'There. Nasty bit's over. You can open your eyes now, flight lieutenant.'

Both Sarah and the medic laughed. 'Sorry, didn't know I'd done so. Is there anything I can do?'

'The patient needs to keep up her fluids – tea would go down well with both of us.'

'I'll ring down to the kitchen and have some brought up, Dr French,' the housekeeper said from behind him. Angus hadn't realised the woman was still in the room.

French dressed and bandaged the injury, which now had seven neat stitches in it, and returned to the sink to wash his hands thoroughly.

'Was it very bad, Sarah?'

'No worse than I expected and a lot better than being carted off to hospital.' She raised her voice and called across to the doctor. 'I don't need an ambulance so I take it you'll cancel it.'

'I'll do that now. Your local chap is Willoughby, isn't he? I'll let him know what happened so he can keep an eye on you. The sutures need to come out in a week or maybe a day or two sooner.'

French walked across still drying his hands on the towel. 'I've heard all about you, Miss Harcourt, you saved a man's leg and quite possibly his life the other week. I'm a general surgeon at the hospital he was sent to, as well as the GP.'

'I'm surprised that my name's been mentioned, but very pleased. I'm hoping to become a medical student myself.'

'I'll write you a glowing reference. According to Doug Willoughby, you know as much as many newly qualified doctors. Any hospital would be mad not to take you on.'

'Thank you, that's very kind of you. I'll definitely put your name down as a reference along with Dr Willoughby. My leg feels much better and so do I. I've been forcing water down my throat ever since this happened.'

'Then I'm sure that a cup of tea will be an improvement. Delighted to have met you, Miss Harcourt. Good luck with your application.' He turned and pointed to a small white envelope on the bedside table. 'Pain relief if you need it.'

As soon as the quack had gone, she started to wriggle towards the edge of the bed. 'I desperately need the loo. I do hope it's a private bathroom behind that door as I doubt that I can hop all the way down the corridor to find another one.'

He leaned in and snatched her up before she could protest. 'I could always hold you over the sink – I'm sure you wouldn't be the first hotel guest to have done that.'

His suggestion had the desired result and she giggled. A waitress arrived then with a loaded tray – not tea this time but coffee and sandwiches and cake. They'd only eaten a couple of hours ago, but the thought was kind.

'The bathroom's behind that door, sir. I'll hold it open for you.'

He put Sarah down beside the WC and then backed out hastily and closed the door firmly behind him. To give her privacy, he moved to the far side of the room before replying to the waitress.

'How did you know we'd prefer coffee to tea?'

'I didn't, I was just told to bring it up. Do you think your young lady will need any assistance?'

'She'll yell if she does. Thank you.' He slipped her a silver threepenny bit and she all but skipped away with her tip clutched in her hand. This was turning out to be a rather expensive outing.

God knows how much two rooms at this swanky place was going to cost him and he certainly didn't have enough on him to pay the bill. He could probably afford one room but he wasn't sure either Sarah or the management would agree.

'Angus, I'm finished, would you be so kind as to come and collect me?'

Her voice carried wonderfully and he was smiling as he pushed open the door. 'I'm going to have to sleep in here with you. You can't go to the bathroom without my help. I'll ask for a camp bed...'

'You can sleep on the same bed as me. I'm quite sure even the vicar wouldn't disapprove in the circumstances. We'll both be fully clothed and we can put a bolster down the middle.'

As he carried her back to the bed, just the mention of clothing, or the lack of it, made his pulse race. 'Well, I'll be fully clothed but as you're minus one trouser leg I don't think you qualify. Do you think I should ask whoever is coming to collect us to call in at Goodwill House for some fresh slacks?'

'No, the less my mother knows about this adventure, the better. The arrival of that stray puppy was fortuitous as it'll keep her busy and stop her worrying.'

He put her gently on the bed and then draped a blanket over her legs.

'Thank you, I know this is embarrassing for both of us but I do appreciate you looking after me. I think we could have been killed so we're lucky to be here relatively unscathed.'

'I'm sorry you were injured. I should have had more sense than to attempt the return journey. For God's sake – I'm a bloody fighter pilot and don't go up in weather like this.'

'Stop blaming yourself and pour me some coffee. I wouldn't mind something to eat as well. All this excitement has made me hungry.'

* * *

Joanna was met halfway down the icy passageway by the puppy who seemed to have made an almost miraculous recovery after just a few hours' sleep and something to eat.

'Well, Lazzy, what a clever little fellow you are. You came to find your mummy. I'll go and fetch your box and then make you comfortable in the kitchen.' She felt quite ridiculous talking to the animal but he seemed to appreciate her rambling as he was licking her hand and trying to lick her face as she picked him up.

'Sarah's stuck in Ramsgate for the night with her handsome chap. I'm glad they are staying somewhere respectable as I don't want there to be any unpleasant gossip. I'd much prefer her to become involved with him rather than go off somewhere and train to be a doctor.' She sighed and kissed the puppy's cold, wet nose. 'Whatever I want, I'll not stand in her way. I just want her to be happy, but do wish she could be content doing what other young ladies of her age do.'

The puppy wriggled and licked and she was quite relieved to put him in his box and then carry him safely in that to the warmth of the kitchen. She wasn't sure exactly where to put the box as she didn't want him to be trodden on if he happened to be out when someone came in in the dark.

'Lady Harcourt, why don't you put his box under the table along with his litter tray?' Eleanor said from behind her, almost making her drop her precious burden.

'You startled me, my dear, I thought all of you were upstairs playing cribbage or something similar.'

'We are, but I've been sent down to make the cocoa. Would you like some?'

'Yes, that would be splendid. I think I'll make a hot-water bottle for him and put it under his blanket. I don't want him to be cold.'

'After being trapped next door, anywhere in the kitchen will seem like paradise to him. Do you have any idea how he got in there or where he came from?'

'I thought perhaps you girls could investigate tomorrow for me. What surprises me the most is the fact that there is a puppy of any sort around in February.'

'I'm not sure if it makes any difference to dogs, my lady. If a bitch comes into season then any dog in the neighbourhood will oblige.'

This was a highly unusual conversation to be having with an unmarried young lady. Joanna was almost tempted to forgo the cocoa but the chocolatey aroma was quite delicious and they'd had a delivery of milk that morning. Cocoa made with water really wasn't very nice at all.

* * *

The following morning, Joanna was up and dressed by six o'clock – to be seen so early was unheard of for her but she was desperate to see how Lazarus had survived the night on his own. She hurried towards the kitchen, expecting to hear piteous whining, yapping, but a worrying silence met her.

Betty didn't come until seven thirty so she would have to get the range burning herself if she wanted a cup of tea before then. Why was it so quiet? She paused outside the door too nervous to open it in case the worst had happened and the poor little thing had perished after all.

She pushed open the door and almost lost her balance as an ecstatic, wriggling puppy threw himself at her ankles. She reached down and scooped him up and this time didn't mind his frantic licks on her face.

With him under her arm, she switched on the light – she wasn't so foolish as to step in without checking there wasn't anything unpleasant waiting for her on the tiles.

The floor was spotless. 'What a good boy you are. I can't let you out as it's far too cold but when Sarah comes home she can take you to the ménage. I hope you like horses as we have three of them here.'

Although there'd been no nasty surprises on the floor, there were several under the table. She was tempted to leave it for Betty to clear up but decided that would be unfair. This was her dog so his mess was her responsibility.

When her housekeeper arrived, she was greeted by a scampering puppy and immediately dropped to her knees so he could stand on his hind legs and lick every bit of her he could reach. 'Oh, my lady, where did he come from? Isn't he sweet? Look at the size of his paws – I reckon he's going to be massive.'

'I don't care how big he is. Before you take off your coat and boots, would you do me an enormous favour? Could you empty his litter tray?' She knew she should do this herself but did so dislike the cold and the smell from the tray.

'Happy to do it. Where's Miss Sarah? Not unwell, I hope.'

'She went to Ramsgate with her flight lieutenant and they were forced to stay overnight as the weather was so bad. Flight Lieutenant Trent is a man I can trust to take care of Sarah and not do anything untoward.'

'I didn't think she was interested in having a boyfriend. She's likely to get her heart broken if she falls for a fighter pilot. My Bert thinks once it all kicks off the Brylcreem boys will be the ones to die first.'

'How very depressing of him to say that. I'm sure it won't be as serious on either side but I'm pleased that she's found herself a young man to go out with. I wouldn't want her to go away to train as a doctor having absolutely no experience of that side of things.'

Betty had made a good point. Sarah was still very young and could easily imagine her feelings for the young man were more than they were. She hoped her daughter wouldn't be heartbroken by this friendship if something went wrong.

13

Sarah couldn't sleep. The pain in her leg was keeping her awake and she didn't want to shift about too often as it would disturb Angus.

'Take one of the tablets, sweetheart, don't be a martyr,' he said from the darkness. He was obviously as wide awake as she was.

'I'm sorry I woke you. Yes, if you'd be so kind as to take me to the loo once more then I'll take one when I get back.'

'I'm glad you stopped drinking pints of water. I'm quite exhausted tracking backwards and forwards.'

'I'm light as a feather, flight lieutenant, so don't you dare complain.' She couldn't imagine any other man making a difficult situation as easy as he did. His humorous comments made her smile and she always responded in kind.

He'd removed his shoes, uniform jacket and tie, but nothing else. He padded around her side of the bed and switched on the small lamp on the table beside her. As this was her third trip, she knew the procedure and put her arm around his neck without being asked.

The hotel had kindly provided them with toothbrushes, tooth powder and fresh towels. He wouldn't be able to shave in the morning and she was rather looking forward to seeing him looking anything but his usual immaculate self.

Would his beard be the same glorious chestnut of his hair? How could she be thinking of such a thing when she was in so much pain? She winced as he put her down but managed to hide it from him.

He carried her back without comment and then handed her two tablets and a glass of water. She swallowed them obediently. Even with the water they tasted vile, and she guessed they were something considerably stronger than aspirin.

He tucked her into the extra blankets supplied by the housekeeper before clambering onto the bed and settling down himself. She shivered. Even with the blankets she was still cold or perhaps residual shock was making her think she was?

Then his arms were around her, her bottom was pulled close to his middle. He pushed her hair aside and kissed the back of her neck. A surge of unusual heat travelled like lightning around her body. She relaxed into his embrace and let the morphine do its work.

* * *

She woke with an unpleasant taste in her mouth and an inability to concentrate. For a moment she couldn't register her surroundings. Surely not? She'd spent the night in a man's arms and even if they were fully clothed, she wasn't entirely sure that her mother would approve.

'Morning, how's the leg? Give me a moment and I'll take you to the bathroom.' Angus yawned loudly, extricated his arm from beneath her waist and rolled away. She heard his feet thump on the ground.

'I'm not desperate for a pee but if you could pour me a glass of water I'd be grateful. Opioids are wonderful for pain but the after-effects aren't very pleasant.' Her voice sounded hoarse and talking was painful.

There was the gurgle of water going into a glass. 'You'll need to sit up, sweetheart, you can't drink it lying flat.'

Pushing herself upright was a struggle. Her limbs were as uncoordinated as a newborn foal and even the slightest movement sent shafts of agony down her leg.

'Here, let me help you.' He slid one arm around her back and then smoothly moved her. 'I think you've got a temperature. I'm going to call the doctor. I think it's likely you'll have to go into hospital after all.'

'I've also got a sore throat, headache and everywhere aches. Coincidental, but I think the fever is caused by a common cold. Before you ring, would you mind awfully showing me the wound?'

'Drink your water whilst I scrub up – that's what you medics call it, isn't it?'

The fact that he accepted her diagnosis without comment, treated her as if she was indeed someone qualified to know about these things, made her like him more. She drank the water, replaced the glass, and braced herself for what was going to be painful.

He was surprisingly gentle and when he removed the dressing they both sighed with relief. There was no sign of infection, the skin was the colour it should be, no inflammation at all and no heat. The doctor had left half a dozen clean dressings and he deftly re-bandaged her leg.

'Whilst you're having a freshen up and so on I'll see if the kitchen can send us up some breakfast. I don't know when transport will be here but it might be in the next hour.'

'Golly, it's only half past six. It'll still be dark outside and I've no wish to travel until it's fully light.'

After washing her face and hands, cleaning her teeth and doing the best she could with her hair, she was ready to return to the bedroom. By holding on to the sink, she was able to hop, slowly and painfully, to the door and open it.

'Angus, I'm ready. You can have the bathroom now.'

'I'm coming. Breakfast will be here in ten minutes. I didn't know what you wanted so I ordered for you.'

When she was safely back on the bed with her leg outstretched, she settled back with a sigh. Moving about was horrible and she dreaded the journey back. Heaven knows how she was going to get into the cab of a lorry – even Angus would have difficulty lifting her up that high without causing her pain.

She could hear him splashing about in the bathroom even with the door closed. In the flurry to get her to the loo, she'd not had time to see what colour his beard was. She wondered if he'd been called ginger nut at school. She'd ask him when next they talked about their families. Swallowing was becoming increasingly painful and she'd sneezed several times already into her handkerchief.

The waitress arrived with their breakfast and she croaked that the girl should come in as he was still busy.

'Good morning, Miss Harcourt, you don't sound too clever. There's a nasty head cold going around – I reckon you've got that.'

'It all smells absolutely delicious, but I really can't manage to swallow anything like toast, bacon or fried bread.'

He'd heard her and took the tray from the waitress and put it on the top of the chest of drawers. 'I ordered scrambled eggs for both of us. Bread and butter for you and toast for me.'

She sneezed half a dozen times and he tossed her his handkerchief. 'Sod's law that you should catch a cold at the same time as injuring your leg. At least you can stay in bed without a guilty conscience.'

'I've been worrying about not being able to look after the horses possibly for weeks. Bates and his son no longer work for us and Mummy has never liked horses.'

'Get a couple of the girls to do it. I should think there must be at least one who is capable of feeding and mucking out.'

By the time the transport arrived an hour later – fortunately a staff car and not a lorry – she was feeling so wretched she made no objection to being bundled up in rugs and carried through the hotel like a parcel. She'd intended to insist that the bill from the doctor was sent to her, that she paid half the hotel bill, but the combination of a vile cold and her leg injury rendered her incapable of thinking straight.

* * *

Angus had told the quack to send the bill to him but French had insisted there was to be no charge. The hotel had been happy to take the notes he'd had; he'd left them an IOU for the balance and promised to send somebody down with it.

He'd also telephoned Lady Harcourt and told her the true state of affairs. She'd been remarkably calm about everything and assured him both her daughter and the horses would be taken care of.

It was appreciably warmer and the snow was already beginning to thaw. Good news in some ways, but it meant the Jerries would be active again in the Channel. Hitler had declared merchant vessels were fair game and his subs were causing havoc with the convoys.

'Thank you for coming, Jimmy, much appreciated. I'll sit in the back.' Although the medic had seemed unconcerned about Sarah having a high temperature, he'd told her mother to arrange for the local chap to visit sometime today just to be sure.

'You'll be pleased to know, Angus, that the Hillman's now back at the base and will be running again very soon. It wasn't as badly pranged as you'd feared.'

Climbing the hill this morning in a more powerful car was uneventful. He carried Sarah in through the front door of her home and was greeted by her mother as well as all the other residents, including the housekeeper.

'Follow me, flight lieutenant, her room's ready,' Lady Harcourt said brightly, but he could see she was worried as she viewed the fever-flushed girl he was carrying so carefully in his arms.

The housekeeper took over as soon as he put Sarah on her bed. The room wasn't warm, a meagre fire in the grate, and although there was a radiator it was stone cold.

Sarah smiled, albeit somewhat feebly, at him. 'Thanks. I hope you don't catch my cold.'

'I rarely catch anything. Rest and recuperate. I'll come and see you when I get another couple of hours free.'

'No, stay way until I'm germ-free. Doesn't matter if I'm ill, but you've got a war to fight.'

'I'm not flying, just supervising. It'll be different in a few weeks.' He touched her hair briefly and then strode out. No time for sentimentality – he'd been absent from his post for too long.

* * *

Jimmy filled him in with what he'd missed – not much of any importance, really. 'Just a couple of Blenheims on reconnaissance flights and the Hurries have practised scrambling. Seems extravagant to keep two squadrons of fighters here just to protect Canterbury Cathedral.'

'The Archbishop of Canterbury is the most important Church of England cleric, at least I think he is. All cathedrals are important, but St Paul's and this one hold a sentimental place in the hearts of Englishmen.'

Jimmy grinned. 'I don't suppose many Englishmen give a damn about cathedrals, it's Englishwomen who care about things like that. I'm afraid the WAAF will be getting their travel warrants next week. Not what you wanted to hear when Miss Harcourt is out of action.'

'It's the taxpayers' money being wasted by having them idle here when they could be doing something useful elsewhere. I'm sure Lady Harcourt will find a suitable replacement for her daughter until she's back on her feet.'

'Bloody bad luck her getting injured like that. Still, better than you in the circumstances.'

Tony was pleased to have him back. 'Had no idea how much you did about the place, old boy, been tearing my hair out this morning trying to keep up with all the paperwork.'

'Sorry about my absence but even more so about the Hillman.'

'Water under the bridge, my friend. How is the young lady? Nasty business – you take as much time as you need to go and see her. By the way, there's an official-looking letter on your desk. I think your posting might have come through.'

A few weeks ago, he'd have been overjoyed he was about to be sent somewhere he could use his training, but now he was dismayed he might have to leave so soon. He'd been eagerly anticipating getting to know Sarah better and possibly persuading her to consider herself his real girlfriend and that they might have a future together one day. After holding her in his arms all night, however innocently, he realised she was beginning to mean a lot more to him than a girlfriend.

'Right, sir, I'll have a deco. I take it you've heard about your posting if I've heard about mine.'

He shook his head. 'Not a dicky bird, so maybe I jumped the gun and it's something else entirely. To tell you the truth, I'd be absolutely buggered if you left before I did.'

The telephones were ringing constantly. The three weeks of comparative peace at Manston were over and he had a nasty feeling life was about to get a hell of a lot busier.

Angus worked flat out all day dealing with admin tasks – requests for twenty-four-hour passes, permissions to leave the base for an evening, requests to see the local medic, as well as the usual tedious stuff about stores, spare parts and so on.

It wasn't until the blackout blinds were drawn and he was the only one left at his desk that he remembered the unopened letter. He checked the time. Eight o'clock – he hoped it wasn't too late to ring and find out how Sarah was doing.

The operator connected him. A voice he didn't recognise answered. 'Goodwill House. How can I help you?'

'Flight Lieutenant Trent here. How's Miss Harcourt?'

'The doctor came this afternoon and said she's poorly with a nasty head cold. Her leg isn't infected. She said to tell you, sir, if you called, that she's doing well and doesn't want you to come until she's no longer contagious.'

'Thank you. Please convey my best wishes. I'll telephone tomorrow for an update.'

He disconnected and then thought he should have asked about the puppy, asked if they'd managed to find someone to take care of the horses, but he wasn't going to ring back. Whatever her wishes, he would take her a gift of some sort tomorrow if he got a spare moment.

Finally, he picked up the letter knife and slit the buff envelope. It was indeed news of his posting. His eyes widened and for a moment he couldn't assimilate what he was reading. He read it a second and third time and then put the letter down. What he needed was a stiff drink with his chums and, from the sounds of merriment coming down the corridor, they were already enjoying themselves in the makeshift officers' mess.

He put the letter back into the envelope and safely inside his jacket. No doubt he'd want to read it again – more than once. Did Tony know the contents? Would they have told him?

It took him several minutes to bring the five of them up to speed with

Sarah's progress. 'Tony, meet your replacement. I'm now a squadron leader and am to take over as CO, as well as leading the squadron when necessary.'

* * *

By the middle of February, the snow had gone and Sarah was fully recovered from both her head cold and the leg injury. Dr Willoughby had come to remove the stitches and was sure that she wouldn't have a scar.

'You'll be glad to be fully fit and able to exercise your horses. I don't envy you taking them out for the first time after they've been confined for so long.'

'I've been able to lunge them as well as turn them into the ménage this week. To tell you the truth, I can't wait to gallop around the countryside again. The house is so quiet now the girls have gone, but our new lodgers should be arriving any day.'

'Land girls, if I'm not mistaken?'

'Yes, there should be at least six of them. They'll be working as a team on the three farms in this area. Actually, I'm surprised they're being sent here as only one of the men has been conscripted so far and none have volunteered.'

'Lord Harcourt was completely against ploughing up your park in order to plant potatoes – has your mother agreed to do so now?'

'The man from the Ministry of Agriculture gave her no choice. Either she agreed or there would be a fine. Our new boarders might well be working here as well as on our other farms.' She flexed her leg and was happy with it. 'By the way, you might well hear from the Royal Free in London as I sent off my application the other day. Dr French and you, as well as the brigade, are down as my references.'

'I'm sure they won't hesitate to offer you a place. I hope they can see you're the perfect candidate for a bursary.'

He picked up his bag and she escorted him to the front door. There was the pattering of feet behind her and the puppy skittered across the boards in his eagerness to greet her.

'This must be the famous puppy you rescued. He's got a lot of wolfhound in him. I hope Lady Harcourt can manage a dog that size when you're not here to exercise it.'

'I hope so, too. I've also got to make arrangements for the horses before I leave. If we've got land girls living with us then I'm hoping that one of them can do it.'

She reached down and picked Lazzy up by his scruff. He wriggled around in her grip and licked her chin. 'Come on, naughty boy, back to the kitchen. I'm sure Betty has a treat for you.'

The housekeeper was looking for her errant charge. 'Sorry, Miss Sarah, he's learned to open the door if it's not properly latched.'

'Betty, has your husband said anything else about when the land girls are coming?'

'My Bert says the land girls will be living here as long as they remain in the Land Army. Goodwill House is in the middle of the three farms they'll be working at and it's no more than a couple of miles in any direction.'

'That's just the news I wanted. It also means we've got room for another four girls if WAAF, ATS or any other service personnel want somewhere to live.'

'Is your young man coming today?'

Sarah rather liked hearing Angus referred to as 'her young man'. Spending the night with him, seeing how kind and honourable he was, had made her reconsider her opinion on having a boyfriend of her own.

He'd called twice and they'd talked for ages and the more time she spent with him, even just remotely, the better she liked him. If only she was a few years older, had more experience of the outside world, then it would be more straightforward. Did she have real feelings for him or was it just having someone of her very own to share things with that she found so appealing?

'He's frightfully busy getting used to his new position and I saw him two days ago. I wonder if he's the youngest squadron leader in the RAF? Did you know he flew over the house yesterday and did a victory roll just for me?'

'I think everybody in the village knew. He's ever so good-looking and I'm not surprised you like him.'

'I don't like him because he's handsome, but I must say it does help, but because he's kind, intelligent, funny and brave. What I don't understand is why he's going out with me when he could have any girl he wanted.'

'Go on with you, Miss Sarah. You're the perfect match. I wonder if any babies you have will be red-headed like him.'

'Golly, we're not even engaged. Please don't talk about babies and certainly not to Mummy. She'd already be planning the wedding and he's not even asked me to marry him.' She laughed. 'We scarcely know each other, far too early to even talk about anything permanent.'

Betty wouldn't let the subject drop. 'Go on, Miss Sarah, would you say yes if he did?'

'I'm determined to become a doctor and I can't be a wife and mother at the same time so obviously I would say no to anyone who might ask me in the next five years.'

She shuddered at the thought of what her father would say if he heard her talking about such things to a servant. Daddy was old-fashioned and believed in the separation of the classes. Discussing such personal matters with a member of staff would never have happened if he was at home but things were different now and she needed someone to talk to.

The puppy wriggled to get down and she clung onto him until they were safely in the kitchen and the door was closed. 'Do you know of anybody in the village who would like to earn a few extra shillings by helping out here when we need them? There are families with the man of the house in France as well as those with their men at sea. Do you think any one of them would be interested?'

'I reckon they'd bite your hand off. They don't get much from the government to make ends meet. Those with young children can't take jobs in the factories or the services because of the nippers.'

'It's going to be too much for Mummy and you to manage possibly as many as ten boarders. We've been lucky because the WAAF girls didn't have to work so were really no trouble at all.'

The telephone jangled noisily. Sarah hurried into the hall and picked it up. 'Sarah Harcourt speaking. How can I help you?'

'Bert Smith here, Miss Harcourt. Them girls will be arriving tomorrow. Can you take them?'

'Absolutely. Do you know how many we'll be getting?'

'There's six expected but I ain't too sure if they'll all be arriving.'

He didn't say goodbye and the line went dead. She'd rather liked Bert when he first married Betty, but he'd turned into a bad-tempered, abrupt man and she didn't envy the girls working under his control.

Six boarders? These girls wouldn't be doing household chores like the WAAF, they'd be too tired after working on the fields all day. This was going to make a lot of extra work for Betty and herself and she just hoped Mummy would do more as well. She was pleased the huge, empty house would be doing something helpful for a change and the money would make things easier.

14

Joanna had never been so busy. The WVS and WI meetings postponed during the bad weather had now been rescheduled. As most of the ladies concerned were in both groups, she decided it made sense to hold the meetings consecutively and to hold them at Goodwill House.

WI members had no uniform and only she, as the chair of the WVS, had a green herringbone tweed suit, red blouse and hat. There were also green overalls but so far none of the women had volunteered to wear them. As these had to be purchased, it was hardly surprising the ladies of the village didn't want to spend some of their precious shillings on something they didn't really like.

She went in search of her daughter, confident the doctor would have finished removing the stitches by now and Sarah would be able to talk to her. She discovered her in the kitchen with Betty.

'I just came to remind both of you that later this afternoon the WI and WVS meetings will be taking place here. Can you light both fires in the drawing room and make sure there are biscuits and tea available?'

'I've already taken care of the fires, my lady. I was able to buy two packets of digestives at Raven's. I don't like going into that shop as his cat sleeps on top of the open bags of rice. I think I was lucky to find any biscuits considering deliveries to the village have been so delayed recently.'

'Well done, Betty. I do hope your young man isn't thinking of coming this afternoon, darling, because as a member of both groups you should be there and not gallivanting around the countryside with him.'

'I expect you've noticed, Mummy, that I'm dressed for riding. I've got three horses to exercise before I can attend any meetings. As far as I know, Angus isn't coming. By the way, we should be getting the land girls tomorrow.'

Joanna frowned. 'I know the wretched animals have to be exercised but please don't come to the drawing room smelling of the stables.'

'I wouldn't dream of it. I can't believe how much Lazzy has grown since you found him. He also appears to know his way around a horse so I'm thinking maybe he came from a farm with horses.'

'My Bert said that they had a litter of cross-breed puppies at the kennels. Do you think he might have come from there?'

'I'm certainly not going to ask. He belongs to us now and I defy anyone to say differently. I've got several letters to write and telephone calls to make. Perhaps you could bring me a coffee and a sandwich of some sort for luncheon, Betty?'

There was a loud knock on the front door as Joanna was about to duck down the passageway to her own sitting room but instead she hurried across to open it.

'Morning, my lady, quite a bundle for you today. I reckon everything's been held up by the weather,' the village postman said cheerfully as he handed over a dozen assorted envelopes.

She saw there were three from David. The flimsy blue airmail envelopes were easily distinguished from the others. Her throat constricted and it was as if a weight had settled on her chest. Her darling daughter had sent off her application for a scholarship to train to be a doctor at the Royal Free Hospital in London. What if her husband had written to say he forbade her to do any such thing?

Maybe she would leave those letters until another time. After all, one of them had already taken over a month to arrive so it would hardly matter if she left them for another day or two. She had far more important things to do than read letters.

The first of them being to write the agenda for the WVS meeting. She rather thought that she'd been a less than satisfactory wife, an adequate mother, but was an excellent committee member. Planning what her group was intending to contribute when the fighting really started, when shortages of everything were widespread, when bombs were dropped and people lost their homes, was the one time she was confident in her abilities and knew that she was doing a valuable job.

* * *

Angus had put a metaphorical rocket up the backsides of the builders and finally things were moving on at speed. The enlarged and improved officers' accommodation, mess and so on would be completed and ready for occupation in two weeks. The underground fuel storage facility would be filled in the next day or two and they now had half a dozen bowsers ready to refuel any kites that arrived from the continent once the balloon went up over there.

He'd caught the men listening to Lord Haw-Haw's nightly broadcast yesterday evening. That man was seeking to undermine public confidence but as far as he could see none of his chaps took it seriously and listened because they thought the man's strange use of English funny. There was no point in banning the broadcast – better to encourage the men to listen and laugh.

He'd managed to requisition a battered motorbike from the motor pool and now used this to zoom around the base keeping an eye on things. Every day, lorries trundled in with spare parts, furniture, miscellaneous items as well as spare uniform, and the vast quantities of food and drink required for the hundreds living there.

They were also getting things delivered by air – which made perfect sense as they were an RAF base. The Avro Ansons, or Annies as they were often called, had no difficulty landing on the massive runway and they were unloaded, refuelled and back in the air in a commendably short space of time. This was at his insistence as he wanted the men involved to get practice with a rapid turnaround.

All too soon, fighters would be landing here to refuel before returning to the fray. No doubt damaged bombers would use the strip on their return from raids over Europe and hope to be patched up before continuing to their home base.

Dressed in his sheepskin jacket, flying boots, helmet, gauntlets and goggles, as always when he was about to take a trip on his motorbike, he stepped out to the welcome sight of builders looking industrious for a change. Tradesmen weren't immune from conscription and most of the blokes were either too young to shave, or too old to be working at all.

Only twenty-one to twenty-eight-year-olds had been drafted so far, so presumably the missing thirty-year-olds had volunteered. Nobody would be conscripted into the RAF – it was a volunteer-only service. Many of the men working here were regulars like himself but there were a few that signed up already qualified and experienced mechanics. Those who worked as orderlies, catering and other routine tasks had only required the basic training before being posted.

Of course, all the flyers were regulars. Those that had volunteered last September wouldn't be arriving at any base for months. It had taken two years for him to be ready for active service. Somehow he doubted, when things got going, if the poor sods joining the RAF would get a fraction of that experience before being sent to fight.

Being a flyer was a high-risk occupation but he was more than ready to fight for king and country – even more so now he had Sarah in his life. Hitler had to be stopped and being at war with Germany was the only way to do this.

He parked the bike each night on its stand outside the admin block. The only protection from the elements was half a tarpaulin chucked over it. So far it had kicked into life every time. He was heading for the far end of the base, to the building where the flight controllers worked, when he swerved, put his foot down and just avoided going over the handlebars.

To the right of him, where the base bordered the extensive grounds of Goodwill House, a massive horse flew over the six-foot hedge and, scarcely checking its stride, galloped towards him. It had to be Sarah. He'd known she could ride but this was the first time he'd seen her in action.

His mouth was dry and his heart was still thudding uncomfortably. He wasn't sure of the etiquette when it came to motorbikes and equines but to be on the safe side he turned off the engine and kicked it onto its stand. She was in full control of the beast and without her seeming to do anything at all it settled into a canter. By the time she was close enough to hear him, it was walking.

'That's a magnificent horse, and you're an excellent rider. I take it you've jumped that hedge before.'

She leaned over and patted the sweating neck of the gelding, kicked her feet out of the stirrup irons and dropped smoothly to the ground before answering. 'Actually, I haven't. It was what you might call a leap of faith. Don't look so horrified, I did know it was grass and not concrete. I thought you would be a rider as you come from a similar background to mine.'

'I do ride, but reluctantly. Not something I'm good at or enjoy.'

She looped the reins over her arm. 'I need to walk him until he's cool. I don't expect you to keep me company. I just rode this way on impulse. I've got two more horses to exercise, so can't hang about too long.'

'I'll walk with you for a bit. The bike will be safe enough here. I'm assuming you had your stitches out or you wouldn't be riding.'

'This morning. I really wanted to tell you that I sent my application in the day before yesterday. Did you manage to speak to your uncle?'

'Christ, I completely forgot. I'm so sorry. I'll telephone him when I get back to the office later. I don't suppose your letter will have reached his desk yet.'

'I don't suppose it'll reach his desk at all. He's head of surgery, isn't he? I shouldn't think he has anything to do with medical students.'

'Only when they begin to specialise. However, he is on the board of the hospital and any bursary recipients are decided by all of them.'

'Then please do speak to him when you get a moment.'

'Are you quite sure your horse won't bolt when a kite comes in? We're expecting a couple of Ansons any minute.'

'He's bombproof. I wouldn't bring my mare here as she's a bit skittish.' They were walking along the grass towards the new blocks that were almost complete. 'It all looks very splendid. When do you think you'll be moving into your new accommodation?'

'As you can see, the windows are just being glazed and the interior's being finished. No more than a couple of weeks, I should think.' He pointed to the other large new building. 'That's the extra overnight accommodation and so on for any squadrons that are temporarily based here.'

She looked suitably impressed. Even with a mud-splattered face, she was still lovely. 'I can't get away until the weekend. I thought we could go to London. Take in a show, or failing that, the cinema. We don't have to stay overnight if your mother would disapprove.'

'I'd absolutely love to but I'm going to be frantically busy as the new paying guests start arriving from tomorrow. Could we go to Hastings instead? That would be an adventure for me and it wouldn't mean staying away.'

'Then that's what we'll do. I'm sorry, sweetheart, but I'd better get on. Can't be seen to be shirking now I'm in charge. The place doesn't seem the same without Tony even though he did bugger all.' She laughed as he'd hoped.

'I liked him and so did Mummy. She's rather disappointed that another older officer hasn't replaced him.'

'Tony had a bit of a reputation with the ladies so good thing he's not here.'

'Will you give me a leg-up? Be easier than letting down the stirrup leather.' She turned her back, bent her leg, and he hoisted her into the saddle.

'What time can I collect you on Saturday?'

'Late morning – I need to do the horses and so on first. Bye.'

He'd been going to suggest that this time she use the gate to leave but she was off, heading straight for the hedge. He held his breath as the horse soared over the barrier with a foot to spare. There was a spontaneous round of applause from behind him and he only then became aware that they'd gathered quite an audience in the short time she'd been on the base.

He would have loved to take her to a smart hotel, to the theatre, but was relieved she wasn't able to go. The hotel bill from their last excursion had made a serious dent in his wallet. If he didn't have a small annuity from a long-defunct aunt, he wouldn't be able to take her out at all this month. Things should improve after his promotion as it had included a substantial increase in pay.

As he returned to his mundane duties, his mind often drifted to Sarah.

He was forced to admit that she now meant a great deal to him and he was in serious danger of falling in love with her. He hadn't intended to get so involved and her being so young just made things more difficult.

His mouth curved. To hell with it, there was a war on, he'd see her as often as he could whilst he was still stationed here and see where it went.

* * *

Sarah rode out on the other hunter for an hour and a half and then got her mare into the shafts of the gig. The harness had needed a lot of elbow grease and saddle soap to restore it but, although old, she was confident it wouldn't fall apart at an inopportune moment.

So far, she'd only driven around the estate, not wanting to risk meeting motorised traffic until she was sure Starlight wouldn't shy and misbehave and tip them both into a ditch. She was about to clamber onto the seat when Betty called her.

'Can I come with you, Miss Sarah? I've got errands to run for your mother and it'll be a lot quicker in that carriage.'

'I'm not sure how Starlight will react when we meet other vehicles. She won't bolt, but she might be a bit lively.'

'You know I like horses, and I trust you to keep me safe. I've been watching you driving the gig about the place and I've been waiting for an opportunity to get a ride in it with you.'

'Here we go then. Literally, Betty, hang on to your hat.'

After releasing the brake, she clicked her tongue and snapped the whip above Starlight's ears. Her horse responded immediately and threw her weight into the collar. The gig rolled forward smoothly. She kept her to a brisk walk until they were safely onto the road and then pushed the mare into a trot.

'My word, this is fun. The last time I was in an open carriage was when I was helping with the harvest years ago and we used to go to the fields in the back of the hay cart.'

'Once I'm certain Starlight is safe, I want to teach my mother to drive her. It would make her life so much easier being able to get to the village and back in this.'

'I shouldn't bother, Miss Sarah. Even if you persuaded her to take the reins, she wouldn't harness your mare. Why don't you teach me instead? I'll be here even when you go in September – or whenever it is – and I was thinking I'd like to look after the horses and the poultry.'

'I was going to say you wouldn't have time but if we're taking on some extra help in the house then you probably would. Your Bert wasn't very helpful about the girls coming tomorrow. In fact, I don't think he knows anything about them apart from their names and he didn't even give me those.'

'He certainly hasn't said anything to me. I have a nasty feeling none of them are country girls, so I doubt they'll be able to help with exercising the horses. Anybody can muck out and feed once they know what's what.'

Whilst Betty went to the post office, the ironmonger and the butcher, Sarah had time to find somewhere she could turn the carriage. It had taken a fraction of the time to reach the village in the gig, but the disadvantages soon became apparent. There was nowhere safe to leave the vehicle unattended as even the High Street was too narrow to allow a lorry to pass without terrifying the mare.

What they needed were usable bicycles for coming here and then the gig could possibly be used by the land girls so they didn't have to walk. There would be plenty of places to put Starlight whilst they were working. She was pretty sure that one of the farms still used horses and the others definitely had stables and barns.

Tomorrow she'd take the girls to see where they'd be working and make sure there'd be no objection to them arriving in the gig, rather than on foot. On the return journey, a lorry full of noisy soldiers approached. The driver, seeing her, slowed down immediately and with a cheerful wave drove past, somehow managing not even to change gear whilst he did so.

'Good girl, Starlight, that wasn't so terrifying, was it? As long as other road users are as polite as that soldier, I don't think they'll be any problems with her.'

She looked around with interest, enjoying seeing the minor road that led to the village from a different angle. Betty interrupted her thoughts.

'My Bert doesn't want the first girls starting until they've all arrived. He said he's not going to go through the basics more than once.'

'Then that should give me time to show them how to look after the horses, harness Starlight and drive the gig. I just hope at least two of them are happy to work with her.'

'If they've signed on for the Land Army, they must be interested in animals and such, don't you think?'

'Good point. Forgive me for saying so, Betty, but I'm really glad they won't be working with your husband all the time. Why has he been put in charge of them, do you know?'

Fortunately, Betty didn't take offence at her criticism of her husband.

'It was his idea to apply so he got lumbered with the job. We could have had two of them staying with us, but he wouldn't hear of it. The lady who's in charge was ever so delighted to have them stay all together. There'll be other teams, but these will just be for his lordship's farms.'

'That's what I thought. I'm going to have to rush if I'm going to get Star put away and get cleaned up for the meetings.'

'Joan and Val are hoping to be taken on here. They can't manage on the pittance the War Office gives them now their hubbies are with the BEF in France.'

'That would be ideal as Mummy knows them already.'

* * *

Sarah slipped into the drawing room just as the first meeting, the WI, was starting. Mrs Thomas was in charge, which meant Mummy was sitting with the others ready to be told what was happening and what they were supposed to be doing. As always, the ladies had brought with them the knitting, sewing or crocheting they were doing for the war effort. No idle hands allowed at a WI meeting.

'You are late, Sarah Harcourt. I would expect someone from your background to understand the importance of punctuality,' Mrs Thomas said scathingly.

Several of the women murmured their agreement but she did get some sympathetic looks from the younger members. 'I apologise for my tardiness, Mrs Thomas.' She should have left it there but the woman's sneer prompted her to continue to speak. 'I can assure you I haven't been sitting around twiddling my thumbs. I have three horses to exercise and take care of as well as other duties here. I'm also not an official member...'

'Sarah, please sit down. You're holding up the meeting and we've a lot to discuss today,' her mother said sternly.

Sarah felt her cheeks turning red and hid her face from the other women. Why was her mother so different when she was in charge of the WVS?

* * *

The ladies of the WI decided they would help the Red Cross and St John pack comfort parcels for the soldiers serving overseas. This was something she was already involved with and therefore volunteered to be the go-between as she was already an active member of St John. There was also discussion about the cleaning rota at the church, which wasn't anything to do with the WI. As all those involved were actually present it seemed sensible to deal with that important problem before they took a break for tea and biscuits.

Sarah and Betty left the ladies chatting. Mummy moved to the far end of the drawing room to have an informal interview with the two ladies who wanted to work here. Neither of them had babies but they had three children each at the village school. Presumably there was a neighbour on hand to let them in when they returned, as their mothers wouldn't be back when school finished in half an hour.

Not every woman – despite being urged to by the vicar, Mrs Thomas and Mummy – had joined the WVS, but all of them were members of the WI. Sarah was pretty sure that when the meetings were held in the village there was a much bigger turnout. Tea over, all the biscuits consumed, the second meeting began. She thought also the fact that those not in the WVS would have been obliged to stay might have had something to do with it.

'Ladies, I'm pleased to tell you that we now have an excellent selection of clean, mended, ready-to-wear clothes to be donated to families in need. We also have boxes of toys, books and even some essential items for new mothers. I know the war started six months ago and, apart from many of our menfolk being away from home either in the Royal or

Merchant Navy, the army or RAF, so far, thank the Lord, no civilian has died.'

'Excuse me, my lady, I beg to differ,' Mrs Thomas interrupted officiously. 'My sister lives in London and said that there have been hundreds of fatalities caused by the blackout. I believe we can consider them war casualties, don't you?'

'Very true, Mrs Thomas, thank you so much for pointing it out. However, what I was about to mention was the fact that as our village and Ramsgate are so close to Manston and the Channel that it's inevitable that we'll be targeted by the Luftwaffe eventually. I want to know if everybody has somewhere safe to go when the air raid siren sounds?'

Sarah was now paying full attention and realised that these meetings weren't as boring as she'd thought. This was a useful discussion as it soon became apparent that the Anderson shelters provided by the government to those who could afford to pay for them hadn't been, in every case, successfully fitted out. Others who had no private shelter would have to use the public shelters, little better than sheds, provided by the parish council. Several of the ladies said that they had no intention of going down into theirs as it was damp and smelly. They intended to hide under the stairs.

Today she was going to insist that Mummy came down to the shelter in the cellar and that she knew where everything was.

15

Joanna made copious notes and by the end of the meeting knew exactly who needed help to make their shelters safe. Some had opted for Morrison shelters – a large metal table under which children could sleep and be protected if a bomb fell on the house.

Joan and Valerie, both sensible and reliable women, were now part of the staff. They were prepared to do whatever was needed as long as their work schedule fitted around the children's school attendance.

It was almost dark by the time everyone had gone home. 'That went well, don't you think, darling?'

'Yes, it did. Pity Lazzy interrupted the meeting and then disgraced himself on the rug. Mrs Thomas was horrified.' Sarah was laughing as she recalled the incident.

'Naughty boy, you aren't allowed in the drawing room again until you can control your bladder.' The puppy rolled on his back in a most undignified fashion and waved his legs in the air. She reached down and rubbed his belly. 'I have three letters as yet unread from your father. I'm rather dreading opening them.'

'It doesn't matter what he says or wants as he's not in a position to know if we follow his orders.'

'Sarah, I don't know why you're speaking so disrespectfully. He is Lord

Harcourt, whose lineage goes back for hundreds of years...'

'I know that, Mummy, but can't you see the war has changed everything? I'm an adult now, both physically and mentally, if not legally, and have my own opinions. He would be horrified that we have a dog in the house, are taking in paying guests and that I have a squadron leader for a boyfriend.' Sarah continued even more forcefully. 'I'm proud of the changes we've made and we couldn't have continued to pay our bills if we hadn't decided to be a boarding house.'

Joanna smiled. 'Good heavens, my dear, there's no need to be so cross. I agree that we've done what we had to. However, I'm not sure which your father would object to most – the fact that we've taken in lodgers or that you've actually got a boyfriend of any sort. Did you see him this morning when you went on your ride?'

'I did and we're going to Hastings for the day on Saturday.'

Joanna was sad that her daughter no longer felt she needed to ask permission or approval for her actions. Things would be so different if David was here. He would make her listen and there wouldn't be this gadding about all over the place in a car with a young man considerably older than her. Squadron Leader Trent was a gentleman and she was almost certain he wouldn't expect Sarah to do anything she shouldn't.

Intimacy of any sort was something she knew little about. She'd married almost straight from school and her mother had just told her that what happened between her and David would produce babies. Exactly how this miracle took place wasn't discussed and her wedding night had been a startling and unpleasant revelation.

David had stopped visiting her at all after the doctor had told them further children would be impossible. To give him his due, he'd never blamed her for not giving him an heir. She frowned as she recalled a conversation that she'd had with him just before he was recalled to his regiment last year.

He'd told her that if anything happened to him, the title would go to a second cousin but the estates and house would come to her and Sarah. He'd seemed remarkably unbothered at the prospect of his own demise.

'Mummy, you're daydreaming. I asked you if there's anywhere particular that you think we should visit when we go.'

'To be honest, darling, I've rarely been to Hastings. Your father didn't like it. We did go to town quite frequently so he could visit his lawyers and his bank. Of course, he dealt with a local branch for day-to-day matters. It's those people who are being so difficult and refusing to give me any information about our finances.'

'We can manage with what we've got as long as we take in at least six girls. Heaven knows what would happen if we needed anything repairing or replacing.'

'That's not your worry, darling. If you do manage to get a bursary or scholarship of some sort and go to London in September then I'll manage perfectly well here with Betty and the other ladies from the village.'

Brave words, but Joanna knew her own limitations and without her daughter's support and company feared she wouldn't be able to cope.

* * *

Angus scarcely had a moment to himself for the next few days. The Blenheims were flying regular patrols over the Channel in an attempt to keep the German U-boats at bay. They were also doing brief reconnaissance flights into the low countries to see what Hitler was up to. The squadrons of Hurries went up a couple of times to enact mock dogfights. Neither he nor any of the blokes had fired a bullet in anger and no amount of friendly dogfights could really prepare them for what was coming. He led one flight and Jimmy the other.

They now had a fully functioning NAAFI van that would be invaluable when there were more kites on the base. When the men couldn't get back to the mess they could get tea and a wad from the van. He'd been summoned to the blower an hour ago and told he was now going to have accommodation, ablutions and mess for a contingent of WAAF. It would help if the bigwigs would make their bloody minds up.

So far, the benefits of being in charge were his promotion to squadron leader, the extra pay, and the fact that he could give himself permission to leave the base for a day. He was making sure all the blokes also got regular time off as he was damn sure in the not too distant future everyone would be permanently on duty. The new adjutant, Flight Lieutenant Barry

Simmons, was a couple of years older than him and also a regular. He'd had a nasty prang which had left him blind in one eye and therefore not fit to fly. He was proving an excellent second in command.

'Enjoy yourself, Angus. You're looking a bit jaded and a day out with your pretty young filly is exactly what you need.'

'Don't bugger everything up whilst I'm out. There's a delivery of parts for the Hurries coming sometime today in an Annie, but nothing else of note.'

'Good show – we need to have everything in place because once it kicks off, Manston will be pretty damn busy.'

'As long as the Hillman doesn't die on me, I'll be back before lights out.'

* * *

Sarah must've seen him coming down the drive as she was waiting when he pulled up. He'd only known her a few weeks, but he could see a change in her. She carried herself more confidently, even had a splash of red lipstick on today, and he rather thought he might have been the reason for this.

'I'm so looking forward to having lunch out with you, Angus, but we've got to be back before eight as there's nobody else to do the horses.'

'That's a shame, I was hoping we might have dinner as well. Let's get going as our time is obviously limited. What about these land girls? I thought they'd be here by now and able to help out.'

She reached the passenger door before he could open it for her. He loved this determination to be independent, to not rely on anyone but herself.

He'd left the engine running so there was no danger of the Hillman refusing to start. The sun was out, the snow had gone, he had a lovely young lady at his side, so why wasn't he feeling on top of the world? He glanced sideways as he negotiated the entrance to the drive. She was looking at him speculatively.

'If you've changed your mind about taking me out, that's fine. I won't be offended, but for some reason you obviously are.'

He stopped the car, pulled on the handbrake and turned to face her. 'Of course I haven't changed my mind. I'm not offended – whatever gave you that idea? I intended to open the door for you, as a gentleman should, but you beat me to it and that somewhat surprised me.'

'Oh, is that all? I'm afraid I'm not familiar with the etiquette of car doors. I thought my saying I had to be back early had upset you.'

'Etiquette of car doors? I love that idea. I'll make sure I've filled you in on everything I know about doors of all sorts by the time we reach Hastings. Perish the thought that your ignorance of such weighty matters will make me look disapproving again.'

Her smile was everything he'd hoped. 'I might be the daughter of a minor aristocrat but I honestly think sometimes that I've been born into the wrong family – perhaps there was some mix-up at the hospital and my mother brought home the wrong baby.'

'Hospital? You weren't born in the ancestral pile?'

'Actually, I was born in a very expensive and exclusive clinic somewhere in London. My parents were living in Mayfair then.'

'I did wonder why you don't look like your mother and now you've explained the mystery to me. The real Sarah Harcourt is growing up elsewhere. Mind you,' he said as he engaged the gears and pulled away smoothly, 'that doesn't really wash, you know. Any baby born at an exclusive clinic will be the progeny of an upper-class family.'

'I can remember Mummy saying she was surprised there were the wives of incredibly rich industrialists having their babies there. So you see, it's perfectly possible I'm really the daughter of an ordinary family which is why I don't like all the rules associated with my position and am so much happier being able to be myself.'

'To return to something more sensible. I asked you when the land girls are coming and you didn't tell me.'

'Didn't I tell you? They aren't coming for a while. Instead, I've some very hush-hush and exciting news. We're to host a family from France. They recently arrived in Ramsgate by boat and the mayor has asked us to accommodate them until they can find something more permanent.'

He glanced across at her, intrigued by this snippet of information. Could these be refugees or diplomats coming to set up a link between France and England?

'How the hell did the mayor know you were offering accommodation?'

'Mrs Thomas, the dreadful woman who runs the WI, is related to him somehow. She must have mentioned it. Although we can't understand why they didn't put them all up at the hotel we went to. All very mysterious and very exciting. We only heard last night so really I should be at home helping to get the rooms ready.'

He slowed to allow a herd of cows to cross the road and she continued her story.

'Mummy's thrilled because she can practise her French. They arrive tomorrow morning, but the tricky thing is we don't actually know how many of them there are or if any of them are infants. Betty has been searching the attics for small beds, cradles and so on just in case.'

'Good luck with them. By the way, in case you're wondering, I rang my uncle but couldn't speak to him. I left a message with his secretary but so far he's not returned my call. I take it you've not heard anything?'

'Goodness me, I don't expect to hear for several weeks. I'm not thinking about it. I don't suppose you know anybody who would like to buy or permanently borrow two magnificent hunters, do you? Starlight, my mare, will be really useful when petrol becomes rationed but the others are just extra work for no return.'

'I might know somebody who would have them, but it would be a problem getting them there. My sister's brother-in-law is one of the red-coated brigade and hunters of that quality are not easy to come by.'

'Exactly where would they have to go?'

'Surrey, somewhere near Guildford, I think.'

'That's about a hundred miles from here. I could ride them there in three days.'

He laughed, thinking this was another joke, but she was serious.

'Both geldings are fit, I've been exercising them every day and they can easily cover thirty-five miles a day and continue to do so for days without causing them undue stress.'

'All right – let's suppose this chap wants your horses and you decide to ride them. Where will you spend the nights? How will you feed them? I think thirty-five miles a day is pushing it – don't forget how short the days still are. What if it snows again or rains?'

'Don't worry about it, Angus, we don't even know if this man wants the geldings. I thought we were going to talk about doors?' She nodded solemnly before continuing. 'I know a gentleman is supposed to hold a door open for a lady, but kindly explain to me the etiquette for a revolving door such as one might encounter at a grand hotel?'

She was irresistible when she was like this and he pushed aside his unease about her ludicrous suggestion that she could actually take the horses herself.

For the remainder of the journey they talked mainly nonsense and when they arrived at the outskirts of the town they were both relaxed and enjoying each other's company.

'Shall we head for the coast? Or is there somewhere else we should see?'

'Hastings and St Leonards used to be a very fashionable resort in Regency times. I think the advent of the train changed all that and they now cater for day trippers from London. Not that there will be many of those in the winter or probably in the summer either now there's a war on.'

'That doesn't answer my question, sweetheart. I need to know where I'm going.'

'Then head for the beach – I do remember being sadly disappointed there was no sand. It's pebbles and very uncomfortable to walk on. What I did enjoy was the horror with which my parents viewed the lines of washing tied between the fishing boats. They thought it frightfully vulgar.'

'One of the chaps told me Hastings used to be one of the Cinque Ports, which would have made it a significant town in the past. Didn't William the Conqueror land somewhere near here? There was certainly a Battle of Hastings at which Harold received an arrow through his eye.'

'You're right and I'm sure there are rows of tall black wooden fishing huts where the men store their nets and so on. I don't suppose there's a lot of fishing going on at the moment or if we can even get near the beach.'

They were forced to park in a side street and walk the rest of the way because of the army restrictions on motorised vehicles. Everywhere you looked there was evidence of the war. Not only were the shops, restaurants, cafés and hotels striped with brown paper in the windows but there were hundreds of sandbags and signs pointing to communal shelters.

He scarcely noticed these sorts of changes and she didn't comment either. It wouldn't be long before all this preparation would be put to the test.

He took her hand and was pleased she didn't pull hers away. They were both wearing gloves so there was no actual skin contact. Things were moving fast; he was ready for the next step, but was she too young to make a commitment to him?

'Golly, you can see France today. It makes you realise just how vulnerable England is if Hitler wants to invade.'

'He's got to conquer the whole of northern Europe before he can think about coming here. Let's not worry about it today.'

She grabbed his arm with her free hand. 'Look, it's just as I remember. I know we can't go on the beach but do you mind awfully if we walk along the promenade? It's hideously windy but invigorating.'

He put his arm around her waist and drew her closer to him. 'I think I'm going to have to hang on to you in case you get swept away.'

She pressed closer and looked up at him, her eyes shining, and he couldn't resist the temptation. He pressed his lips against hers, tasting her lipstick. To his delight and astonishment, she stepped into his embrace and rested her head against his shoulder. It was as if he'd been waiting for this all his life. She belonged in his arms and he closed his eyes and revelled in the moment.

He didn't attempt to kiss her again. No need to rush things, for she was so very young, after all. 'I shouldn't have done that, sweetheart, but you're incredibly lovely and the more time I spend with you, the harder I'm finding it to keep my distance. I know you're not comfortable with physical intimacy.'

She sighed audibly and then swivelled and leaned back so she was looking up at him with his arms around her. 'I didn't think I was and I didn't know that you realised that.' Her smile was enchanting and he moved a little closer to the precipice which once fallen over would be impossible to climb back up. He really didn't want to fall in love with her but he rather thought that horse had bolted. She was everything he'd dreamed of – brave, intelligent, funny, kind and also the most beautiful girl in the world.

'How do you feel about what happened?'

'I enjoyed it. That was my first kiss and I'm so glad it was you. Whatever happens in the future, Angus, I'll always remember you.'

'I'm rather hoping that your future includes me.'

Her eyes widened. 'Are you saying that you want to be more than just a casual boyfriend? We've only known each other a few weeks and this is only the second time we've been out.'

'I kissed you. As far as I'm concerned, a gentleman doesn't kiss a young woman unless his intentions are honourable.' No sooner had he spoken than he regretted his pomposity. He sounded like his father, not a young, red-blooded RAF officer.

She stretched up on tiptoes and pressed a fleeting kiss on his mouth then laughed. How he loved to hear her laugh – it was joyous and infectious.

'I love the fact that you're so old-fashioned but honestly, dearest Angus, you don't have to worry about my sensitivities. I want to enjoy these weeks we've got together and am looking forward to being kissed several more times before either of us is forced to leave.' She batted her eyelids at him and pouted provocatively. 'However, I can assure you that I don't intend to sleep with you. I'm sufficiently old-fashioned to think that's something better kept until the wedding night.'

'We'd better find somewhere to eat lunch before this conversation gets out of hand. I was being an arse – forgive me – I've absolutely no intention of marrying you. Do you feel more comfortable now?'

'Absolutely, Squadron Leader Trent, as that fits my plans perfectly. I've absolutely no intention of marrying you either – well – at least not until I'm a qualified doctor. If you're still alive, I might consider your proposal then.'

He swept her off her feet and held her in mid-air. 'I've never known anyone like you, Sarah Harcourt, and find you, in equal measures, both irresistible and impossible. Shall we agree that we're not getting married and just enjoy what we do have?'

'Put me down, Angus, you're making me look quite ridiculous.'

He did so and slung his arm around her shoulder. She made no objection. He wanted to punch the air, shout out his excitement to all those they passed. There was no need to say anything else – she was falling in love with him too.

16

Sarah felt as if she'd just swallowed a mouthful of sherbet. Her insides were fizzing and for some reason the sun seemed brighter, the sky bluer and having Angus beside her was the best thing in the world. Had she fallen in love with him? She wasn't entirely sure how this should feel – but if it meant wanting him to kiss her again, to smile at her in that toe-curling way, that she'd never been happier than she was at this moment – then she was in love. He was the kindest, most supportive person she knew and this was more important to her than his good looks.

'If we walk along Marine Parade towards the pier with the pavilion then I'm pretty sure we'll come to the Queen's Hotel. It isn't that far. It's a huge white building, five stories high, and I think we'll probably see the Union Jack flying from the roof before we get there.'

'That sounds perfect. I hope we can get a table as if it's got so many rooms the residents might well have reserved them all.'

'I don't suppose there are many residents or visitors now. Not just because of the war, but because it's still far too cold to wander along the parade.'

'It's always possible it's been taken over by the army, navy or RAF. The War Office can commandeer any building they want. I'm pretty sure several hotels are now used to train WAAF recruits.'

'It really doesn't matter if we can't get a splendid lunch in a grand hotel. I'll be happy eating fish and chips on a bench somewhere. In fact, I'm having such a lovely time I really don't mind if we just have a sandwich and a cup of tea.'

His arm tightened and she looked up at him. 'Why are you enjoying yourself so much?'

'I just love being with you. Going out with a boyfriend is something I never expected to do. I always imagined that I'd be introduced to somebody suitable by my parents and that would be that. I'm quite sure they never went out like this before they were married.'

Everything in her life had changed since Daddy had dashed off to France. She'd grown up and fallen in love with Angus.

'I feel the same way, sweetheart. I've had a few girlfriends but this is the first time…' He hesitated and she realised he was nervous for some reason.

'The first time? Don't leave me in suspense – tell me what you were going to say.'

'I'm falling in love with you. No, dammit, I am in love with you.'

She couldn't keep back her squeal of delight. She flung her arms around his neck and he kissed her for the second time. This was quite different. His lips were hard, demanding almost, and spirals of pleasure raced through her until her head was spinning.

They were attracting far too much disapproving attention from passers-by and the muttered comments finally made them both draw back from the embrace.

'I didn't even like you very much when we first met but it was inevitable that when I got to know you better that I'd fall in love with you. Why does this happen so fast? I don't really understand.'

'I don't think we're meant to understand it, darling, that's what makes it so magical. Come on, I can see the hotel just ahead. We'll try there first and if we can't get a table we'll go in search of fish and chips. Having feelings for each other really complicates things. I don't quite know how we're going to manage this but at the moment I don't care.'

'I agree. I also think it better we don't tell anyone. Mummy would start talking about wedding dates, bottom drawers and so on. I don't see why we can't be in love but still continue with our plans. I do want to be a wife one day – hopefully yours – but the next five years are going to be devoted to becoming a doctor.'

'I don't expect you to give up your dream for me. Let's not talk about the future – let's just enjoy the moment.'

They crossed the road and ran past the low white wall that bordered the front of the hotel and then up the steps. There was a uniformed doorman who touched his cap to Angus and held the door open.

The interior was disappointing. The furniture looked tired, the carpets were faded and she thought the Royal in Ramsgate far superior, although half the size. There was a sprinkling of rather dejected-looking guests. 'I'm sure they'll have plenty of room in the dining room but honestly, I really don't want to eat here. I doubt that the food will be any better than the decor.'

'Too late, the maître d' is rushing towards us with a look of expectancy on his face. Do you have the heart to disappoint him?'

'Today I couldn't disappoint anybody and especially not this poor old man. He looks a decade past retirement.'

'Good afternoon, sir, miss, have you come for lunch?'

'We have, but would like to see the menu first. Perhaps we could have coffee whilst we look?'

'Certainly. If you would care to follow me, I'll take you to the coffee lounge. It has an excellent view of the coast – as does the dining room.'

They'd scarcely had time to remove their coats before a young waitress appeared with the tray. 'Here you are, got the decent stuff too. I won't be a tick; I've just got to fetch you a couple of menus. You're in luck today. They've got some smashing Dover sole, freshly caught.'

Sarah poured the coffee and it was indeed the good stuff. 'Fresh Dover sole? I'm absolutely going to eat here if that's what we can have. I can't remember the last time I had some really delicious fresh fish.'

'Doesn't the fishmonger's van call at your house? He comes to the base twice a week and although we've never had anything as expensive as Dover sole, the fish is always excellent and almost flapping it's so fresh.'

'He stopped coming when we couldn't pay the bill. Very embarrassing for Mummy and as soon as we've got a full house again that'll be the first bill to be paid. We're slowly clearing all our debts and I can't tell you how lovely it is to be able to go into the village and purchase what we need without worrying about not being able to settle the bill at the end of the month.'

'It seems incredible to me that someone of your status, living in the biggest house in the neighbourhood, is struggling to pay their way.'

'I rather think that the family money was lost during the depression a few years ago. Daddy never said anything, he's far too proud to admit even to his own wife that there's no money.'

The menus arrived and they chose Dover sole. It was just as delicious as she'd hoped and cooked simply with just butter and lemon. Heaven knows where they'd got a lemon from, as she hadn't seen one in any of the three grocers' shops in the village since the war started.

'I don't have any room for dessert, but if you want one, Angus, I'm happy to watch you eat it.'

'What about a compromise? We could have another jug of coffee and see if they've got any *petit four*?'

'Yes, I could just squeeze in a few mouthfuls of something sweet. The coffee was certainly the good stuff. I can't believe it's getting dark already. We mustn't be too long, as after our last night-time drive I'm a bit nervous about travelling in the blackout in that Hillman.'

She was torn. She didn't want to drive in the dark but didn't want this wonderful day with Angus to end either.

* * *

Joanna felt there was no need for her to inspect the rooms made ready for the French family arriving tonight. She trusted Betty and the two village ladies to have done what was needed. When she'd been told how much she was to be paid by these temporary guests, she'd been quite overwhelmed by what this family was going to pay for their brief stay. These French émigrés must be wealthy and had managed to bring their money with them. If they were so desperate to flee from Hitler, she rather thought they might be Jewish as, from all reports she'd read, the Germans were treating them really badly.

France so far hadn't been invaded but, from what she saw in the papers and heard on the news, it was only a matter of time before they owned the whole of Europe. The very thought of jackbooted Nazi soldiers marching through London filled her with absolute horror. The English were an independent nation and wouldn't accept being ruled by Germans.

She was fussing the puppy, loving him more each day that passed. The two of them were now inseparable. 'Well, young man, what do you think about it? How would you feel if Hitler invaded England?'

The dog rolled on his back and waved his legs in the air and she laughed. 'Exactly so, I think that would be safest for all of us. Absolute surrender on the surface but resistance behind the scenes.' Then she gasped and the puppy yelped when she inadvertently squeezed him too hard.

If Hitler and his storm troopers came to England it would mean the BEF had been defeated and that David would either be a prisoner of war or dead. Her hands were clammy, her stomach lurched. She realised she hadn't thought about her husband at all since he'd sent the letters. In fact, they remained unread in her dressing table drawer.

What if he forbade Sarah to take a scholarship and begin her medical training? No – that wasn't what she'd asked him at all. She'd said that Sarah was intending to become a nurse, which was quite different. Even Mrs Thomas, chairperson of the WI, said that girls like Sarah, who had completed every single practical examination and written test for the St John Ambulance, were already as knowledgeable as many trained nurses. Did this mean her daughter would be able to step straight into a position at the hospital without having to do the three years' training?

She hurried upstairs and removed the letters from under the handkerchiefs where she'd hidden them. Thinking about it now, she wondered why her daughter hadn't asked what had been in them – perhaps she no longer thought about her father either.

She opened each of them and checked the dates and then put them in order. The first was just the usual uninformative sort of thing he always wrote. He said he was fine, that he'd been having dinner with his friends, that it was cold and so on but nothing of any interest. Of course, he couldn't tell her what was actually happening as that would be censored before she received the letter.

The second one was more of the same, thanked her for her letters, but again nothing of importance. She hadn't told him about taking in paying guests, and had no intention of doing so, otherwise they could talk about that.

However, the third one was quite different in tone and content.

Dear Joanna,

I was dismayed to hear that our daughter has decided to abandon her hopes of becoming a doctor in order to be something that in reality is no more than a nursing servant. I won't hear of it. For her to have become a doctor would have been something we could be proud of – being a nurse, even in a time of war, is not something a Harcourt should even consider.

You obviously are now cognisant of our financial situation and realise there's no possibility of Sarah taking up a place at Oxford. She will remain at Goodwill House with you until I return. Then I shall find her a suitable husband. I give my consent for her to continue to work with the brigade, the Red Cross, WVS and WI.

I categorically forbid her to become a nurse or to join any other of the armed services in any capacity. As I'm not there then you must refuse to sign the parental consent form in my stead.

She read the letter once more and then screwed it up and tossed it into the flames. As far as she was concerned this particular piece of correspondence had never arrived.

* * *

On the drive back, it began to rain, and visibility deteriorated so rapidly Angus had to stop Sarah from trying to engage his attention. 'Sorry, sweetheart, need to concentrate. The road's slippery and it's dark. We don't want to end up in the ditch – I don't think this poor old thing would recover from a second prang.' His main concern was keeping his darling girl safe but he thought it best not to keep reminding her of the accident.

'You don't know the road, which doesn't help. Why don't you let me drive as I'm more familiar with the area than you are?'

'I'm a fighter pilot...'

'I can't see that makes any difference when you're driving a car. I could always get out and walk in front waving a red flag if you like. I did offer once before, remember?'

'God, I'm not going that slowly, am I? Please shut up and let me get you home safely.'

'I've had an absolutely splendid time. I'm going to sleep now as otherwise I'll keep talking to you.'

She wriggled a bit in her seat and then sighed and her breathing became slow and regular. His lips curved in the darkness. That was another thing they had in common – the ability to fall asleep instantly. He thought this would help both of them in their future careers. She, as a medical student, would be working impossibly long hours and he, once things got going, might well be on permanent duty waiting to be scrambled.

Having someone else to think about, to plan for, was a new experience for him. Up until now he'd thought only of himself and the men he commanded. Now things were different. He'd not been joking when he'd said he saw them being together in the future. Was it too soon to ask her to marry him? With his ring on her finger, he'd be certain she wouldn't be snatched up by one of the doctors she'd come into contact with once she left for London.

It wouldn't be right to tie her to him when she wasn't even eighteen. He would have to rely on the strength of their feelings for each other to keep her from becoming involved with anyone else. Anyway, he might well go for a burton and he certainly didn't want her to feel obliged to grieve for him if that happened.

No, they must just make the most of the time they had and pray that would be enough to maintain a relationship that was inevitably going to be reduced to the occasional telephone call and letter.

The first squadron of the Royal Canadian Air Force were on their way and he rather thought that every pilot was going to be essential if they were to hold off the invasion. The Aussies were already here, as were the Kiwis.

The Luftwaffe had practised their lethal skills on the poor sods in

Spain, whereas none of the RAF had fought in earnest yet. He thanked God he hadn't been forced to become a bomber pilot. Killing civilians, which was bound to happen, wasn't something he'd be comfortable with. Somehow shooting down a German doing the same job as him didn't seem quite as bad.

Sarah woke as they turned into the drive. 'Golly, I feel much better now. I wonder if the French family have arrived? When will I see you again?'

'I've no idea. There's someone from the War Office coming to inspect the new accommodation and check that we're ready to fight when necessary. I'm going to be on duty most of the time until then. I'll telephone when I know I've got a few hours free.'

'There's a social in the village hall next week. I don't think there's been one since you arrived last year but, now the weather's improved a little, the parish council has decided to start holding them again once a month.'

'I've not been to one of those for years. I seem to remember they have card games for the elderly, dancing and silly games for everyone else. Is that what happens here?'

'Absolutely. I've only been to one as my father didn't approve of me mingling with the village folk. I went to the last one which was just before Christmas. Such fun, and especially as most of the men, and some of the women, dash off to the pub at regular intervals. Only tea and soft drinks available at one of these events.'

'Then that's a date. I'll walk you to the door.'

He'd expected her to refuse but they both knew this was an opportunity for them to exchange another kiss. Trying to do so in the confines of the Hillman didn't appeal to him and from the speed with which she exited the car she was in agreement.

He took her hand and together they hurried into the shelter of the portico. He didn't need to reach out for her as she was in his arms the moment they were out of the rain.

'I'm so glad I probably won't be going away until September at the earliest. That should give us six months to be together.'

'There's always the possibility I'll be posted elsewhere before then. Being the commanding officer at Manston doesn't necessarily mean I'll remain here.'

'I know that. Also, if I can't get financial help then I can't go to London. I've spoken to my brigade commander and he told me that as I've completed all the sections in the training manual, I could walk straight into nursing without becoming a student. I'd be working as an auxiliary until I'd taken the necessary exams but I'm sure it wouldn't take me long to become a fully qualified SRN.'

'Are you trying to tell me in a roundabout way that you wouldn't wait until the autumn if you're going to become a nurse?'

'I could leave next month as you only have to be seventeen and a half to become a student nurse. I'm hoping it won't be necessary but I'm determined to serve in a medical capacity during this war and if I can't be a doctor, then I'll be a nurse.'

'Presumably you won't make a decision until you've heard from the Royal Free?'

'I won't – which gives us a few weeks to enjoy each other's company. I'd better go in as if our new guests aren't here, they could arrive at any moment and it wouldn't look too good finding us canoodling outside the front door.'

He didn't need telling a second time. He pulled her hard against him, wanting to feel every inch of her, but couldn't as there was the thickness of his uniform jacket and greatcoat between them.

The kiss was even more passionate than the second one. He ran the tip of his tongue experimentally along her closed lips but she didn't respond by opening her mouth and allowing him access. Too soon to move things on to such an intimate level.

She broke the embrace by gently pressing on his chest and with reluctance he released her.

'Thank you for an absolutely wonderful day. I know you're going to be busy during the week but I might ride over and say hello if I get a moment. If not, will you collect Mummy and I or shall we meet you at the village hall on Saturday night?'

It took him a few seconds to find his voice. 'Don't ride to the base – it's far too dangerous and I can't risk any adverse comments about my command at the moment.'

'I didn't realise my coming on horseback had caused adverse comments. Goodnight, Angus.'

She'd opened the front door and vanished inside before he could apologise. He hadn't intended to criticise her and hadn't realised until he'd spoken that he'd not appreciated her unexpected appearance the other week.

Manston was an active RAF base and girlfriends and horses had no place there.

17

Joanna had hoped the new arrivals would come before Betty left for the day or at least after Sarah came back from her jaunt to Hastings. Despite the fact that she'd been to numerous social events, had entertained at Goodwill House, these occasions had always been with David at her side.

She paced nervously in the drawing room, trying to convince herself that she was quite capable of dealing with anything and certainly something as simple as welcoming their new guests. She'd inspected the rooms twice already and was more than happy with how they looked. The drawing room was pleasantly warm, there was ample coal and logs to keep the fires burning as long as necessary.

The breakfast parlour was being used as the dining room as it was a sensible size and far easier to keep heated. This was also sparkling, with the matching walnut furniture freshly polished, the table laid with the rarely used, best china, silverware and crystal. All she had to do was – what did she have to do in order to serve their dinner?

She sent up a fervent prayer to the Almighty, begging him to send her daughter back in time to serve the meal, otherwise it would be an unmitigated disaster. She then sent up a second prayer apologising for her first, as she thought God might not appreciate being asked to intervene in something so trivial when there was a war on.

Then she thought she heard a car crunch to a halt outside. Her heart was hammering. Was this Sarah or the French family? She could hardly pull back the curtains in order to look as that would reveal light and break the blackout regulations.

She braced herself for the knock on the door but there was none so she must have been mistaken. She was a mature woman, capable and intelligent – she was being quite ridiculous.

'I am Lady Joanna Harcourt, I am the most important person in the neighbourhood. I've nothing to be nervous about.' She spoke the words aloud and Lazzy, who'd been sleeping soundly at the other end of the house, must have heard her and thought she was talking to him.

The puppy began to yap loudly and she had no option but to rush to the kitchen to quieten him. The French family hadn't been asked if they were agreeable to staying in a house with pets and they might change their minds and go elsewhere.

'Quiet, naughty boy, I'm coming. You know you mustn't bark. It's very bad manners.'

The dog was throwing himself enthusiastically against the kitchen door and on opening it he hurled himself at her, whining and wriggling ecstatically as if they'd been apart for days and not an hour or two.

'Come here, you almost knocked me over. Now, don't keep licking my face, it's most unhygienic and I spent half an hour putting on my lipstick and powder.'

'Then you'll have to do it again, Mummy, as he's removed most of it,' Sarah said from behind her. 'Let me have him, he probably needs to go out if he's been asleep. I take it I'm in time to greet the new guests and more importantly to serve them an unburnt dinner.'

'I won't ask what you were doing so long outside with your handsome young man but I heard a car pull up a considerable time ago.'

Sarah wandered off laughing, but didn't answer. Joanna wasn't sure if she was happy for her daughter to be on kissing terms with this young man or whether she was worried things were moving too fast.

Maybe a romantic entanglement was exactly what was needed to keep Sarah at home. Unless she was able to persuade Betty to become a live-in housekeeper, running Goodwill House on her own was going to be difficult but if Sarah could do something life-changing then so could she.

* * *

Sarah let the puppy nose around in the dark to do his business whilst she checked the three horses had sufficient hay and water to last them until the morning. She hoped Angus would remember to contact the person he'd mentioned who might like the two hunters.

She shouldn't have been cross with him for telling her off about riding to the base because he was absolutely right. She had treated it as a bit of a lark and there was nothing at all amusing about Manston and its purpose.

There was barely time for her to wash her face and hands and tidy her hair before the much-anticipated knock on the door. There was no sign of her mother but she was happy to answer the door as her schoolgirl French was perfectly adequate for the purpose.

Before she could open it, she had to close all the doors that led into the various rooms and turn out the grand hall light. Why did they refer to it always as the 'grand hall'? Silly, really, as it wasn't at all grand – she supposed it was to distinguish it from the smaller hall in the Elizabethan part of the house and the other in the Victorian wing.

Fortunately, the switch for the main light was adjacent to the front door, which made things so much easier. She plunged the space into darkness and allowed a few moments for her eyes to adjust to the feeble light from her torch. These were indeed her visitors. There were four of them and no sign of whoever had arranged this temporary stay. Neither was there any sign of their luggage. She must suppose it was still in the car and they expected a servant to come out and fetch it for them. They were in for an unpleasant surprise if they thought the size of the house was an indication of the wealth within.

'*Bonsoir, monsieur, madame, rendez-vous chez nous. Je m'appelle Sarah Harcourt.*'

'Good evening, Miss Harcourt, thank you for welcoming us into your home. Your accent is passable for an English girl.' A tall, dark gentleman ushered three smaller figures – their sex indistinguishable under their outdoor garments – into the hall. His English was impeccable but she disliked him already for his sneering comments about her French.

'As only my mother, Lady Harcourt, and I speak any French at all it's fortuitous that you all speak English. Would you care to introduce your family, sir? Or do you wish me to take you to your rooms first?'

The anonymous trio huddled together, looking around nervously, and appeared to be waiting for permission to speak or even move.

'Have someone fetch our luggage and put the car under cover.' He was looking around, obviously expecting a servant to rush to do his bidding.

She was about to say something extremely impolite to this arrogant Frenchman when Mummy appeared, looking every inch an aristocrat.

'There is no one here to fetch and carry for you, monsieur. Do you really think an English aristocrat would take in paying lodgers such as yourself unless we were in financial straits?'

He was about to answer but her mother turned her back on him and smiled warmly at the nervous group. 'Madame, you have delightful rooms upstairs. Come with me and I'll show you where everything is. No doubt your husband is capable of bringing in your baggage whilst you get settled. Dinner will be ready for you in half an hour.'

The still-unidentified silent trio followed obediently, leaving Sarah with the head of their household, who was obviously unimpressed by this turn of events.

'Miss Harcourt, I was under the impression we were to be staying in the most prestigious house in this part of Kent. Am I to understand that you expect us to do menial tasks? We might as well have moved into a hotel.'

Sarah bit her tongue; she was tempted to tell him to do exactly that. 'No, sir, we have a housekeeper and three other part-time indoor staff. What we don't have are any living in. Your laundry, cleaning and meals will be provided, as explained to you when you made the arrangements to come here.

'This is the home of Lord and Lady Harcourt. Lord Harcourt is presently serving as a major in the infantry with the BEF helping to protect your country. I can assure you that if he was here then you wouldn't be. We just wish to do what we can for any unfortunate immigrants who've been obliged to flee their home.'

'You are perfectly capable of fetching our suitcases...'

'I am, but I won't be doing it. I'm sure they'll come to no harm left overnight in your car. If you wish it to be put under cover, there is a perfectly adequate barn where our Bentley is currently seeing out the war.'

Politely she held out her torch. 'Please remember to turn out that light when you go outside. Excuse me, I have dinner to attend to.'

She didn't wait to see if he stormed upstairs to harangue his miserable family or if he went out to fetch their belongings himself. What a thoroughly objectionable person he was, and as he hadn't bothered to identify himself she couldn't come to any conclusion about why he should have departed his own country so precipitously.

Hopefully, Mummy would learn more from the wife and children whilst she was upstairs with them. Thank goodness there were three bedrooms available as well as the sitting room. If she was the wife, she would definitely want to sleep on her own. Their two offspring had been female, that much had been clear from their clothes when they were creeping up the stairs. From their size, she thought they were probably around ten and twelve – but she might be wrong as the woman was quite small herself.

There was leek and potato soup to start the meal, game pie for the main course and apple crumble for dessert. This would possibly not be appreciated by the guests as they might be expecting elaborate meals. Betty was a super cook and had got everything ready and all it needed was to be cooked.

Once the crumble and pie were in the hot oven, she put the water on for the vegetables and pushed the saucepan of soup over the slow ring of the Aga. This item was the last extravagant thing her father had bought and as far as Betty was concerned it was worth every pound spent. Not only did it cook whatever you wanted brilliantly, it also heated the water for the kitchen, scullery and the downstairs cloakroom.

The only drawback was that if the wind was in the wrong direction it failed to function at all, but fortunately that didn't happen very often.

There was a large boiler which should have heated the upstairs water and the radiators but when that had failed to function it hadn't been mended. She could scarcely remember it being warm in the house in winter but she supposed it must have been when she was a toddler.

Appetising smells filled the kitchen and if this family complained about the food then they would be making a fuss for the sake of it. They wouldn't get better anywhere and certainly not for the price they were paying.

'Everything smells quite wonderful, darling, will it be ready soon? I'm hoping once they're fed they might cheer up a bit.'

'I really didn't like the man – he expected me to go out and fetch his luggage. I told him to get it himself or leave it in the car.'

'Good for you. I'd have done the same. I don't think madame or the girls speak English. Although I did speak French to them, and I know my French is perfectly comprehensible, but they still didn't answer.'

'I think they're terrified of him. I'm more inclined to think him a German spy than a refugee.' She dropped the metal ladle with a clatter on the floor, causing the puppy to yap excitedly. 'Gosh, maybe they are German and not French. That would explain why the woman and the children didn't answer you – they couldn't understand French or English.'

'You have an overactive imagination, darling, as if he was a spy he wouldn't make himself so objectionable, now would he?'

'A double bluff, perhaps? I was just being silly. The soup's ready so I hope the family are too. Shall I just take it and the bread and put it in the breakfast parlour and let them find their own way?'

'I told them dinner would be served at six thirty and it's exactly that now. I'm not running up and down stairs after them. If they don't come down then it's their fault if the food is cold.'

'Please go and tell them at least that I'm serving the soup. Even if we don't like him, I do feel sorry for his wife and daughters, and they look as if they could do with a good meal. All three of them are far too thin.'

She carefully poured the soup into the warmed tureen and put the matching lid on. She then placed it on the waiting tray along with the basket of fresh bread. The butter was already on the table, as were the soup bowls and ladle for serving.

With hindsight, it might have been better to warm the dishes, because then if the family was slow arriving the soup wouldn't be as unpalatable. The dinner plates were in the warming oven along with the potatoes, carrots and cabbage. There was also home-made redcurrant jelly as a condiment and an extra jug of the delicious gravy the pheasant, partridge and rabbit were cooked in.

The house was ominously silent – not even any movement from upstairs to show the family were coming to eat. Did they expect her to put it on a tray and carry it up to them? That wasn't part of the arrangement.

As expected, the temporary dining room was empty. It looked as it should and they certainly couldn't complain about not being treated well when they saw the beautiful, almost translucent, porcelain service that was being used for the first time in living memory as far as she knew.

She was about to collect the soup bowls and take them back to be dunked in hot water to warm them when she heard the welcome sound of voices approaching. She hastily retreated through the door that led to the kitchen, leaving the family to enter through the main door. There was no wine – that hadn't been included – but there was a jug of water.

'Here we are, Monsieur Ducray, just in time. All your meals will be served in here although morning coffee and afternoon tea will be in the drawing room.'

Again, there wasn't a peep from the females but he spoke as loudly as before. 'Are we to serve ourselves? Do you not have even a housemaid?'

'As I explained earlier, Monsieur Ducray, we have no live-in staff so your evening meal will be served as it is now. Breakfast, luncheon and everything else you will have a member of my staff to attend to you. I hardly think it appropriate that either myself or my daughter wait on you.'

Finally, Madame Ducray spoke. '*Bernard, s'il te plaît, ne fais pas d'histoires. Cela semble délicieux et les filles et moi avons tellement faim.*'

So madame thought the soup looked delicious, she and the girls were hungry and she didn't want him to make a scene. Good for her – he needed to be told he was ill-mannered.

She shouldn't eavesdrop but wanted to hear what they thought. She was pleasantly surprised as even the pernickety husband praised the leek and potato soup.

'Sarah,' her mother whispered loudly from the other end of the passageway, 'leave them to eat and don't stand there listening.'

She hurried back and followed her mother into the kitchen. 'Why didn't they come down until you told them to?'

'They were busy unpacking. Monsieur did fetch the luggage. Such a good idea to give them all three bedrooms as madame has taken one, the girls are adjacent to her, and monsieur is in the one on the other side of the sitting room. I know we thought them dissatisfied with their accommodation but I rather think they're very happy to be here now they've seen they've got four rooms to themselves.'

'At least we know they are definitely French. I wish the organisers had told us why they've come to England in such a hurry. I still think there's more to this than we know and I'm determined to find out.'

'We don't want to offend them. The money we get from their two weeks here is an absolute godsend. I can't tell you how much it means to me to be able to walk into the village knowing I can pay my accounts at the end of the month.'

When Sarah returned to collect the soup tureen and used cutlery and crockery, the atmosphere was definitely lighter than it had been on her last visit.

'I'm glad you enjoyed the soup.' As the tureen had been scraped clean this was obviously the case. All the bread had also been eaten.

'I'll bring your main course now. It's game pie – would you like me to plate your meal or bring in the dishes and let you help yourself?' She addressed her question to him as she still thought his wife didn't speak English.

'If it's as delicious as the soup then please allow us to help ourselves,' he said. 'I can't tell you how long it is since we ate anything quite as good. If our meals are going to be of this standard then I fear you're going to find it hard to get rid of us.'

She almost dropped the tray and looked at him more closely. Maybe she'd misjudged him and just fatigue and worry had made him so unpleasant. 'Betty, who does all the catering, is an excellent cook. Your meals will not always be as elaborate as this one – we wanted to make your first evening a memorable one – but I can assure you everything you get will be equally delicious.' She paused, not sure if this was the time to mention ration books. 'As you know, a lot of food is now rationed here, so you might not get the variety of dishes that you're used to.'

'I hesitate to ask, mademoiselle, but my wife and I would really enjoy a glass of wine with the main course. This, of course, will be an extra expense. I was rather hoping that a house of this substance might have a wine cellar.'

'We do, but to be honest only my father ever went down there so I've no idea how much there is or what's worth drinking.'

'If you would permit me to accompany you, I'd be happy to pick out something that would complement our dinner perfectly.'

She was about to refuse as the last thing she wanted to do was wander about in the bowels of the house with this man, but when he smiled he looked quite different – approachable, almost – so she reconsidered.

'I'll ask my mother if that's permissible and if she agrees then I'll come and fetch you.'

When she asked, her mother nodded vigorously. 'What an excellent idea, I'm sure after a few glasses of wine they will feel so much better. I know where the key's hidden. Shall I take him down as you've got to take in the trays?'

'No, I know how much you dislike being underground. You haven't even visited the shelter Daddy made for us in one of the cellars. I've told you it's perfectly comfortable and a lot better than the Anderson shelters the villagers are going to have to use.'

'Then I'll take in the food and try and speak with Madame Ducray. I still don't know the names of the girls and hopefully I'll also find that out whilst you're gone.'

'It's a good thing that Betty made us a separate pie as the whole of this one is going in to them. The vegetables are already in their dishes, the gravy's in the jug and the pie's on the table. I'll take one tray and you bring the rest on the other. Hopefully, it won't take us long to find some wine. I'm pretty sure red wine would be best with game pie but that will be horribly cold and it should be at room temperature.'

The food was received with enthusiasm – it certainly smelled wonderful. 'I've got the key and there's electric light down there so we don't need our torches.'

'Do we need to put on outdoor garments?'

'We won't be down there long.'

She led the way; their feet clattered loudly on the stone steps and she shivered as they reached the bottom. She flicked on the light switch. It didn't seem quite so dismal when you could see where you were going. Having this bad-tempered man so close behind her made her a little uncomfortable but she pushed these thoughts aside.

'We turn right here, and then it's straight ahead. These cellars ramble about under most of the building. I've always hated coming down here as I was terrified I'd get lost. We've got a very swish air-raid shelter down here but I sincerely hope you don't need to use it whilst you're here.'

She paused and pointed to the door. 'It's through there. It has an underground passage that leads into the grounds so in the unlikely event that the house takes a direct hit we'd still be able to get out.'

18

Angus was fed up to the back teeth with builders, subordinates and generally being in charge of Manston. He was a young, active member of the RAF and shouldn't be tied to a desk job. A squadron of Hurries screamed overhead as they did their daily patrol of Canterbury and in that moment he decided to put in for a transfer.

There must be dozens of older men who could no longer fly who would be better equipped to take over. Tony hadn't been up to the task but he was certain there were others who would be. Every pilot was going to be needed soon. The poor buggers who'd volunteered last September were going to be thrown into combat with sod all hours in their logbooks. A flyer of his experience would be essential to lead these new blokes.

His promotion to squadron leader was dependent on him being CO at Manston but he would happily return to being a flight lieutenant if it meant he was stationed somewhere he could lead every sortie and do what he was trained for.

Manston was part of Fighter Command Group 11 and orders came from there, but being the closest base to the coast they were going to be targeted by the Luftwaffe. Any bomber that was driven off by fighters and failed to reach their targets inland – like Hornchurch, Debden or Kenley – would drop their bombs on Manston on the way back.

They had dozens of anti-aircraft positions surrounding the base, numerous ditches into which flyers could dive if they couldn't reach a shelter, but ground crew and anyone working in the huddle of buildings would be sitting ducks.

He swallowed a nasty taste in his mouth as he thought that his request for a transfer might be considered as cowardice – that he lacked moral fibre – but the reverse was true. He was far more likely to go for a burton in the air than he would be footling around telling others what to do.

Leaving the woman he loved would be a wrench, but there was a war on and all men had to put duty first.

The man from the Air Ministry had arrived in a taxi Anson and stayed for an hour before flying off to inspect somewhere else. Manston was now fully operational as far as the bigwigs were concerned and they were to expect an influx of personnel over the next week or two.

He completed his transfer request and put it in the pouch of letters and documents to be taken directly to Bentley Priory, the gloomy headquarters of fighter command. He'd commandeered the Hillman to take Sarah to the social that evening.

He felt a jab of guilt that he'd not even spoken to her on the telephone during the past week. He had good news for her about the horses. His sister had found a home for them and was sending a horsebox to collect them as soon as it could be arranged.

Some of the chaps had fiancées, wives even, but the majority of the men were just out to have a good time. As long as they made sure they took French letters with them, he wasn't going to interfere.

Much as he'd like to make love to Sarah, he wasn't going to seduce her into bed. He loved her and hoped that one day they would marry but their lives were on separate paths at the moment and their relationship must remain more or less platonic.

The mood amongst the chaps was buoyant as it had been reported in the paper that three hundred British prisoners of war had been rescued in a daring raid on a German tanker hiding in a Norwegian fjord. These poor blighters had been captured from ships sunk by the *Graf Spee*. On balance, he and Jimmy had decided they'd rather be shot out of the sky than drowned in the sea.

He pulled up outside Goodwill House, hoping his passengers would be on the porch waiting for him. They weren't. He knocked and shouted but the only response he got was from the puppy yapping somewhere.

Where the hell were they? After several fruitless minutes banging and shouting he was forced to accept that they'd gone without him. This didn't improve his temper, which was already frayed because he'd had to deal with several annoying administrative problems which had delayed him.

He knew where the village hall was and it would only take him ten minutes to get there. He was tempted to abandon the evening and return to base but thought that would be childish.

The battered lorry from the base was parked outside the hall, which he'd expected, but there was also a large saloon car, which he hadn't.

This event, as all were nowadays, was being held late afternoon so at least the guests could arrive in daylight even if they would have to depart in the blackout. The laughter and music coming from inside lifted his spirits a little. It was amazing how people were able to forget there was a war on and enjoy themselves at something as simple as a village social.

The blackouts were already drawn, which was a wise precaution. He pushed open the door and the racket made him smile. The doors leading into the hall were open and he could see some sort of silly game in progress which was causing a great deal of hilarity. He wasn't sure children's games were quite his thing but he was prepared to join in if Sarah wanted him to.

There was a trestle table behind which sat two smiling village women. 'Good afternoon, squadron leader, your young lady was somewhat put out by your tardiness. Please put your sixpence in the tin and take a peg and raffle tickets from the bowl.'

How in God's name did they know about Sarah?

He did as asked, but was mystified by this request. The other lady pointed to a pencil securely tied with string to a nail hammered into the trestle. 'Write your name on one side of the raffle ticket. Then attach it to your overcoat and hand it in to the two boys over there. Then, when you give them the other half of the ticket on your departure they'll be able to find it for you without difficulty.'

He grinned and nodded. 'Ingenious. Thank you. How did Lady Harcourt and her daughter get here? I hope they didn't walk.'

'No, they have a charming French gentleman and his family staying with them and he drove them here.' The speaker exchanged a smile with her friend before continuing. 'I think they are quite puzzled by what's happening here this afternoon. I don't think they have anything similar in France.'

After handing in his greatcoat and other belongings to the spotty youths in charge of the cloakroom, he headed for the party. He paused in the doorway, scanning the crowd for Sarah and her mother, and this mysterious French family.

'Angus, I'm sorry I didn't wait for you but Monsieur Ducray offered to bring us and it would have seemed impolite not to accept.' Sarah appeared at his side, looking beautiful in a floral frock that fitted closely over the bosom and flared out in a full skirt. It suited her admirably.

'I should have called and told you I was going to be late. This looks fun – what exactly's going on?'

'Have you never played musical chairs? What a miserable childhood you must have had.' Her smile made him regret his decision to keep his distance. 'Mind you, I've only ever played this once and that was last year when I came to my first social.'

'I thought these sorts of games were for the children but there are as many adults involved as little ones.'

'You'll note that the grown-ups let the children sit down first before fighting for the remining empty chairs. It's all very silly, but terrific fun. Would you prefer to join the more sedate group playing whist at the far end of the hall?'

She was standing so close to him he was able to speak directly to her without anyone else overhearing. 'What I'd prefer to do, sweetheart, is kiss you but I think I'd better not.'

Something flashed in her eyes and then her arms were around his neck and he couldn't resist. He kissed her thoroughly, barely managing to remain within the bounds of decency. Why had she decided to announce their involvement so publicly?

* * *

Joanna was enjoying her conversation with Mrs Thomas, who was being remarkably polite this afternoon. They had managed to talk for fifteen minutes without either of them getting irritated with each other.

'My word, I thought better of your daughter, Lady Harcourt. Even the village girls don't behave so inappropriately in public.'

She turned and saw her daughter in the arms of her squadron leader whilst he kissed her and they were attracting a great deal of attention. This was hardly surprising, as not only were they the most attractive couple in the hall, he could be considered the most eligible bachelor and she the most eligible young lady.

What had possessed Sarah to display her partiality so publicly?

'As everybody is well aware they are serious about each other, I can see no harm in them exchanging a kiss here or anywhere else. If you look carefully, Mrs Thomas, you will see that there's not a single disapproving face in here apart from yours.'

She made her way through the riotous game players – the only ones not watching this embrace – and arrived at her daughter's side just as they came up for air.

'I take it that congratulations are in order? I hardly think, Squadron Leader Trent, that you would behave as you have in full view of the entire village if you had not just become engaged.'

She knew perfectly well they hadn't but thought it would no harm for them to be forced to explain their inappropriate behaviour.

'My lady, if I thought Sarah would accept my proposal then I would go down on one knee here and now.'

'How do you know what I will say if you don't ask the question?'

Her daughter was calling his bluff. He rose to the occasion and with a blinding smile dropped dramatically to one knee and spoke in a voice loud enough to be heard from one end of the hall to the other.

'Miss Harcourt, would you do me the honour of becoming my wife? Will you make me the happiest of men?'

Whether she or Sarah was more astonished by his behaviour it would be hard to say. Sarah replied quietly.

'I'll give your offer suitable consideration and you will have my answer in a day or two. Now, kindly get up and stop making a complete fool of yourself.'

He was on his feet as smoothly as he descended. 'Then I shall wait with bated breath. Lady Harcourt, please keep your congratulations in hand until I have my answer.'

'Good heavens, young man, I didn't expect you to actually propose. Sarah's going to be a doctor or a nurse and certainly doesn't need a fiancé as well.'

'Mummy, Angus knows that perfectly well. He was just playing to the crowd. Good – musical chairs has finally reached its conclusion and Betty said there would be dancing next. I'm hoping I can do better than I did last time.'

'I'd better go and speak to everybody and say – well, what shall I say? Everybody heard the proposal, but they didn't hear your answer as you didn't speak as if on a parade ground as he did.'

'Tell them that we're going out. Anything else is not their concern.'

* * *

Sarah was enjoying the social, although the constant comments from the other revellers about her relationship with Angus were annoying. A couple of the girls from the village said they would be only too happy to take him on if she wasn't going to marry him.

There were more men in blue and khaki than there were in civilian clothes. Those that weren't in uniform were mostly older men, some of whom would never be called up, while others were still waiting. The British Army was in France at the moment and they didn't really need more conscripts.

'I notice most of the men are popping out for a drink at the pub. I'm quite happy with tea and orange squash but feel free to get a beer if that's what you want.'

'I'm not a big beer drinker myself. I'm a whisky man if given a choice, but not even much of that.'

'My father drinks whisky and there's a decanter in his study, as well as two bottles in his desk drawer. Next time you come I'll make sure you get a glass.'

'That Frenchman is heading this way with his family in tow. Are you going to introduce me?'

'Monsieur and Madame Ducray, allow me to introduce you to my boyfriend, Squadron Leader Trent.'

Hands were shaken and greetings exchanged. 'Mademoiselle, although we have found the experience interesting, an hour and a half is sufficient. I assume that you will be returning in order to serve dinner at the correct time.'

Angus stiffened next to her and she touched his hand. He nodded but his eyes were hard as he stared at the speaker.

'No, I'll be coming back with Squadron Leader Trent but not for another hour. I explained to madame this morning that, because of the social, dinner would be at eight o'clock tonight and not at six.'

She deliberately turned away and smiled a warning at Angus. 'That's the music for a polka. Shall we dance?'

He swept her away and they spun around the floor at breakneck speed and almost collided with others doing the same. After just one turn she realised they had to go after all. 'Has he gone?'

'Yes, they left immediately. You didn't tell me he was so unpleasant. He speaks perfect English, not a trace of an accent, I wonder how that is?'

They threaded their way through the crowd and into the comparative peace of the lobby. 'Would you be kind enough to find my mother and tell her that I've got to leave immediately? I know I said we weren't going for another hour but he can't get in as the house is locked. I'll find our coats – do you have your ticket so I can claim yours as well?'

He handed it over and she rushed to the cloakroom. Scarcely fifteen minutes after the Ducrays had departed, they were in the car and speeding towards home. Mummy had decided to stay and said she would get a lift back from someone when the event ended.

Angus returned to the theme he'd started earlier. 'How did he end up in your house?'

'I'm not exactly sure, but somebody from Ramsgate contacted Mummy and asked if she'd put them up until a permanent arrangement could be made. We weren't told anything about them apart from that they were wealthy.' She smiled in the darkness of the car interior. 'I thought he might be a German spy but he's obviously not as his family's French. They don't speak any English and so far the two girls haven't uttered a word to me and my French is reasonable.'

'France is still unoccupied, as is Belgium, but I don't blame him for getting out. The writing's on the wall and it's only a matter of time before German tanks have overrun the entire continent.'

'What a depressing conversation, and up till now I was having such a good time. Are you going to come in?'

'I'm not leaving you to cook dinner and serve it by yourself. I don't suppose there'll be enough over for us? I haven't had anything since breakfast.'

'There's plenty – it's nothing elaborate tonight. Mixed vegetable soup, omelettes and sauté potatoes followed by apple pie and custard. They also have wine which they pay extra for.'

'Sounds perfect to me. If you cook, I'll serve.'

'In which case you deserve a very large glass of whisky to make the chore seem less onerous.'

'I forgot to tell you. Someone will be coming for the hunters next week. If they prove to be as good as I've said then they'll be happy to buy them.'

'That's the best news I've heard all week. Starlight, my mare, is now content to be driven, so when the land girls finally do arrive then they can use her to get to whatever farm they're working on.'

They pulled into the turning circle and the Ducray car was there but it was empty. 'Where on earth are they? Would you look in the barn and stables? Although heaven knows why they would go there. In fact, that man isn't stupid, so why didn't he ask for the key before he left?'

'God knows. I'll take my torch and have a scout around and see if I can find them.'

She got out the door key and was about to put it into the lock when she realised the door was already open. 'Angus, they must be inside. I'm sure we locked up before we left so I don't know how they managed that.'

He arrived at her side at a run. 'Here, sweetheart, let me go in first. There's something dodgy about all this.'

She was only too happy to slip behind him. Her palms were clammy, her heart pounding, but she would be safe with him here. He pushed open the door and she expected to find lights on at least in the drawing room but the place was silent and dark. If they were in here, they certainly weren't making a noise. The puppy wasn't barking his usual greeting. That was even more disturbing than the lack of human noise.

There was no need to be told to be quiet – it was the sort of situation where one instinctively kept silent.

19

Angus moved into the centre of the grand hall, keeping the feeble beam of his torch pointed towards the parquet floor. Sarah was right to be concerned that the puppy wasn't barking. It had certainly made enough noise earlier that evening when he'd banged on the door.

She was standing close behind him and he could feel her tension. Four people couldn't just vanish into thin air and neither could a puppy. They must all be in the same place.

'Do you think they could be in the cellars? The puppy would have followed them down. That would explain why we can't hear them.'

'I can't think of anywhere else they could be, but why would they go down there? If there'd been an air raid that would be different – I'm certain the girls wouldn't be there willingly as they're far too nervous.'

'I'm pretty sure this isn't a burglary...'

'Burglary? I didn't think of that – could there be robbers creeping about collecting the silver?'

'I just said I'm certain that isn't the case. The Ducrays didn't have a key, so how did they open the front door? This is all very mysterious but I'm sure there's a simple explanation.'

They were talking quietly but their voices still echoed in the empty space. 'I'm going to put the lights on. Why don't you call out? You've certainly got a very loud voice.'

Light flooded the space and it took a few seconds for his eyes to adjust after the darkness. 'I don't know exactly what I should shout. Let's just look for them. Why don't you show me how to get into the cellars?'

They walked through the house switching on the lights as they went. If the missing family had been on the ground floor than they would certainly have both heard and seen them.

'This is the door to the cellars.' She attempted to push it open but it didn't budge. 'This doesn't have a lock – I don't understand how it can be stuck.'

'Here, let me try.' He put his shoulder against it but was as unsuccessful as she'd been. 'They must be down there but God knows why the entire family would want to go into freezing cellars.'

'We can get in from outside. Remember, I told you there's an old smugglers' passageway that comes out behind the clock tower? My father had the shelter built in the cellar with the exit to the passageway. I'm getting a very bad feeling about this. The door opens inwards and the only reason I can think for it not to be moving is because there's something preventing it on the other side.'

She unlocked the back door and for a few seconds they were breaking the blackout – that was the least of his worries at the moment. By the time he'd closed the door she was a distant shape, and he followed the wavering beam of her torch.

He caught up just as she vanished into what looked like impenetrable bushes. 'Daddy had new doors installed. They open from this side – in fact, now I come to think about it, anyone could get into the house this way if they knew about the secret passage.'

The two doors pulled open smoothly and a waft of dank, earthy air enveloped them. 'Right, do you want to go first as you know the way?'

He was speaking to himself as she was already halfway down the narrow, slippery stone steps. The passage was just wide enough for him to walk without turning sideways but the sides were slimy and he was slightly claustrophobic being entombed like this.

Sarah, on the other hand, seemed unfazed by the darkness and was hurrying ahead of him. He increased his pace and almost lost his footing a couple of times as he attempted to keep up with her. The passageway widened slightly and the sides were now constructed of brick and the smell was less oppressive.

'Look, the entrance to the shelter's just ahead. This opens towards us so it would be impossible to block in the same way as the other one. Angus, I forgot to bring my medical bag and I've a horrible feeling I'm going to need it.'

'Let's worry about that once we're in. Won't there be something similar in the shelter?'

'How stupid of me – of course there is – I helped put it together.' They reached the half a dozen steep stone steps. 'You have to stay at the bottom, there's no room to open the door with both of us on the steps.'

'Do you want me to go first? In fact, I think it would be better if I did as we don't know exactly what's going on up there.'

'I've passed all my St John's exams...'

'Bugger your exams.' He reached up and lifted her down and placed her firmly behind him. 'I'm twice your size, sweetheart, and that might be more crucial than being qualified in first aid.'

He lifted the latch and was obliged to walk backwards down the steps in order to open the door. He half-expected to find the missing family in the shelter but it was dark and empty. She pushed past him and he heard her searching for the light switch.

'Angus, I can hear something. It sounds like the girls crying.'

'Find the first aid box. I think we're going to need it.'

His torch was redundant now but he was bloody glad he had his thick greatcoat on. The sound of at least one child sobbing somewhere on the other side of the door wasn't encouraging.

'Here, grab these blankets. If they've been shut in the cellar for half an hour they're going to be cold.'

Sarah didn't need telling to do this as she already had an armful of blankets as well as the first aid box. He flung open the door and the light from the shelter spilled into the inky blackness.

'Wait a minute, Angus, I'll put the light on. The crying isn't coming from this passageway but somewhere near the wine cellar, I think.'

She fumbled along the wall and he heard her push the switch. 'The bulb's gone. That's why it's dark. We're going to need our torches until I can find a replacement.'

'We can see enough from the light in the shelter.' He could see what was blocking the door. Mr Ducray was slumped against it – obviously unconscious.

'I'll see what I can do for him, you go and find the other three. Now is the time to shout as I think they're probably lost. Goodness knows why they didn't stay here or go into the shelter. I showed him where it was.'

She handed him three blankets and then hurried to the far end of the passageway to attend to the man and he ran towards the sound of the children.

'Call out, I'm coming to find you. It's Squadron Leader Trent and Miss Harcourt,' he bellowed and was sure they'd hear him.

He stood still and listened. The crying had stopped. A voice, he thought it the mother, called back.

'*On est près de la cave à vin. Bernard s'est effondré et on n'a pas pu le déplacer. Nous sommes perdus et si froids*.'

He'd forgotten she couldn't speak English and he'd no idea what she'd said. He turned to the crouched figure at the far end of the passageway. 'Sarah,' he yelled, 'what did she just say? How do you say "follow my voice, I'm walking towards you" in French?'

'She said that she's near the wine cellar and they are all very cold. You need to shout this – *marche vers ma voix, je viens te trouver*,' she replied. 'He's still alive, has a faint but regular pulse. I think he's had a stroke or a heart attack perhaps. There's not much I can do apart from put a blanket around him. I'm going to race back and call an ambulance. Can you bring the others through the passageway?'

'I can. You go, I won't be far behind you.'

* * *

Sarah tucked two blankets around the comatose patient and then ran all the way back to the house. As she was asking the operator to connect her to the emergency services, she thought about the puppy. Why hadn't he been yapping?

The ambulance had to come from Ramsgate but she was assured it would be there within half an hour. She paused just long enough to put two kettles on to boil and put out all the hot-water bottles she could find. Once she had two of them filled, she would go back and put them under Mr Ducray's blankets. Then she would stay with him until the ambulance arrived. While she waited for the water, she rushed about in a frenzy tipping coal and logs onto all the fires.

Angus would have to bring the ambulancemen down the same way she'd just come up. It would take at least two of them to move the patient so the door could be opened, but at least they'd be able to bring him out through the house and not be forced to take him back through the underground route.

She was filling the last of the hot-water bottles when the bedraggled and dispirited trio trooped in from outside. 'Here, madame, take this and give one each to your daughters. Go into the drawing room, the fire's burning brightly there. I've put the soup on and Squadron Leader Trent will bring it in to you when it's ready.'

She repeated this in her schoolgirl French and they seemed to understand. They thanked her profusely and the three of them, clutching hot-water bottles beneath their blankets, dashed into the drawing room where she could hear them talking volubly in their native tongue. Odd, as she'd not heard the girls talk before and now they were doing so non-stop.

'I'm going back. The ambulance should be here soon. Bring them down through the passageway.'

The patient hadn't stirred; he wasn't any more awake but he wasn't any worse either. She carefully pushed the hot-water bottles inside his cocoon of blankets. There was nothing else she could do apart from keep an eye on him. She couldn't put him into the recovery position, but as he was propped against the cellar door she thought he wasn't in any danger of choking, and that his airway would remain open.

She was backing down the staircase when there was a faint scuffle behind and she couldn't keep back a squeak of shock. She looked around and saw a very miserable and frightened puppy shivering at her feet.

'So there you are, silly little thing. Whatever are you doing down here? Come on, let me pick you up. I think you'll just about fit inside my coat.'

Lazzy whimpered and snuggled against her. He must have thought he was back in the Victorian wing. No wonder he was in such a state.

The ambulancemen eventually arrived, accompanied by Angus. Briefly, she explained to the men what she'd found, what she'd done and what she thought was wrong. They made short work of transferring Mr Ducray to the canvas stretcher and then Angus opened the door and they carried the patient out to the waiting van.

'I gave the others the soup, bread and butter and left the apple pie and custard on the table in the kitchen where they could help themselves. Is that the puppy I can see sleeping inside your coat?'

'It is. He's fine but he's peed all down my best frock. I suppose I should be grateful that was all he did.'

'Have you any idea what they were doing down there in the first place?'

She carefully put the sleeping puppy into his box under the table before answering. 'Hardly – the patient was unconscious in case you hadn't noticed. I'm just going to change and then I'll speak to madame. It's all quite extraordinary. I see you've put the kettle on again – can you make me a pot of tea and a jug of coffee for the drawing room?'

It took her some time to strip off her soiled frock and then rinse the urine from the front so it wouldn't smell or stain. Dressed in her oldest slacks and two jumpers, she returned downstairs hoping to be able to discover exactly what had happened, why the entire family had been trapped in the cellars.

The drawing room was empty. She hurried into the kitchen where Angus was setting out their supper. 'Where are they?'

'They went upstairs. I suppose she can't ring the hospital to ask for news as she can't speak English.'

'I'll make us both an omelette and put the potatoes on to sauté whilst we have the soup. I see they've left us plenty of apple pie for dessert.'

The puppy appeared from under the table as they finished the last of the pie. She dropped her cutlery. 'I'd better pop him outside before he has an accident. I'll check on the horses and shut the chickens up. I should have done it hours ago; I do hope a fox hasn't got into the barn.'

She didn't bother to put on her boots or coat but raced around outside doing what was necessary. 'I'm just going to wash my hands and then I'll join you for coffee in the drawing room. We might as well make the most of the two fires in there.'

'I've made you coffee but, sorry, sweetheart, I can't stay. I need to be back at the base ASAP.'

'Thank you for staying as long as you have. You being here made things so much easier. We make a good team, don't you think? And by the way, if you were serious about wanting us to become engaged then I don't see why not. Having your ring on my finger will protect me from unwanted advances when I'm training. I'm hoping that knowing I'm waiting for you will make whatever you have to endure over the next year or so more bearable.' As soon as she'd finished, she realised her acceptance had been rather unromantic. What mattered was how much she loved him, not what a good team they were. 'I love you, Angus, and know you love me too.'

His eyes darkened and he reached out for her. She went willingly into his arms and by the time he'd finished kissing her she was hot all over and understood why girls were prepared to do things they really shouldn't when they were in love with a man.

'We'll go into Ramsgate next time I get a few hours free and buy a ring. I love you, darling, and you're quite right, having someone of my own to fight for will make things easier. It doesn't matter how long we have to wait before we can be married – if we both survive to the end of this bloody war then we *will* be married.'

If his arms hadn't been firmly around her waist, she rather felt she might have slithered to the floor in a heap. She was resting her face against his shoulder and giving herself time to recover. 'I'm hoping to hear from the Royal Free in the next few weeks. If they can offer me a scholarship and will take me before I'm eighteen, I'll leave immediately.'

His hold tightened and he kissed the top of her head before gently releasing her. 'I'm glad you've decided to do that, sweetheart. I didn't have time to tell you tonight but I've put in for a transfer. I'm going to give up my promotion and return to being a flight lieutenant so I can do something more constructive than run Manston.'

'Maybe you'll be posted somewhere near London – then we could meet up occasionally. I love you, I didn't want to, but it's too late to change things. You'd better go or you'll have to put yourself on a charge.'

He cupped her face in his hands and kissed her again and then strode off. She didn't go with him – she understood that his mind was now on more important things than her.

As she was checking the door was firmly shut she noticed the spare key, which usually hung on a hook by the door, was missing. At least the mystery of how the family got into the house was explained.

* * *

Joanna went to the pub when the social ended with a group of friends for a few G & Ts before someone kindly drove her home. She was more than a little tiddly but had thoroughly enjoyed herself. David didn't approve of such frivolous entertainment – if she was honest, he didn't approve of anything very much.

Feeling decidedly disloyal, she tottered into the house and went straight upstairs. She was just climbing into bed when something she'd seen, but the significance hadn't registered, made her jump out again.

Snatching up her dressing gown, she shoved her feet into her slippers and rushed across the passageway to burst into Sarah's bedroom.

'Darling, wake up. The Ducrays aren't here – the car has gone.'

Her daughter sat up, instantly awake. 'Just a minute. I'm coming.'

'How could you have gone to bed without them being home? They must have had an accident.'

'No, he had a heart attack but they were here when I went to bed and so was the car.'

Madame Ducray's room was empty, as was the one occupied by the two girls. They checked the wardrobes and all had been cleared. When they looked into his room, everything was as he'd left it, his clothes were still there although the bed, obviously, hadn't been slept in.

'They've run away from him. How extraordinary! Now we'll never know what happened last night and how they all ended up in the cellar.'

'We don't know that he won't recover, darling, and if he does then he can explain. There's nothing we can do tonight but I'll have to contact the people in Ramsgate, those who arranged for them to stay with us, in the morning.'

'I can't help feeling sorry for Monsieur Ducray, Mummy. If he does pull through it will be to find his family has abandoned him. I know he wasn't a very pleasant gentleman but nobody deserves what happened to him.'

Joanna agreed but what stuck her most were the similarities between Monsieur Ducray and David. Both were cold, controlling men and she didn't blame madame for taking the chance to escape. The war had released her from her unhappy marriage and she was determined to make the most of her independence so that when David returned he wouldn't be able to bully her into submission again.

20

Angus was flying regular sorties with the Hurricanes but so far had only encountered a couple of Luftwaffe reconnaissance kites and they'd not hung around to be shot at. Eventually he had a spare couple of hours and purloined the Hillman and set out for Goodwill House. There'd not even been time to have a brief telephone conversation with Sarah since the drama in the cellar.

The adjutant knew where he was going and could contact him if he was needed. He could be back at Manston in ten minutes at a push. He particularly wanted to see her today as her father's horses were being collected. Losing them would be hard as they'd been part of her life for the past few years.

He also wanted to know what had happened with the Ducray family. He passed a smart double horsebox on the road and guessed it contained the hunters. When he arrived, he expected to see the large Rover belonging to the Frenchman, but it wasn't there.

Sarah must've heard him arrive as she waved from the drawing room. The front door opened as he stepped under the portico and she threw herself into his arms. A highly satisfactory five minutes later, he raised his head.

'I'm sorry, darling, I was hoping to get here before they went. Are you very upset?'

'Not at all. The chap they're going to is the master of foxhounds and he took one look at them and made a very generous offer. I'm so glad I spent hours plaiting their manes and tails and polishing their hooves. Daddy won't be happy, but Mummy and I are ecstatic. Not only have we got enough money to keep us going even without having boarders but we also no longer have to feed them. I've got far more time to study my medical books so I'm ready if I get called for an interview.'

'I want all the gen about the French bloke. Did he go for a burton?'

'Come in, I'm just going to have a sandwich for lunch. Mummy and Betty have gone into the village for a WI meeting so I'm on my own. You won't believe what I have to tell you.'

'I'm still waiting to know if he survived and what was actually wrong with him?'

'He had a heart attack but not a serious one. He knocked his head when he collapsed and that's why he was unconscious. Mummy went to see him and he explained what had happened. He went down to get some wine and when he came out of the cellar the puppy dashed down the steps. He refused to go and find it so the girls persuaded their mother to go with them.'

'I think I can guess what happened next. The bulb blew, leaving all of them in the dark, and then Ducray had his heart attack and fell against the door. Not nearly as exciting or mysterious as I thought.'

She was busy buttering bread and as the kettle whistled, he poured the water into the teapot. 'That's not all that happened. Madame and the children abandoned him and stole the car to do so. Nobody knows where they are. He's now in London somewhere. I'm pretty sure he's a spy, not a German one, but for de Gaulle.'

'What makes you think that?'

'It was all very hush-hush and we were told not to discuss anything about the incident with anybody. Two men from the foreign office came and collected his belongings and paid his bill in full so we benefited from that as well.'

'Have you heard anything about your application? I've had no response at all from the Air Ministry about mine. I've been flying most days as one of Jimmy's flight is in hospital with appendicitis.'

'I've been to one meeting of the St John's but it all seems a bit pointless now. I won't be here to minister to anyone injured in an air raid – I'll either be living in a nurses' home or in London.'

'We don't have time to buy a ring today but I promise we'll do it before one of us leaves. It would probably be easier if I could choose it for you – actually I think that's usually how it's done. Do you have any preference?'

'Look, I hope you won't be offended, but I know you can't afford to buy anything expensive. My great-grandmother, my father's mother, left a box of jewellery to be handed down to me. She didn't want Mummy to have it as she wasn't Harcourt blood. Would you mind awfully if we chose something from that?'

'I don't have a family heirloom or I'd give you that. Why don't you fetch the box down whilst I take the tray into the drawing room?'

'Golly, not in there. It's freezing as we don't light the fires now our guests have gone. Take it to the smaller sitting room at the back of the house. I won't be a moment. I told my mother we were engaged and she said she was happy for us but thought it better not to mention it to Daddy.'

'Fine by me. We're not thinking of getting married for years and you'll be of age by then.'

He did as she asked and was glad she'd left him alone to gather his thoughts. Somehow it didn't seem right that the engagement ring came from her side of the family and not his, but as long as she wore a ring, then he was okay with it.

'Look, Angus, I'd no idea there was so much valuable jewellery in this box as I've never bothered to look inside. I should think there's a fortune here – mind you, I doubt anybody's interested in buying precious stones and so on at the moment.'

He put the tray down on the coffee table and went to sit beside her on the chintz-covered sofa. 'Good God! You're not kidding, sweetheart, there's a king's ransom in that box.' He was staring down at a kaleidoscope of precious stones, necklaces, bracelets and rings and even three tiaras. 'If these stones are real then you're a very rich young woman. Don't you realise what that means? You don't need to get a scholarship but could actually take up your place at Oxford and use these to pay for your tuition and living costs.'

'These are heirlooms, I wouldn't be allowed to sell them even for something as practical and necessary as paying for my medical training. However, I am allowed to wear any of them if I want to.' She rummaged around like a toddler in a toy box, treating the fabulous items with total disregard. He loved her for not being impressed by these riches.

'What about this ring? It's not too big, it's an emerald with diamonds around it and set in either platinum or white gold. Shall I see if it fits?'

He took it from her, examined it, and then slipped it over the knuckle of her ring finger. 'It fits perfectly and is exactly right. I wasn't sure about not being able to buy one for you but it would be silly not to use this.'

She turned her hand from side to side, examining the ring. 'I would have loved to have had one that you chose for me but this one will do. Mummy's talking about having a party to celebrate the engagement – what do you think?'

'Why not? Any excuse for a knees-up. How many guests are you going to cater for? Which reminds me, I'd better write to my parents and tell them the good news.'

'Betty and the two ladies from the village will do everything. You can invite whoever you like from the base – there'll certainly be dozens from the village. My father will be incandescent when he gets back and sees half his precious wine has been drunk. I don't think she's writing to him any more so he won't know anything about it, which is probably a good thing.'

'Do you think he wouldn't approve of me?'

'No, it's me he'd be disappointed with. Obviously, he wanted a son and got me instead. To be honest, both Mummy and I have been a lot happier without him here. We were both permanently walking on eggshells, waiting to be shouted at for breaking one of his hundreds of unwritten rules. I suppose we're lucky he didn't believe in physical punishment or we'd have been black and blue.'

'Sounds like a pretty miserable childhood so I'm not surprised you were happier at your boarding school. When was your mother thinking of having this party?'

'As soon as possible. I think that's really why she's gone to the village.

She and Betty will be plundering the three grocery shops for anything that's still available. It'll be a buffet, help-yourself sort of thing, and whatever we can find in the cellar to drink.'

'I'll get hold of some beer – the men will probably prefer to drink that. It can be a farewell party for both of us as well as an engagement do.'

The telephone jangled at the far end of the house. With a rueful smile she put down her sandwich and ran to answer it. He was already on his feet, expecting it to be the base and that he'd have to depart in a hurry. Things were moving on fast, both for him and Sarah and for his career.

'Sit down, it's not for you. It was someone about the land girls. Our farms aren't eligible to get them at the moment – apparently, they don't qualify as we've almost a full complement of workers. That's a bit of a blow so thank goodness we've got the money from the hunters to make ends meet.'

She didn't seem at all worried so he made no comment and let her continue and made a suggestion.

'This is a ridiculously large house for two people to live in. I'm sure if you offered it to the RAF or army they'd be only too happy to commandeer it and use it as a convalescent home or something similar.'

'It's not Mummy's prerogative to dispose of the family home. It makes my going more difficult as I don't really want to leave her rattling about in here on her own with only the puppy for company. Also, she hates horses and until we've got land girls to take care of my mare, the chickens and ducks, I've really got to stay.'

'I might get my posting before you're ready to go.'

'I know, but that doesn't change anything. We're engaged and we love each other. The rest will just have to fall into place.'

* * *

The next few days were spent in party preparations. Sarah had pushed aside all thoughts of becoming a medical student or a nurse for the moment and was just concentrating on helping her mother. One thing she was sure about was her love for Angus and she was ready to show the village and all his friends they were a couple.

The day of the party was Wednesday, 20 March. The weather had improved, which meant Angus and his fellow pilots had been constantly flying sorties over the Channel for the past three weeks and this was the first day most of them were free to attend.

All the guests were aware they would be told on the actual morning of the event and nobody had complained. Being invited to the 'big house' for any sort of shindig was an event not to be missed even with the inconvenience of not actually knowing what day this party was to take place.

'Sarah, do you think we have enough to eat and drink as we don't actually know how many guests we'll have this afternoon?'

'People have been so generous with their time and their rations. We've got enough to feed a small army. The two pins of beer, all the wine we've stolen from the cellar, as well as the orange squash, will be more than adequate, however many people come. I'm so glad the men who played at the dance we went to a few months ago are happy to do the same for Angus and me.'

'Shall we all give the house a final tour just to be sure everything's in place? Do you know, darling, I've lived here for twenty years and this is the first time there's been a big party like this. Imagine actually dancing in the ballroom – so exciting.'

'I don't know how Betty managed to make such a magnificent engagement cake when the ingredients are rationed. I expect this will be the last fruit cake anyone eats until the war's over and these things can be imported safely from wherever they grow. Do currants grow?' She laughed at her nonsense. 'I'm pretty sure currants are shrivelled grapes – or is that sultanas? Anyway, I'm going to enjoy everything. This is how a house like this should be used. It's ridiculous for just two of us to be living here.'

She and Mummy had talked about the cost of the party but the money from the sale of the hunters and from the French family meant they were no longer living on the edge of financial ruin.

'I think everything looks absolutely splendid, darling. You've done wonders getting this organised. I don't know why it is that I can take charge of the WVS but find making any decisions about our lives and the house so difficult. I rather think I relied on your father too much in the past.'

'It wasn't a case of you relying on him, Mummy, he was a very controlling sort of man and didn't let either of us have opinions of our own.'

Her mother's shocked expression brought home to her just how significant her casual use of the past tense had been. 'I'm sorry, slip of the tongue. It's just that life's so different, so much better for both of us, without him here. I don't think you ever really loved him, did you? Not the way I love Angus.'

'I've never really thought about it. When an actual lord asked me to marry him of course I didn't hesitate. I wish you'd been able to meet my parents, they would have loved you. Unfortunately, they both died before you were old enough to ask about them. David didn't want me to have anything more to do with them, which I found extremely difficult, but they accepted that was how it should be as they weren't in his social class.'

They completed the inspection and everything was as it should be. At least her mother hadn't denied that things were better without the man of the house around. 'I wish I'd been able to meet at least one of my grandparents, or any other family member for that matter. Daddy never spoke about his mother – I don't even know if she's alive or dead.'

'Actually, the Dowager Lady Harcourt, as far as I know, is still alive and well but she lives in the south of France. She didn't approve of David's choice of bride and refused to attend our wedding. She must be in her late sixties now so she could have died. I don't suppose I'll ever know.'

'I hope if she's living that she doesn't find herself under German rule.'

'Whatever do you mean? The BEF and the French army will keep Hitler under control. Please don't say anything so dispiriting on such a happy day.'

'I'm sorry, you're right. The house looks wonderful and this is the last time there's likely to be any sort of party here for a long time.' She saw her mother about to contradict and stepped in quickly. 'No, there won't be a wedding. I think you should know that we've no intention of getting married until the war's over and I'm a doctor – whichever comes first.'

'Good heavens, child, the war will be over long before you qualify. It takes five years to become a doctor, doesn't it? Everybody says Hitler will be defeated before Christmas.'

As Sarah had promised not to spoil the occasion by mentioning anything depressing, she didn't say what she was thinking – that the war might very well be over by Christmas, but it wasn't going to be Christmas 1940, and possibly not the following one either. It had hardly started as yet and Hitler was going to want to invade Britain at some point but she was resigned to this like most other people.

She'd decided not to wear one of her more expensive gowns but something simpler as she didn't want to make any of the guests feel underdressed. Angus would be in his best blues so she'd found something that would complement his uniform.

Her hair was pinned up in a French pleat, she was wearing a smudge of red lipstick and a dusting of powder. She examined her face from every angle in the dressing table mirror. She looked different. Older, wiser and considerably thinner.

The frock she was wearing was dark blue with white spots – very fashionable – and had a nipped-in waist, full skirt and what was called a shirt front. She might be thinner in the face but she certainly wasn't in the bosom department. The bodice was rather tight and she sincerely hoped the buttons didn't pop open when she was dancing.

It might well be years before she and Angus could celebrate their actual marriage so she was going to enjoy this engagement party and make sure everyone else did too.

21

Joanna had received another two letters from David but had pushed them into a drawer in her dressing table without reading them. As long as she didn't know what he was writing, she wouldn't feel obligated to follow his orders. She just hoped he would think the postal service was to blame and that their letters were being lost in transit.

If he knew any of the things that had been done in his absence, he would be furious; even from France she rather thought he might be able to cause her and Sarah a lot of unhappiness. If only she was brave – like her daughter – and could truly take charge of her life.

A good wife would have asked his permission before selling the hunters, agreeing to the engagement, taking in boarders and holding a party for the entire neighbourhood. The fact that she was actually allowing them into the house itself was unprecedented. In the past there had been village fêtes and garden parties held on the lawn but nobody, apart from his close friends, had been invited inside.

How was she going to manage when Sarah left? The very idea of being in charge of this huge house, the estate, and everything else that was going on, filled her with terror. She pushed these unpleasant thoughts aside and pinned on a happy smile. Today was for Angus and her darling daughter and she wasn't going to spoil anything by being silly.

She decided to ignore the advice not to dress up too much and was wearing a gown that had been made for her in London. Her clothes had been one thing David had never cut back on. It hadn't occurred to her until now that this was more for him than for her – that he wanted to keep up appearances, not let anybody know that they were in financial difficulties. By ensuring she was dressed in haute couture, despite the crippling cost, everybody would think things were tickety-boo.

Thank goodness the weather was at least dry, if not particularly warm, as most of the guests would be walking from the village. Those that had cars were David's friends and she'd deliberately not invited them. It belatedly occurred to her that one of his cronies was bound to hear about the activities at Goodwill House and would no doubt write to him.

She glanced nervously at her dressing table. Perhaps he already knew and had written forbidding the engagement and everything else. If she didn't actually read those words on the paper then she could pretend she was in ignorance of his demands. Heaven knows what would happen when he came back – if he came back. At the moment she was forced to admit she hoped he wouldn't. Not that she wanted him dead – of course she didn't – but life was so much easier and happier with him on the other side of the Channel.

Downstairs there was the distant sound of the musicians tuning up, Betty was marshalling her troops and everywhere seemed very jolly. The hothouse had fallen into disrepair years ago so the floral arrangements were daffodils from the garden and foliage from the woods, but none the worse for that.

'My lady, isn't this grand?' Betty said as she gestured expansively to the cluster of children's balloons tied in bunches around the grand hall. 'I've never seen the like. People will be arriving at any moment. Miss Sarah and her young man are in the ballroom.'

'It's all so very exciting. Remember, you and your team are guests at the party as well as everything else. Make sure you have time to enjoy yourself. This isn't a formal event but something for everyone. I do hope I didn't miss people off the guest list who will be offended.'

'I'm sure you didn't. All the members of the WI and WVS, along with their hubbies, will be here. I think it's a good thing the kiddies aren't coming too as with so much free alcohol available I reckon there'll be a lot of men a bit worse for wear before the end of it.'

'I do hope the ladies don't refrain from drinking – there's some absolutely splendid wine just for them. I even unearthed three bottles of sherry and I do know that several of them enjoy a glass of that.'

* * *

Angus had been amazed how different Goodwill House seemed just by putting dozens of simple flower arrangements and bunches of balloons around the place.

'What do you think? I can't believe I'm actually going to dance with you in here.'

'I don't imagine that anybody coming to our party, sweetheart, will ever have danced in an actual ballroom. I certainly haven't. Are you having party games as well as dancing?'

For a moment she thought he was serious but then laughed. 'Actually, I don't see why we shouldn't. Blind man's buff, hide-and-seek – both those would be fun but I don't think musical chairs would go down too well.'

'Idiot girl – come on – let's have a practice run.' He looked over at the trio from the base. 'What about a waltz?'

They could hardly refuse their commanding officer and the ballroom was filled with music. He drew her into his arms and then they danced. He'd waltzed with her before but somehow being in this place made it even more special. They made the perfect couple and for a few blissful moments he was able to forget the war, the fact that they would soon be parted, and revel in the joy of holding the woman he loved close to his heart.

'There you both are. We need to be in the hall to greet our guests. People are beginning to arrive.'

'Yes, Mummy, we're coming.' Sarah's smile was sufficient compensation for the dance being interrupted.

'I thought this was an informal sort of do. A greeting line?'

'Angus, don't be a spoilsport. There isn't going to be a line like a wedding or a ball; we just have to be visible and ready to say hello as our guests come in.'

'Will there be raffle tickets and clothes pegs handed out like there were at the social?'

'For a fighter pilot, Squadron Leader Trent, you're remarkably unobservant. There are rows of trestle tables down each side of the hall. I worked out there's more than enough room for over a hundred coats and I don't think there'll be that many.'

'Anyone from the base will be travelling in the lorry so I doubt they'll wear their greatcoats. I did notice the trestles, but didn't register the reason for them being there. Being dim is far worse than being unobservant.'

He kept his arm firmly around her waist as they hurried down the draughty passageway and into the hall. 'Good God – when did the notices appear? Surely I didn't miss those as well?'

'One of Betty's team of helpers put them up after you arrived. Our guests need to know where the lavatories are, also where the bar is. Everything else I'm sure they'll find for themselves.'

'Actually, I was referring to the ones with the big arrows pointing to the trestles, saying "Coats On Here". I suppose making things clear is easier than having to repeat yourself a dozen times.'

He loved these discussions he had with her – they were definitely on the same wavelength and shared a similar sense of the ridiculous.

The front door couldn't be left open or the hall would be impossibly cold. She told him there was another notice pinned to it telling people to come in. The sudden influx of guests, dozens and dozens of them, made him smile. In between nodding and smiling to everybody he drew her aside to share his observation.

'I think they must have walked up here in a crocodile, like a school trip to the park. I wish I'd seen it.'

'I'm sure you're right. Now, from the sound of it your lot are arriving.'

There was no need to remain in the hall for more than half an hour as by then everybody was there. The tables were laden with neatly arranged coats; the bar was the busiest place but everywhere else was pleasantly full of happy partygoers. Surprisingly, they'd received very few congratulations, and this bothered him.

'Sarah, why aren't people mentioning our engagement? I thought this was supposed to be a celebration for us.'

'I asked Mummy not to make a big thing of it. I'm sure everybody knows but equally they know that I'm going to be going away shortly. It's unusual for a couple to become engaged and not have a wedding date planned.'

'Everything about our relationship is unusual. I'm surprised you haven't heard from the Royal Free – do you want me to get hold of my uncle and ask him what's going on?' She looked away but not quick enough. 'What's wrong? You're upset. Tell me, I'm on your side, whatever it is.'

'We're not getting any land girls after all – at least not for the next few months – so I can't leave even if I'm offered a place. My mother can't manage on her own.'

'Does it have to be land girls?'

'It does really as I need somebody to take care of the livestock and my mare.'

'There must be a youngster in the village, somebody who's just left school and is too young to be conscripted, who'd be only too happy to work here. Didn't you say selling the hunters meant you didn't actually have to take in lodgers for a while?'

'It's not just that. I don't think she'll cope by herself in this huge house. Would you like to live here on your own? I certainly wouldn't – it's bad enough with both of us.'

'We're getting some WAAF after all – we need more catering staff, admin help, and it seems there might be some trained drivers coming at some point. Did you know they are even training girls to be ground crew?'

'I didn't but it makes sense. I really like the six we had initially and it's a shame they couldn't have stayed as they'd already made friends with everybody. I thought you were building accommodation for them?'

'We've got a Nissen hut fully equipped with its own ablutions but so far we've not got a recreation room or anywhere for them to eat. We don't want them fraternising with the airmen as that's a recipe for disaster.'

'So if you get the girls before these other things are completed they could come here? That would solve a problem and hopefully the land girls will be forthcoming by the end of the year.'

'We haven't got a drink as yet – do you want one?'

'No, I'd much rather dance with you again.'

They made their way, hand in hand, to the crowded ballroom, where

Angus's men were much in evidence. He was forced to relinquish his partner several times which gave him the opportunity to watch her dancing. She was without doubt the most beautiful girl in the ballroom and he didn't think he was just biased because he was in love with her. She positively sparkled and it didn't matter who she danced with, she gave them her undivided attention.

'There you are, Angus. We've not danced together – as your future mother-in-law I think you're obligated to do so.'

'It will be my absolute pleasure, my lady...'

'I refuse to be addressed by my title. My name's Joanna, as you very well know. Hurry up, I see Mrs Thomas approaching at speed and I refuse to give up my partner to her.'

* * *

Sarah was almost glad when the last guest finally departed. 'I'm going to change, Mummy, and then I have to do the horses and chickens. I can't believe Betty and her ladies managed to wash up everything before they left. Thank goodness they shared the food that was left over or we'd be eating it for days.'

'Take the puppy with you as he hasn't been out all day. I expect we'll be finding unpleasant surprises in unlikely corners because of that.'

'I let him out once and I'm sure Betty did too, so all tickety-boo on that front. I'm absolutely exhausted but I loved every minute. Why don't you change into something less elaborate and then we can put our feet up in the sitting room? I didn't eat much so I'll make us an omelette if you like.'

'Thank you, darling, I'm really getting too old for all this nonsense.'

'You're in your mid-thirties and if you say that you're old again I'll throw something at you.'

'I'd rather you didn't. I'll be in the sitting room when you've made us something to eat.'

Her mother had drifted about the place looking elegant but hadn't lifted a finger to do anything useful. By rights, she should be the one making the supper. Heaven knows how she'd get on if they actually did have half a dozen boarders and there was no one there to help her in the evenings.

Perhaps when she went into the village tomorrow she'd put a card in the newsagent's window asking if there was anybody interested in a part-time outside job; she would also advertise for a live-in maid. If there were boys looking for work there must be girls doing the same. There were no factories within walking distance and at fourteen years old they weren't able to volunteer for any of the services.

* * *

By the end of the month she'd managed to find a brother and sister, twins of fourteen years of age. They'd been sent to live with their grandmother in the village when their mother had died in a tragic accident caused by the blackout. The unfortunate woman had been run over by a bus in the darkness. There apparently was no father in the picture.

Liza and Joe had been desperate to escape from their new home and their grandmother was equally pleased to be rid of them. Joe knew nothing at all about horses, chickens, ducks or geese but within a few days was competent and confident taking care of them. Liza had been doing housework, cooking and laundry since she was old enough to reach the sink. She too was proving to be the perfect fit.

The two of them had taken over the attic rooms used for live-in servants many years ago. Sarah had been worried about putting them in somewhere so unappealing.

'We ain't used to anything fussy, miss, we shared a bed with our ma and a bog with a dozen others,' Liza had said when she was shown the new accommodation. 'I reckon we've died and gone to heaven being here. We'll make it ever so cosy and we won't let you down.'

Within a week of their arrival, Sarah wondered how they'd ever managed without the twins.

Angus rarely got more than an hour or two free so he just drove to her and they spent what time they had in the sitting room that was previously used by the paying guests. He telephoned as often as he could and those moments spent talking or together were precious.

'I spoke to my uncle yesterday and he's certain your application never arrived or he would have seen it by now as you're applying for a bursary,' he'd told her in one of his flying visits.

'Golly, I really should have done that myself – not contacted your uncle, of course – but checked they actually got it. I'll do it again this afternoon. I've got so little to do now that I'm attending WI and WVS meetings with my mother just to fill in the time.'

Angus handed her a piece of paper with a name and address scribbled on it. 'He said send it to him directly. He was encouraging, not to say enthusiastic, about reading it and bringing you in for an interview. He said if you've passed all the St John's exams then you're already qualified to work on the wards. They have several nurses doing exactly that – they just have to do a year's practical experience and then they can take their SRN examination.'

'I really want to become a doctor, not a nurse.' She hesitated and then decided to tell him what she planned if she didn't get the finances she needed to study and live in London. 'I'm going to sell the jewellery. I won't tell my mother and once either she or my father discover what I've done it will be a *fait accompli* and too late to do anything about it.'

He wasn't dismayed by her announcement but agreed with her. It had taken her these weeks to make the hard choice but she was sure it was the right one. Keeping her mother in the dark was difficult but there was no other option.

'That's the right decision. I promised you a night out in London. Why don't we combine the two things? I'm going to give myself a forty-eight-hour pass as I've not had more than a few hours away from the base for weeks.'

'That sounds absolutely spiffing. I'll get my application off and then hopefully I'll get an interview soon. Then we can do all three things whilst we're in town. I read somewhere that it's going to be impossible to see *Gone with the Wind* as all the seats have been booked. Do you think that the fact there's now meat rationing will make it difficult to get a decent meal?'

'I doubt it. If you've got the money then you can get anything. I'm absolutely rolling in it at the moment as I'm not a big drinker and that's where most of the men spend their meagre wages.'

'I'll have the money from the jewellery so I'll be even richer. Shall we book into the Savoy or the Ritz? We might never have the chance to do anything like this again for years. I'm certain I'll be a medical student as I was offered a place at Oxford. So I can't see me not being accepted at the Royal Free if I can pay my own way.'

'Two rooms will be prohibitive even for us.' He took her hands and she guessed what he was going to ask. Did she want to share a room with him? Yes – but sharing a bed wouldn't be right.

'Then book one and you can sleep on the floor.'

'Excellent. We'll have to masquerade as a married couple. They won't let us share otherwise.'

'I'll spin my engagement ring around. How incredibly *risqué* of us!'

He flashed one of his toe-curling smiles and her stomach clenched. It was a good thing she trusted him as if he looked like that when they were alone she might not be able to resist.

22

Joanna was enjoying being a lady of leisure again and having both Betty and Liza to do the things she'd rather not do. She wasn't entirely sure allowing Sarah and Angus to spend time alone upstairs in the guest sitting room was a sensible idea.

He was a virile and attractive young man and her daughter was completely inexperienced with men of any sort – which was exactly as it should be for a young lady from her background.

The only thing that neither of the indoor staff were prepared to do was answer the telephone. Therefore, she had no alternative but to answer the noisy thing herself.

'Good afternoon, Lady Harcourt speaking. How can I be of help?'

'I apologise for intruding, my lady, but Squadron Leader Trent is needed back at the base urgently.'

'Then I shall fetch him immediately. Goodbye.'

An emergency at the base couldn't be good news. She prayed none of the young men, the brave pilots, had crashed their aircraft. There was no need to knock on the door as, quite rightly, it had been left open.

'Angus, you're required at the base. An emergency of some sort.'

'Thank you, Joanna, I'm on my way.'

He nodded, but scarcely acknowledged her presence, and was down the stairs two at a time. The front door slammed scarcely a minute after she'd called his name.

She waited for Sarah to join her. 'I hope nothing serious has called him away.'

'He'll ring and tell me if he can. By the way, my application never arrived so I'm going to do it again and then ride down to the village and post it.'

Joanna was forced to admit that Sarah was no longer under her control, did exactly as she pleased, and whatever was said to her would be ignored unless it was something she agreed with. There was a war on and things were going to be dangerous for those actively involved in fighting it. However, in her opinion, this didn't mean standards should be lowered at Goodwill House. From now on, they could sit in the drawing room and not come up here where temptation might well overtake their scruples.

* * *

Angus drove at a reckless speed to the base, fearing the worst. He would only be recalled under the direst circumstances. There were none of his kites up and he was dammed sure he'd have heard if a plane had crashed as the base was less than a mile away as the crow flew.

He fell out of the Hillman, leaving the engine running and the door open, and tore into the building. He yelled at the clerk in the main office.

'What's wrong? Why am I needed so urgently?'

The airman scrambled to his feet and shook his head. 'No idea, sir, I didn't send for you.'

'Then who the hell did? For Christ's sake, I only leave here for a couple of hours a week and don't expect to be called back on a fool's errand.'

'There you are, old boy, sorry to drag you away from your little popsy but this is only a flying visit.' The speaker was a wing commander with a terrifying walrus moustache. 'Flying visit? Good, what?'

Angus took a steadying breath and barely restrained himself from punching his superior officer on the nose. To give himself a few more moments to recover his temper he turned to the nervous airman watching from the office door. 'Deal with the Hillman.'

'Yes, sir.'

'Wing commander, to what do we owe the honour of this unexpected visit?'

'Shall we go to the mess? I could do with a snifter.'

The new officers' mess and billets could be accessed from a door at the rear of the admin building.

The last thing he wanted was a drink with this buffoon but he had no option. He supposed he'd better find out why the old fool had come to Manston. He still didn't have his name and was damned if he was going to ask. He'd address him as sir and then he wouldn't need to know.

'I say, old boy, I've heard that this new building is a wizard show. Wanted to see it for myself after hearing the gen about it.'

Surely he hadn't been dragged back just to show the new premises? He glanced across at the apron and saw an Annie parked there. Presumably, this unwanted visitor had arrived in that.

'We're very happy with our new accommodation, sir. Everything's in place for when the balloon goes up. There are hundreds of brown jobs manning the guns around the perimeter and I have a nasty feeling they're going to be essential fairly soon.'

Angus led the way into the mess and was relieved to find there were only a couple of blokes in there. He didn't want to give the impression his men were spending more time drinking than preparing for battle – although that was probably the case.

He got the wing commander a large whisky and ordered himself a coffee. He told the men not to drink when they were on duty and he couldn't expect them to follow the rules if he didn't.

'I don't want to hurry you, sir, but it will be too dark to fly soon unless you've got an RAF flyer and not an ATA pilot.'

'Good thinking, my boy. I was sent to sound you out about your request for a transfer. Are you quite sure you want to leave this cushy number and take command of an active squadron of fighters?'

'Absolutely certain. I'm an experienced flyer and wasted here. Being CO somewhere like this isn't a posting for a young man unless he's no longer able to fly. I appreciate being given this opportunity, but I've done as much as I can here and somebody else can take over. If I have a choice, I'd prefer to join a squadron of Spits.'

'We'll see what we can do, old bean. You do realise you'll lose your promotion. You only got the rank of squadron leader in order to be in charge here.'

'I understand and I'm happy to return to being a flight lieutenant. When am I likely to get my posting?'

'There's a newly formed squadron of Spits in need of a commander and you'll be stationed at Hornchurch. Half of them are raw recruits.'

'That will suit me perfectly. God willing, I'll have time to give them some flying experience before things kick off. I take it that my transfer's imminent?'

'April eighteenth – you've had no leave since you arrived here last November. You'll depart from Manston on the eighth. You've done a splendid job, but you're right. Men of your calibre are needed in the front line.'

This bloke wasn't the nitwit Angus had thought he was. He obviously had the pukka gen about Manston and his role in things here. His annoyance at being called away from Sarah's arms had coloured his judgement.

'Thank you, that's excellent news. My fiancée will be a medical student in London so being at Hornchurch might mean we can meet up occasionally.'

'Becoming a doctor? A girl? Good for her – we need all men and women to do their bit if we're going to keep the jackboots out of England. Did you know there are now a few women ATA pilots? Not seen one myself, but don't see why they shouldn't be used to collect and deliver kites to bases.'

Again Angus was surprised by his companion. He'd not expected someone like him to be so forward-looking. 'I'll look out for one. We're getting a WAAF contingent here soon. Girls are being trained to drive all the heavy vehicles as well as vans and cars. The more women doing these sorts of tasks, the more men that are released for active duty.'

'Jolly good show. Must be off – toodle-pip, old boy. Good luck with the new posting.'

As soon as the Annie took off, Angus headed for his office and asked to be connected to Goodwill House. Sarah answered immediately. He gave her the good news and was shocked that she wasn't as happy as he was.

'I'm sorry, but you leaving so soon isn't something I can celebrate. I know we'll have some time together in London first, but what then?' She didn't wait for his answer. 'Then I'll be here and not able to see you at all.'

'You'll be in London. Until things get lively, I'll get plenty of free time...'

'I can't start my training until I'm eighteen and that's not until September.'

'My uncle's aware of your age but that didn't put him off. I'm sure he'll get the board to enrol you as soon as you want to go. You're better qualified than most of the applicants and he's well aware that having someone like you working at the Royal Free will be a godsend when the bombs start dropping.'

He pushed aside the fact that if bombs were dropping in London then they would also be dropping on the woman he loved.

* * *

Sarah had detected a nervousness, a change in her mother since the last time Angus had been at the house. Was this just a normal mother-and-daughter thing? When a girl fell in love and started to put her fiancé before her parents then things were bound to change. Maybe the distance between them was caused by having secrets – she hadn't told Mummy about selling the heirlooms and had no intention of doing so.

She was waiting expectantly for a letter from the Royal Free as, until she got her interview, she couldn't finalise the trip with Angus. If the letter didn't come today then she'd have to make a second trip as his tenure at Manston would be over soon.

None of these things would be happening if it wasn't for the war and the fact that her father was no longer dictating her every move.

It hardly seemed possible that in a little over three months she'd met and fallen in love with the man she intended to marry one day. Even more amazing was that from having absolutely no interest in boys or men she was now engaged to one. The fact that they wouldn't be sleeping together was immaterial as they would be sharing a room and leaving the village together.

It really didn't matter what anyone said as she wouldn't be here to listen to it. There was little point pretending nobody would know as village gossip would soon spread the word that she and Angus had gone to London.

It would be Mummy who had to live with the scandal and was this really fair? This needed further thought. Much as she loved Angus and wanted to share everything with him, there was no rush. Once she'd left home, nobody would know what she was doing and her behaviour wouldn't embarrass her mother.

She was teaching Joe to ride as Starlight would need exercising until the land girls eventually turned up. He was proving an apt pupil and would be waiting right now for his next lesson in the ménage.

'Miss, would you look at that?' Joe was watching Lazzy gambolling around Star and she was nudging the puppy, ears pricked, and enjoying the interaction as much as the dog.

'I'm so glad the two of them are such good pals. I was worried Star would miss her stablemates as she's never been on her own.'

'That little bugger's out here most of the time. Her ladyship don't seem as interested in him no more.'

'I'm sure she is, but he's better off out here with you. Right, Joe, are you ready? I see Star's tacked up so shall we get on with the lesson?'

Joe was about her height so had no problem mounting as the mare was only just over fifteen hands high. He was a natural and already had an excellent seat.

Two hours later, the horse was rubbed down and happily munching hay from her manger and Joe was cleaning out the barn where the chickens, ducks and geese lived. Sarah returned to the house and hastily washed and changed as she was due in the village at two o'clock for a St John meeting. Today she was instructing the cadets in the use of bandages and splints.

Angus was meeting her for tea at Milly's, the café in the village, after her engagement. She couldn't see if he was already inside as the windows were steamed up. The bell rang as she stepped in.

'There you are, darling, I've ordered for both of us.' Angus was on his feet and came to meet her. She tilted her head for his kiss.

'I'm sorry, a small contretemps with two of the cadets and a box of bandages. All tickety-boo now.'

He helped her off with her coat and then hung it over the back of her chair.

'First time I've seen you in the grey St John's uniform. Can't say I like it.'

'Not flattering, is it?'

Conversation had resumed and she was no longer the focus of half a dozen disapproving village matrons. He had bagged their usual table, one tucked away in a corner where they could talk without fear of being overheard.

'Do you think the ladies were staring at me? I can't think what I've done to ruffle their feathers.'

'Sit down, there's something I have to tell you.'

From his expression, whatever it was wasn't good news. 'Are you being transferred without leave?'

He reached across the table and took her hands. 'Worse than that, sweetheart. I'm needed immediately at Hornchurch as my squadron of Spits is arriving earlier than expected. I do have leave, but only three days starting tomorrow.'

'That's a shame. But I'll still come with you as planned.' Somehow she managed to hide her devastation that he was going on active duty so soon.

'I'm sorry, but that's not all. It's on the cards that we'll be sent overseas as soon as the new bods have settled in.'

She blinked back her tears. 'Then we'll go to London tomorrow. I wasn't sure about sleeping with you but now I am. You might be killed. I might never see you again. I don't want you to go away before we've shared everything.'

'If you were of age, I'd apply for a special licence and we could get married, but I'm certain your mother wouldn't give her permission.'

'I'm not sure she can. I think permission has to be from the man of the house.'

The jolly waitress arrived with their tea. 'There you are, ducks – scones, jam and butter plus two slices of Victoria sandwich freshly made today.'

'Can we settle the bill now, please? In case you're busy when we have to leave.'

'Bless you, I'll get it right away.'

Despite the bad news, Sarah's appetite didn't desert her and everything was consumed. She'd forgotten about the critical looks from the other tea drinkers and scrambled into the trusty Hillman keen to sort out the details of their trip.

'I'll book somewhere splendid for two nights and pick you up at ten tomorrow. I was hoping you'd agree to come with me and asked Jimmy to act as our chauffeur and take us to Ramsgate station.'

This was a huge decision and she'd made it so suddenly. What if she got pregnant? What if he was killed? She needed to consider what she'd said but knew he'd abide by whatever she wanted and not try and tempt her into bed.

As they turned into the drive, she saw a very smart car, it looked like a Rolls, parked outside the house. 'We've got visitors. I don't like the look of this, Angus. Will you come in with me?'

23

When Joanna heard the heavy knocking on the front door, she thought it might be a telegram from David trying to find out why she hadn't been writing to him.

Liza was now the designated door opener and enjoyed the responsibility. She'd been instructed to ask whoever it was to remain outside until she'd checked if the visitor was allowed to enter. The girl forgot to knock on the sitting room door and burst in, eyes wide, so excited she could barely form a coherent sentence.

'My lady, it's another lady outside. She's got a man what drives her car in a peaked cap and blue uniform as well as a snooty-looking lady in black. I ain't seen her, but there's a load of luggage coming out of the car so I reckon she's come to stay.'

'Goodness me – it must be the Dowager Lady Harcourt – my mother-in-law. Quickly, Liza, find Betty and tell her to prepare the guest suite. Then fetch your brother to help bring in the trunks and cases. You must go with Betty and light the fires upstairs and also in the drawing room.'

The girl raced off and Joanna followed her to the hall. 'Welcome to my home, ma'am, an unexpected visit indeed.'

This was the woman who'd refused to attend her own son's wedding and now expected to be taken in and treated like royalty. Was this David's doing? Was this his way of taking control of her again? The Dowager was elegantly dressed but her clothes were out of date, her skirt almost Edwardian in length. She looked exactly like David – although it was her husband who actually looked exactly like his mother. This meant Sarah was a younger replica of her grandmother.

'Where is my son? He wouldn't keep me standing here. The house is in need of redecoration and refurbishment and is unpleasantly cold.'

'I don't arrange for fires to be lit in any rooms that aren't being used. We've been asked to be cautious with our use of fuel. David is in France with the army and has been since last September. The only room with a fire is my sitting room – would you care to join me there or do you wish to go up to your apartment?'

'What I would like is a pot of English tea. The French are incapable of making tea the way it should be done.'

The front door was wide open and Joe and the chauffeur began to bring in the luggage. 'Leave it here and bring in the rest then the door can be closed. The housekeeper will direct you to the correct apartment.'

'Yes, my lady, I understand,' the chauffeur said with a grin. The older woman in black just stood, mouth pursed, disliking everything she saw.

When Joanna turned round, she was alone. The wretched woman had already stalked off as if she owned the house. She detoured to the kitchen and found Liza laying up a tea tray using the best china.

'Bring some of the biscuits Betty made this morning. The Dowager Lady Harcourt is obviously intending to remain here for the duration of the war.'

'Blimey, two Lady Harcourts. It ain't half confusing as I never knew even one lady before I come here.'

'I'm sure you'll get used to it – we're all going to have to adjust to the changes.'

'Do I have to curtsy to her like what you do for the king?'

'I'm sure she'd like you to, but it's absolutely not required. You and your brother will treat her with the same respect you treat me.'

'That's all right, then. I'll bring the tea just as soon as I can find those blooming biscuits.'

It was no surprise to Joanna that her chair was now occupied by the other Lady Harcourt. There was little she could do about it as she could hardly tip the woman out bodily.

'The tea will be here in a moment. From the amount of luggage you have with you, I assume you're thinking of staying here for several weeks. I have to tell you that I'm expecting six WAAF to arrive in a week or two. They will be boarding here. I hope that won't be an inconvenience to you?' The more inconvenience she could cause this woman, the happier she'd be. If she could make the Dowager really uncomfortable then maybe she'd go somewhere else.

'How very patriotic of you, my dear, but I'm certain they will be no bother to me. I assume they'll not be dining with us or sitting in here.'

'Actually, mother-in-law, this is my private sitting room. You will have full use of the drawing room but I prefer to keep this for myself and my daughter.'

Joanna was pleased with how so far she'd held her own with this obnoxious woman. She now understood why David was the man he was – he would have received little or no affection from his mother.

* * *

Angus followed Sarah up the steps and into the house. There were three suitcases and a trunk waiting to be taken upstairs. Whoever had arrived obviously intended to make their stay a long one.

'Look at the labels on the cases, they're from French towns. I know exactly who this is – it's my grandmother. Until a few weeks ago I thought I had no relatives apart from my parents.'

'Then I don't need to act as your bodyguard?'

She laughed and stood on tiptoe to kiss him briefly. 'I can't wait to meet her; however autocratic and unpleasant she is, I'm determined to like her. I didn't even know I had a grandmother until recently. I'm actually pleased I have another relative. It makes no difference to our plans – I'll be waiting to leave at ten as we've arranged.'

'I might not be able to get a room at either the Ritz or the Savoy – does that matter?'

'Are you asking me if I'll refuse to come if we can't stay at one of the swishest hotels in town? I'd prefer not to be in somewhere infested with bed lice and fleas...'

He kissed her again. 'Idiot girl. Go and meet your grandmother and I'll see you tomorrow.'

This would be his last night at Manston and he was aware Jimmy was arranging a bash in the mess. Heavy drinking wasn't something he enjoyed and he intended to stick to a pint of bitter. Tomorrow was too important to ruin with a hangover. God knows when he'd have another chance to spend the night with her even if it was platonically.

Was he being selfish asking her to go away with him when a long-lost relative had just appeared? He was in two minds to cancel the whole thing but couldn't bring himself to do so. He loved her too much and God knows when he'd see her again if he was posted overseas.

The new CO should have arrived a week before Angus left but, because of the change to his posting, Manston was going to be without a commanding officer for a week. Jimmy was perfectly capable of running the place for a few days and the adjutant would take care of day-to-day things. He'd left everything shipshape and thought he'd done a damn good job in the few weeks he'd been in charge.

His kitbag was packed, his uniform no longer showed the insignia of a squadron leader, all he had to do now was get through the evening's jollity and he had three days and two nights to spend with Sarah. Just being with her would be enough and in some ways he hoped she would have changed her mind about sleeping with him.

* * *

With a clear head, unlike most of the chaps, Angus tossed his bag onto the rear seat of the Hillman and hopped in beside an AC1. Jimmy must have delegated his role as chauffeur because of his hangover.

'Do you know where Goodwill House is?'

'Yes, sir. Be quicker to go across country but I doubt this old car could cope.'

Angus half-expected that the arrival of the second Lady Harcourt might mean Sarah wouldn't come with him. But she was waiting, looking smart in a burgundy coat, with not a small suitcase as he'd expected, but two large ones. She smiled brightly, but he wasn't convinced.

'We'll have plenty of time for a cup of tea before the train arrives. I like the new coat and I've never seen you in a hat before – unexpected, but it suits you.'

He hadn't bothered to get out, had spoken through the wound-down window. He didn't make the mistake of going out to open the door and had shaken his head when his driver had been about to do so. She was unusually quiet during the short journey to the station and her bright smile had been false.

He thanked the airman and watched him drive away with a slight pang of regret. He'd enjoyed his stay at Manston and would miss some of the chaps, Jimmy especially. He wondered if he'd ever see him again.

'I'll just dump our things in the luggage office and then we can go in search of a cuppa. Why don't you get your ticket whilst I do that?'

She smiled sadly. 'I think I'd better buy a single. I don't want to talk about it now – I'll tell you what happened last night over breakfast. I haven't eaten since yesterday lunchtime.'

He put his arm around her shoulders and hugged her. 'Bugger the bags and your ticket. There's a bench over there. Let's sit on it and you can tell me right now.'

'I look just like my grandmother but I sincerely hope I'm not anything like her in character. She's an absolutely vile woman and already terrorising my mother. When I told them I was going to London with you, Mummy was somewhat taken aback but would have been all right about it. She knows we will sleep separately. However, my grandmother told me I was a disgrace, that no decent girl would spend a night with a man she wasn't married to. She then said if I left today then I shouldn't come back.'

'For God's sake, that's appalling. Didn't your mother contradict her? Speak up for you?'

'She did try but was silenced by the tirade coming from that horrible person. I don't have any regrets about leaving as I doubt I'd have stayed anyway with her there. I am worried about leaving my mother to deal with her without me for support.'

This made things awkward and he felt guilty for taking Sarah away and making things difficult for her mother too.

'I'm sure your mother will fight back when she's ready. Don't forget she spent the last twenty years being the perfect, obedient wife to your father. You can't expect her to change overnight.'

'I don't blame her. I'm going to miss her most dreadfully but I can write to her and telephone occasionally. I'm quite sure that woman won't lower herself to pick up the telephone when it rings.'

'You don't have to come – I'll understand if you've changed your mind.'

She was already nestling against his shoulder and he had his arm around her. She twisted and looked at him.

'I love you and I'm an adult and can make my own decisions. Don't worry, I've got it all planned. If you don't mind, when we get to London and have booked into whatever hotel you've reserved for us, I'm going to the Royal Free. I'm hoping, even though it's the middle of the academic year, that I can join the current cohort of medical students because of my St John's qualifications.'

'Have you brought the jewellery with you?'

'I have. That will be our second job. Should we go to somewhere like Hatton Garden or find a more disreputable pawn shop somewhere else?'

'Do you have anything to prove they are yours to sell?'

'Actually, I do. I found a letter from my great-grandmother in the bottom of the box stating the jewellery belongs to the daughter of the current Lady Harcourt. As my father was an only child the box was kept for me. It doesn't say that I have to keep them, just that they are mine.'

'Then Hatton Garden. You'll get a better price there.'

* * *

Until she'd told Angus what she intended to do, she hadn't really clarified her thoughts. Speaking them out loud made it easier to see that she'd made the only decision in the circumstances.

'This isn't how it should have been but it's how it is. I just wish you were old enough to get married without having anybody's permission.'

'It's a good thing I'm not, as I would have said no. The last thing we should do is get married at the moment. It will be so much easier for both of us to consolidate our careers if we don't have any legal ties.'

'Legal ties? I'm a regular in the RAF – I couldn't leave even if I wanted to. As for consolidating my career, circumstances will shape that, not me.'

She wasn't offended by his comment but nodded. 'Of course you are. I knew that really and was just talking about myself. You don't mind that I wouldn't marry you right now even if I was able to?'

'Why should I? As long as we're still engaged, I know that when the time's right you will be my wife, I'm okay with that. The wind from the Channel is making sitting here unpleasant. Let's get ourselves sorted out, find a café and not worry about the future.'

'I don't care what anybody thinks, even if they look down their noses at us, as long as we can spend the next three days together. I wore this hat because it makes me look older.'

'It does, and hopefully it'll do the trick.'

'Who are we going to be? Not Mr and Mrs Smith, I hope.'

'I just thought I'd sign in as Flight Lieutenant Trent and Mrs Trent – it's almost true, isn't it?'

'Are you sorry you're not a squadron leader any more? You were just getting used to having the extra pay and now you'll be back to the old amount. '

'In fact, because I don't drink or smoke, unlike most the other chaps, I don't run up a massive bar bill every month. I'll actually be in charge of a squadron, just not with the rank of squadron leader.'

Whilst she purchased her ticket, he put their bags into the left luggage office. She noticed there was a station café. She couldn't see much through the steamed-up windows so pushed open the door an inch or two and an appetising smell of hot toast and bacon drifted out.

He strode up to her. 'The bloke in the left luggage recommended this place. It would appear people come up from the town just to eat here. Shall we go in? We've got just under an hour before the London train arrives.'

'By that time it'll be almost lunchtime – it's already nearly eleven o'clock. We'll call this meal brunch and then we won't need to eat again until dinner tonight. Did you reserve a table at the Ritz?'

'Better than that, sweetheart. There's an afternoon tea dance today and

I've reserved a table for us. What could be better than dancing, plus tea and cakes to go with it?'

'I doubt that I'll get to the Royal Free and to Hatton Garden before the dance.'

'We've got all day tomorrow to do that and most of Friday; I don't have to be at the base until five.'

'Then I'll stop worrying about what might or might not happen and just enjoy your company.'

The café was half-full, but then it was still early and the breakfast eaters would have gone and the lunch eaters had yet to arrive. A waitress in black, with a white apron and frilly cap, beamed at them.

'Table for two? Just coffee or do you want to eat?'

'We'd like a hot meal if that's possible – neither of us had breakfast and we won't be eating again until late this afternoon.' She'd answered automatically when really she should have allowed Angus to reply, but he was unbothered by her taking over. He was really the most wonderful man and she was so lucky to have him in her life.

'Then I'll put you where the tablecloths are – they're the ones for diners.'

She was about to remove the pins that held her hat in place when she stopped. None of the women had taken theirs off.

'It's going to be very odd eating a meal with a hat on, but if everyone else is doing so I'd better do the same.' He took her coat and hung it on the coat stand by the door along with his own greatcoat, the two gas masks and the other outdoor paraphernalia they both had with them.

They settled for cottage pie with vegetables and then apple crumble and custard for dessert. They decided to have a pot of tea to drink with the meal and coffee afterwards. The waitress had assured them it was the real stuff and not the dreaded Camp, which came out of a bottle and looked like gravy browning – it didn't taste much better either.

As they were finishing the delicious meal, he handed her a small leather box. 'I didn't buy you an engagement ring so I've bought your wedding ring in advance. I'd like you to wear that, then you can have your engagement ring showing as well. Perhaps you can keep it on a chain around your neck until we actually get married.'

Surreptitiously, she removed her engagement ring with her hand under the table and then pushed the wedding ring on first. 'That's absolutely perfect, thank you so much. Let's pretend we've just got married and are going on a honeymoon before you get posted away. It will make it seem more romantic.'

'We'll start right away – get into character before we get to the hotel where we might be under some scrutiny.'

Fortunately, the train steamed into the station, alerting them to the fact it would be steaming out again within fifteen minutes. The first-class carriage was already occupied by a businessman in pinstripes and bowler hat – travelling late to his workplace in London for some reason – and a portly matron in burgundy tweed.

Angus didn't put their belongings in the overhead rack but piled the two cases and then his kitbag on the seat beside them. They hadn't bothered to put on coats so he folded these neatly on top of the pile of luggage.

'You will have to move those, young man, if anybody else comes into the compartment. There might well be others who booked seats in first class.' The middle-aged woman stared pointedly at the two seats he'd obstructed. The businessman kept his head in his paper and didn't even look up.

'I'll move everything if I have to, ma'am, but I think putting all three items in the overhead rack might well cause it to collapse. We didn't have time to put our belongings in the guard's van.'

Sarah decided to add authenticity to the story. 'We've just got married and are going to London for a three-day honeymoon before my husband takes up a new posting at Hornchurch.'

Sarah knew her radiant smile was enough to convince anyone of the truth of her statement. She loved Angus, they were engaged, and one day she would be his wife.

24

Joanna wanted to believe Sarah wouldn't actually go through with it and leave with Angus so spent a relatively untroubled night, although deep down she knew her daughter would do exactly what she wanted regardless of her or anyone else's opinion. Her mother-in-law was a nightmare but she supposed she'd get used to her in time.

Betty no longer came in at weekends as Liza and her brother Joe took care of everything apart from the cooking of dinner, which Sarah did.

'Morning, ma'am, miss is out with her horse and the puppy's gone with her. How do we do breakfast now things have changed?'

'We'll use the breakfast parlour for the Dowager Lady Harcourt but Sarah and I will continue to eat in the kitchen as it's more convenient. She will use the drawing room, not the sitting room. There's no need for you to make up fires, clean and so on, in any of the rooms that she uses as she has her own staff to do that.'

'I don't mean to speak out of turn, ma'am, but those two what you just mentioned have told us we've got to move out of our rooms so they can have them. That ain't right, is it?'

'It certainly isn't. How did you prevent them from invading your domain?'

'We locked the doors and played the wireless what you borrowed us ever so loud so we couldn't hear them shouting.'

'Good for you. I'll speak to them myself as I expect they'll be down at any moment. There are half a dozen perfectly usable rooms in the attic and they'll have to do what you did with yours. My mother-in-law will pay for any changes as I'm certainly not going to.'

She really shouldn't be discussing this with Liza but she liked the girl and knew she was loyal to a fault, that she and her brother considered Goodwill House their home – the first decent one they'd had in years, if ever.

'Righty ho, ma'am, we're snug as a bug in a rug up there and we ain't budging from there not for no one.'

'And neither should you. My mother-in-law arrived uninvited so must fit in around my arrangements and not the other way round.'

'She's a terror and no mistake. She'll keep us on our toes, I reckon.' Liza busied herself at the Aga and Joanna took her usual place at the table.

'I expect Betty showed the new members of staff where everything is yesterday when she was here so you should be able to get on uninterrupted. Just toast and tea for me today.'

She finished her breakfast and wondered why Sarah hadn't come in as she usually did after doing the horses. Oddly, Joe, who enjoyed his breakfast, hadn't come in either. The kitchen clock showed the time to be almost ten. She was about to go and investigate the absence of her daughter and the boy when a bell rang loudly outside in the kitchen passageway.

These were connected to all the main rooms of the house but hadn't been used since she'd lived there and, until now, she hadn't known they still worked.

'Liza, would you be kind enough to have a look and see where the Dowager is ringing from.'

'Gordon Bennett! Whatever next?' The girl poked her head outside the kitchen door. 'It's the dining room, ma'am.'

'Oh dear, I suppose I'd better go and explain to my mother-in-law how things are done in this house. Would you be kind enough to take a tray of tea and some freshly made toast into the breakfast parlour? Lady Harcourt won't need anything else this morning.'

She walked briskly through the house and into the icy dining room where her mother-in-law was siting, back straight, mouth pursed, at the massive table.

'Mother-in-law, your breakfast and your other meals will be served in the breakfast parlour. Obviously, we don't use the dining room, which can seat more than forty, to just serve one. Secondly, please don't pull the bell strap as the people working here are employees, not servants – there is a difference, you know.'

The Dowager remained exactly where she was, her expression glacial, and said nothing. Joanna thought she might as well get the accommodation of the new staff sorted out now as well.

'I think I also need to make it quite clear that as far as I'm concerned the two staff that you employ are responsible for your well-being, your laundry and your rooms. There is adequate accommodation in the attics for both of them but they will have to organise the furniture and so on themselves. What they won't be doing is evicting Liza and Joe.'

'I am as entitled to live here as you are. I expect to be treated with respect and my dresser and my chauffeur are not employed to do menial tasks.'

'Then I suggest that you find some staff of your own who are prepared to do so. I didn't invite you here and as you haven't communicated in any way with your son for the past twenty years then I doubt that he would want you here either. I won't turn you away but if you wish to remain under this roof you will abide by my rules.'

Her head was spinning, she felt sick, but she'd said what she wanted to say and was proud of herself. As she crossed the hall, she heard a car driving away and flew to the window. She recognised it immediately – it was the Hillman – Sarah had ignored everything that had been said and gone to spend the weekend with her fiancé.

She should have stood up for her daughter against her grandmother's outburst. She admired Sarah for being confident enough to follow her own wishes, even with the threat of not being allowed to return hanging over her. Of course, this wasn't the case as Goodwill House was her home, however reprehensibly she'd behaved.

Joanna returned to the kitchen and was surprised to find it empty.

There was a letter addressed to her lying in the middle of the table and she recognised at once that it was Sarah's writing.

Mummy,

I am most dreadfully sorry but I can't live under the same roof as that woman. The fact that you didn't contradict anything she said about me being a disgrace to the name, to not being allowed to return here, can only mean that you agreed with her.

Don't worry, I won't come back to embarrass you. I shall spend three days with my fiancé and then hope to take up my place at the Royal Free. I will write to you when I have an address you can respond to.

I do love you but you have let me down badly.

Sarah

She read it through twice more before the words fully registered. Whilst she'd been dealing with the Dowager, her daughter had left, possibly forever. This was all her fault – she'd driven Sarah away and forced her to choose between Angus and her family.

She now understood why Liza and her brother had gone elsewhere whilst she read the letter. They must have known and helped Sarah leave. She slumped onto a chair and dropped her head into her hands, unable to take in what had happened.

'We're that sorry, ma'am, but we couldn't tell you,' Liza said as she made the tea and toast for the unwanted guest.

'That's all right, I understand. Sarah would have gone anyway in the next few weeks to start her medical training. I just wish it hadn't been like this.'

'Don't you fret, ma'am, she ain't gone for good. She'll be in touch soon enough and then you can nip up to London to see her.'

'Thank you, that's exactly what I thought. Joe, you can come in, I won't bite your head off.' He'd been hiding behind the pantry door but now emerged looking somewhat sheepish. 'I've made it quite clear that you will remain in your own rooms. Also, Lady Harcourt is responsible for arranging her own staff to take care of her personal needs.'

'We ain't seen neither of them snooty two since last night. I reckon they might have abandoned ship.'

'They ain't taken the car, Joe, so if they've gone then they'd have had to walk.'

'Please take that tray to the breakfast parlour. Hopefully, my mother-in-law will have deigned to move because if she hasn't, she won't get any breakfast.'

* * *

It was April and only six months since David had been recalled to serve with the BEF. How much Joanna's life had changed in half a year. Her daughter had grown up and started a life of her own and she was happy for her but was going to miss her dreadfully. She had discovered the estate was in financial difficulties but by taking in paying guests and selling the hunters she thought they would be able to keep afloat.

The arrival of her mother-in-law from the south of France wasn't ideal, but it was just possible that over the next few weeks they might find a middle ground. At least she wouldn't be entirely alone. A letter had arrived yesterday from Victory House in London confirming the arrival of six WAAF at the end of the month. They would be staying until Manston completed the necessary arrangements for the girls to live on the base permanently.

Sarah wasn't the only one who had grown up, who had found her feet. Before war was declared last September, the only thing Joanna had done of any use was running the WVS – but now look at her.

* * *

Angus was only too happy to join in the play-acting. There was nothing he'd like better than to be Sarah's actual husband. Anyway, the story of being on honeymoon was received as truth and by the time they got off the train in London he almost believed it himself.

'I can't carry your suitcases as well as my kitbag. What the hell have you got in them? They feel like a ton of bricks.'

'Not bricks, books mostly. Dr Willoughby gave me half a dozen medical volumes that will be essential, so it seems, to know from cover to cover if I'm going to complete my medical training. Let's get a porter and then a taxi rather than the underground.'

'Absolutely – I'm amazed you got them out of the house let alone into the car without my help.'

'Years of looking after horses has made me stronger than I look. I'm so excited I feel as if I've drunk a whole bottle of fizzy pop.'

He wasn't going to ask if her excitement was at the thought of being with him for three days or because she was about to embark on a new, independent life fulfilling her childhood dream of becoming a doctor.

They found a decrepit porter who on being given two shillings for his trouble happily went in search of a cab for them. On arrival at the Ritz, they were greeted less than enthusiastically. They were told by a sniffy assistant hotel manager that their room wouldn't be available until the afternoon.

'I'm well aware of that fact. I was told we could store our luggage until then. We have a table booked for the tea dance this afternoon.'

The young man, his hair slicked back, and barely able to see through his pebble glasses, showed little interest in any of this information. Then Sarah stepped up to him and smiled winningly.

'We've just got married. This is our honeymoon – we've saved up for ages to be able to pay to stay at this wonderful hotel. Being at the Ritz is like being a princess in a fairy tale.'

This was laying it on a bit thick but the man lapped it up. 'Congratulations on your nuptials, Mrs Trent. I'll have a bootboy put your luggage somewhere safe until this afternoon.'

She winked at him and Angus hid his smile behind his hand. Ten minutes later they rushed out of the hotel like children escaping into a playground at break time. 'I've got the jewellery box in my handbag. Shall we head for Hatton Garden?'

'Hatton Garden is somewhere between Gray's Inn Road and Farringdon Road. About two miles to walk, which is a bit far. Shall we catch a bus or go on the underground?'

'A bus every time – you don't see anything apart from people's backs on the underground. Even if it's quicker, I'd much prefer to be able to see London.'

They walked down to the Mall and caught a bus that took them along the Strand, then got out at Fleet Street. All he'd noticed was that London seemed dingy with its piles of sandbags at every corner, taped windows and depressed-looking pedestrians walking along, heads down, gas masks over their shoulders.

'There are more service people on the streets than there are civilians which I suppose is only to be expected.'

'A lot of RAF blue, khaki, but not many sailors. I suppose the poor souls are the ones doing all the work for us at the moment. I can't imagine anything worse than being in a submarine.'

He smiled at her non sequitur. 'Then it's a good thing you don't have to be a submariner. I'd rather be a flyer than a sailor. Look – that's Hatton Garden. Which jewellers are we going to try?'

They stopped whilst she got out the leather box with the gold filigree fastening. With scant regard for the contents, she turned it over and pointed.

'There's a name embossed on the bottom and I think I saw a place with the same name just now so that would be a good place to start.'

She walked in with such confidence, every inch the daughter of an aristocrat, and the two salespeople immediately rushed to attend to her. When she told them she was hoping to sell family pieces that she'd inherited, they were only slightly less keen to see to her needs. They were ushered into an office with thick, luxurious carpet and a large leather-topped desk. They were left alone whilst the buyer was fetched from somewhere in the bowels of the building.

'It might be better not to sell everything at once, sweetheart, just a couple of pieces and the rest can go in a safe-deposit box at my bank. That way you can just get out something every now and again and sell it.'

'That's a good idea. I don't have a bank account – I just have a post office savings book. I was going to put whatever I got today into that.' She put the box on the table and flipped open the lid. 'I really dislike tiaras so I'll try to sell those. There are three of them and they're full of excellent diamonds. I know a little about carats and clarity but not much about the cut.'

Sarah had been right. She was offered a fabulous amount of money but wisely she hesitated as if not sure whether to accept.

'Mrs Trent, as you say, these stones are of the finest quality but they will have to be remounted. We cannot sell these pieces as they are.'

'I'm not sure. What do you think, darling? Should I accept their offer or try somewhere else?'

Angus was somewhat startled to be addressed as darling but rose to the occasion. 'Perhaps another fifty pounds would be in order?'

The man behind the desk hesitated for a moment and then nodded. 'I'll increase my offer if Mrs Trent will agree to give us first refusal when and if she decides to sell any more pieces.'

'I'm happy to do that. Thank you.'

Angus wasn't comfortable wandering around the streets with so much cash and a vast fortune in precious stones and jewellery. Eventually, they found a post office, paid the money in and then walked to his bank in Holborn where they deposited the box.

'We'd better head back to the hotel,' he said as she paused and looked longingly into the steamed-up window of a café.

'I suppose you're right. Do you think they'll let us go into our room now? I'd really like to be able to change into my posh frock – I want to look my best for such a glamorous occasion.'

'After you flirting so outrageously with that poor man, I'm sure he'll agree to anything you ask.'

* * *

He had ample time to unpack, take a shower and put on his best blues before going down to Palm Court. Sarah was dressed when he emerged from the marble-tiled bathroom in his finery. 'You look spectacular, darling, you'll fit in perfectly in that gown.'

She twirled, making her silky skirt spin out and revealing a froth of petticoats, stocking tops and possibly a glimpse of knicker too.

'I don't expect to be able to wear something like this once I'm a poverty-stricken medical student. I'm not normally a fan of pink, but this colour is called damask rose and I think it's perfect on me. I'll be the belle of the ball.'

For a moment he thought she was paying herself a compliment but then she pouted and fluttered her eyelashes at him. 'You'll be the most beautiful woman at the tea dance, without question. We'd better get a move on if we're not going to be unfashionably late.'

They hurried down the stairs, not wishing to wait for the lift to be summoned. As they turned into the spacious corridor that led to the venue for the dance they could hear the orchestra playing.

'Quickly, Angus, I don't want to miss a minute.'

25

Sarah stopped so suddenly that Angus walked into her, almost sending them both to their knees. 'I'm sorry, did I hurt you, sweetheart?'

'No, I shouldn't have halted like that but I've never seen anything like this. I might come from a grand family but I've had a very sheltered upbringing. This is quite magnificent – look over there, I believe that woman's wearing diamonds and a mink stole.'

'There are half a dozen like her as well as men in tails. Ridiculous in the middle of the afternoon – but that's the upper classes for you.'

'There are only a couple of other men in uniform and certainly no one quite as handsome as you. Shall we find a table or do we have to wait and be told where to go?' A waiter was in fact hurrying towards them.

'Flight Lieutenant and Mrs Trent, follow me and I'll take you to your table.'

The afternoon lived up to everything she'd imagined. The tea was exquisite – cucumber sandwiches, tiny, delicious cakes as well as warm scones with strawberry jam, real cream and butter. The dancing, the music, the singer, all were even better and when the final notes died away she wished it could go on for another hour at least.

'It's dark now but we could still go for a walk if you want. Green Park is just across the way,' he suggested as they followed the other guests from the ballroom. His arm was heavy across her shoulders and for some reason she wanted to shrug it off.

'No walk, thank you, I'm quite worn out after dancing all afternoon. Did you notice there was a photographer? I know he took several pictures of us – do you think we'll be able to buy one of them? I'd really like to have a memento of this afternoon.'

'If you make your way upstairs, I'll find out. I don't have a snap of you and I want one.'

A lot of girls at school had thought of nothing else but making an excellent marriage, walking down the aisle in a stunning white gown, but she'd not been one of them. Things had changed for her and she was now engaged but that didn't mean she had to share his bed.

It took several attempts to insert the key into the lock but eventually she opened the door. Her eyes widened and for a moment she was too surprised to move. There was a magnificent bouquet of spring flowers on the sideboard, a bottle of champagne in a silver ice bucket, and what looked like a box of expensive chocolates.

Had she come to the wrong room? No – her key had opened the door so it must be correct. Had Angus asked for these to be sent up, because she was quite sure he wouldn't be able to pay for them on his modest wages.

She was still dithering in the open doorway when he arrived behind her. 'Good God! No wonder the man was smiling and nodding like a madman.' He put his hand on the small of her back and bundled her into the room. 'Remember, darling, we told them we were on our honeymoon? I think this is a gift from the hotel. I bloody well hope it is because I can't pay for it.'

'Can we send it back? If we haven't touched anything then they can't charge us, can they?'

He strode to the collection of luxury items and triumphantly waved a card. 'With the compliments of the hotel and congratulations on our marriage.'

'How kind of them, but I feel really guilty now for lying.'

'If we hadn't lied then they wouldn't have allowed us to stay. We don't have to drink the champagne tonight; we can leave it until tomorrow.'

As always he sensed her disquiet and smiled reassuringly. 'If we put a couple of pillows down the centre of the bed like we did last time then we can both sleep comfortably and it'll be like each of us being in a single.'

'That would be perfect. It's not that I don't love you, it's just that I'm not sure I'm ready to take this next step.'

'If I have to wait to make love to you until we're married, then so be it. I'm just going to enjoy being in your company, hearing you breathing beside me, imagining what it'll be like when we're actually married sometime in the future.'

Her tension evaporated and in that moment she couldn't have loved him more.

'We have a wireless and I've got a pack of cards. Shall we listen whilst we play? I'm a demon at piquet – do you know how to play it?'

He didn't, but soon picked up the rules and by the end of the evening he actually triumphed a couple of times. 'I really enjoyed that,' he said as he deftly replaced the cards in the box. 'I'm going to ask them to bring us a jug of coffee and a sandwich of some sort – the tea was delicious but hardly substantial.'

'Yes, please. That sounds marvellous.'

She was no longer nervous about being with him as he was a man of his word, he loved her, and if she didn't want to move things on then he'd respect her wishes. They couldn't rearrange the bed until after the room service had come – it would be obvious there was something amiss if a honeymoon couple chose to sleep on either side of a row of pillows.

The coffee duly arrived along with a plate of scrumptious sandwiches – not cucumber this time, thankfully. They cleared the plate and ate half the chocolates, which went perfectly with the coffee.

'If you want to use the bathroom, clean your teeth and so on I'll organise the bed.'

There was ample room on either side of the barricade even for someone as tall and broad as him to sleep comfortably, although she rather thought a fighter pilot could sleep anywhere if necessary. She wasn't quite sure how she'd react when she saw him in his pyjamas but they were so utilitarian, not at all romantic, that she didn't even think about the fact he'd nothing on beneath them.

When she emerged, the main lights were out and only the bedside light on her side was still on. She skipped across and scrambled into bed and then plunged the room into darkness.

'Good night, darling Angus, I'll never forget today. I love you so much.'

'I love you, sweetheart, and know that however long it takes, one day we'll be together.'

* * *

Joanna spent the day hiding from her mother-in-law in the kitchen where she knew the wretched woman wouldn't come. She wasn't exactly frightened of her, more worried that words might be exchanged that would make things untenable. She had no option but to appear in the breakfast parlour for supper – it wasn't called dinner here any more.

Sarah would normally have cooked the meal but today she and Liza had done it.

'Well, my lady, I reckon we've done a smashing job,' Liza said as she dished up the vegetable soup. 'This first with freshly baked bread and then the rabbit pie and apple crumble for afters.'

'Thank you for helping. I'm going in so please bring it through in five minutes.'

The redoubtable woman was already seated and in the correct room this time. 'My servants have left my employ, Joanna. Therefore, your staff will have to take care of my personal needs.'

This wasn't a good start. Joanna took a deep breath and sat before answering. 'I don't have anyone available, mother-in-law.' This wasn't strictly true as the ladies from the village could easily do what was needed.

There was a silence and Liza arrived with the soup and they served themselves and ate without speaking.

'I owe you an apology, Joanna.'

She dropped her spoon in shock at this unexpected announcement.

'I should have let you know I was coming. If you would be kind enough to find me someone to act as my dresser then I can pay her wages. I won't need a chauffeur as the car won't be used.'

This was a start. 'I might know someone who could work during the day but not to live in.'

'Then that will have to do. We all have to make sacrifices during a war, do we not?'

'Yes, we do. There will be more staff here when the WAAF arrive and the house will be noisy and crowded.'

The woman almost smiled. 'Then I must get used to it as I've nowhere else to go.'

'Another thing: my daughter is no concern of yours. This is her home and she can come back whenever she wants.'

'I'm certain David wouldn't have allowed her to even meet that man, let alone run off with him.' Her lips pursed but wisely she refrained from further criticism.

Joanna sighed. She didn't like the Dowager, but maybe they could learn to live together and at least she wouldn't be alone. Life could be a lot worse – she was financially stable, her beloved Sarah had left to become a doctor and soon this huge house would be ringing with the laughter and noise of another group of girls from the WAAF.

She wasn't a courageous woman like her daughter but she was getting more confident and was actually looking forward to running Goodwill House on her own.

BIBLIOGRAPHY

First Light by Geoffrey Wellum
The Home Front by Marion Yass
Wartime Britain by Juliet Gardner
RAF Airfields by Jonathan Falconer
The Wartime Scrapbook by Robert Opie
Britain at War: Unseen Archives by Maureen Hill
Oxford Dictionary of RAF Slang by Eric Partridge
A WAAF at War by Diana Lindo
The WAAF at War by John Frayn Turner
Unseen Hastings and St Leonards by Frederick Crouch
The WAAF by Beryl Escott
The Ramsgate Story by John Huddlestone

ACKNOWLEDGMENTS

I'd like to thank Boldwood for inviting me to join their team of fabulous writers and for making me feel at home and valued from the start.

MORE FROM FENELLA J. MILLER

We hope you enjoyed reading *The War Girls of Goodwill House*. If you did, please leave a review.

If you'd like to gift a copy, this book is also available as an ebook, digital audio download and audiobook CD.

Sign up to Fenella J. Miller's mailing list for news, competitions and updates on future books.

https://bit.ly/FenellaMillerNews

ABOUT THE AUTHOR

Fenella J. Miller is the bestselling writer of historical sagas. She also has a passion for Regency romantic adventures and has published over fifty to great acclaim. Her father was a Yorkshireman and her mother the daughter of a Rajah. She lives in a small village in Essex with her British Shorthair cat.

Follow Fenella on social media:

twitter.com/fenellawriter
facebook.com/fenella.miller

ABOUT BOLDWOOD BOOKS

Boldwood Books is a fiction publishing company seeking out the best stories from around the world.

Find out more at www.boldwoodbooks.com

Sign up to the Book and Tonic newsletter for news, offers and competitions from Boldwood Books!

http://www.bit.ly/bookandtonic

We'd love to hear from you, follow us on social media:

facebook.com/BookandTonic
twitter.com/BoldwoodBooks
instagram.com/BookandTonic

Ingram Content Group UK Ltd.
Milton Keynes UK
UKHW041051050623
422888UK00002B/23

9 781801 628211